GRACE

THE ICE PRINCE

GRACE

THE ICE PRINCE

&

J.L. SCHARF

thistledown press

Library and Archives Canada Cataloguing in Publication

Scharf, J. L. (Joyce Laird), 1958-
Grace & the ice prince / J.L. Scharf.

ISBN 1-897235-09-7

I. Title. II. Title: Grace and the ice prince.

PS8637.C43G73 2006   jC813'.6   C2006-903741-8

Cover painting © Marc Potts
Cover and book design by Jackie Forrie
Author photo by Paul Stewart
Printed and bound in Canada

Thistledown Press Ltd.
633 Main Street
Saskatoon, Saskatchewan, S7H 0J8
www.thistledownpress.com

Thistledown Press gratefully acknowledges the financial assistance of the Canada
Council for the Arts, the Saskatchewan Arts Board, and the Government of
Canada through the Book Publishing Industry Development Program for its
publishing program.

SASKATCHEWAN
ARTS BOARD

 Canadian   Patrimoine
Heritage   canadien

 Canada Council   Conseil des Arts
for the Arts   du Canada

ACKNOWLEDGEMENTS

With special thanks to my editor, R.P. MacIntyre,
as well as Wendy Peterson, and to family and friends
who have been so encouraging.

For Grace, Ian & Lily

Chapter One

In a time and a place when the ways of the world offered more reason and purpose than wonders and surprise, where nothing out of the ordinary ever occurred simply by chance, there lived a slip of a girl named Grace. Fair of face, with sunlit hair and the poise of her namesake, Grace was just shy of her twelfth birthday. Although her life thus far had proved rather uneventful, aside from the commonplace milestones charted from birth to age twelve — first words, first steps, first grade and the like — with Grace there always was a hitch, something unusual that either marred an event or prompted questions. There were little things that happened, oddities that occurred during everyday incidents — Grace simply did everything with her own special twist.

As a baby, Grace's parents had eagerly waited for her first signs of speech as all new parents do. Her first word uttered was not the sentimental favourite of ma or pa, rather "dra." It caused her mother minor embarrassment to be so called, especially when all of the other babies she knew called their mothers mama. Her first steps were not taken in the comfort of the carpeted living room floor but, instead, outside on the front steps encrusted with ice in the middle of winter. A remarkable feat considering that just as her father attempted to retrieve her, he slipped on the very same ice, crashing down the stairs and landing in a heap. On the first day of school she was asked to illustrate her family. Grace drew her parents, herself, and one other. Since Grace was an only child, she was asked to explain the phantom sibling; Grace shrugged her shoulders and replied. "It's my invisible sister." An imaginary friend wasn't so far-fetched for a child at that age, but as she grew older the invisible sister remained in all of her drawings. It was something that unsettled her mother at times, and she hoped Grace would eventually grow out of this phase and accept what may never happen.

Ever hopeful, Grace knew she wouldn't. Deep in her heart she had always wished for a sister or even a brother. She longingly envied the large families of her friends each having a sibling or two or three. Their houses were always overflowing with rambunctious activity — both hostile and friendly — as siblings' activities can be. Secrets shared, sweaters borrowed, and help with homework were simply a person away. Grace cherished the times when she was generously included, despite knowing she was an outsider and not part of their clan. At the end of the day, she would return home alone with her parents to the quiet household made up of three.

Not that she was unhappy at home — just a trifle lonely. Grace lived in a pleasant old house with her own bedroom plus a playroom all to herself, on a tree-lined street, on the edge of a very big city. Cars and buses travelling up and down the boulevard made for quite a busy thoroughfare, and for as long as Grace could remember, her mother had warned her about venturing out front to play. Instead, the back garden and the sanctuary it offered was deemed much more appropriate for outdoor adventures. This suited her just fine; she loved the peace and beauty of the garden away from the bustle of the street and spent many hours there, season after season, welcoming their changes.

The garden was quite large, with beds overflowing with flowers, bushes, and trees. In spring, a sea of tulips and hardy crocuses poked through mounds of melting snow. Solomon seals sprouting delicate bellflowers waved in the breeze and ferns with gentle fronds stood lush and green. Soon after, great pink pompoms of peonies crawling with tiny ants released their sweet fragrance into the garden. In summer, when the air was hot and humid and the sun bright, purple and white phlox burst into bloom attracting butterflies of fancy and gentle ladybugs. As summer drew to a close in anticipation of fall, black-eyed rudbeckias stood defiantly tall among chrysanthemums. Tall trees lined the surrounding fences giving the garden welcome shade during the day. A thick, green hedge along one edge towered overhead; standing on tiptoes with arms outstretched, Grace could not touch the top leaves.

As the last foliage fell from the trees and brisk winds blew through their branches, Grace stared out her second-floor bedroom window searching the skies for the first signs of snow. Sometimes the skies offered only a tease, a mere flutter of flakes, which melted at the ground's touch. Eventually, the season advanced and winter could no longer be held at bay, clouds released their snowy loads and the fall garden suddenly became winter white. Trees glistened, their boughs weighted with tapered icicles. Drifting snow sculpted the ground creating a snowscape of hills and valleys set sparkling by the rays of the winter sun. A wand of winter magic waved throughout and left little untouched. Even the panes of Grace's window seemingly etched by an illustrator's hand became a frosty portrait of the wintry world outside. The garden was truly a private place, and although quite beautiful at times, it was still a place where she found herself alone. Time and time again.

On a cold, bright afternoon, Grace gazed through her window at the garden below. She unconsciously tugged on her left ear, a habit she had developed early on as a child when contemplating important decisions or absent-mindedly daydreaming. Grace was born with a small tag on her lobe. Curious about its origin, she asked her parents. They assured her it was a special birthmark — a pearl they called it — passed down through generations. It didn't really bother her, and didn't prevent her from getting her ears pierced; she hardly paid it any mind. However, it did offer a distraction when lost in thought, as now, staring out at the snow.

Sunlight bounced off white snow and made her squint. Every gust of wind sent snowflakes swirling in the wind until they rested again on hard-packed mounds. Even as a small child, the winter scenes that lay outside had always fascinated and intrigued her. Grace embraced all the beauty of the winter wonderland, and wished in her heart to be granted a place in such spectacular scenery. She knew, truth be told, the garden was not a welcoming place even in all this splendour. Cold, wet, and pierced by harsh winds — this was no place for a young girl, especially not without the proper attire of boots, a down suit, hat, scarf, and possibly a balaclava.

Grace left her post at the window and went on to other important distractions. Her CD collection had suffered a catastrophe: the case had toppled off her desk and disks lay haphazardly strewn on the floor. How she hated having to pick things up. It was so much easier to let her mother tidy up — or the housekeeper who came in once a week. Lately, her mother had begun to protest that Grace was old enough to tend to chores on her own, especially those concerning her room. There was a book report to finish, e-mails to send to friends, phone calls to make. And as night finally fell, the darkness of the sky spread out over the snow to change the landscape again.

After a few chapters of her latest read — a page-turning adventure novel set in exotic places — Grace switched off her light and snuggled deeply into the soft folds of her down duvet. Light spilled in from the transom window above her door and cast shadows ever so softly about her room. Curtains now drawn, hung motionless inside the frames of her windows shielding the night sky, and blocking the brightness sent by the full winter moon. In the dimness, Grace glanced about trying to make sense of shapes and figures that would share her sleep that night. Out of focus furniture stood without definition; figurines and stuffed animals sat in grey silhouette, their faces masked and without expression.

"Whatever," she yawned and drew up her covers. As she closed her eyes, the room disappeared and she quietly, gently slipped into sleep.

She dreamed the dreams of adventure: the same dreams that came to her over and over again had occurred more frequently of late. Strange and mysterious creatures appeared and faraway places shimmered into view hazily sketched. A storm was raging — a frenzied storm — with winds howling in an opaque, white squall. Someone was calling to her, calling her name over and over again. Always a feeling of great urgency accompanied these dreams and she could feel her heart racing as she succumbed to sleep. And just when she was about to drift into an even deeper slumber where dreams would not be remembered, she was pulled back — back into consciousness, back into her world; back into her room.

At first a distant tapping disturbed her silent surroundings. Growing stronger, the sound roused her awake and when she opened her eyes, her room materialized back into view. Grace uncurled in bed, sat up on her elbows and perused the shadows to pinpoint the source of what had caused her to wake. She cocked her head and strained to listen but the harder she tried, the fainter the sound. The moon now hung lower, sending through a sliver of light where the shade had separated from the window and where the tapping seemed to originate. Coaxed out of bed, Grace tiptoed toward the intrusive moonbeam, stopped mid-step and listened again. The tapping fell completely silent. Puzzled, Grace wrinkled her brow, then shrugged her shoulders and turned back toward her bed.

The moonbeam caught her eye once more and curiosity struck. Venturing toward the window she reached to draw the shade, but abruptly snatched back her hand. She wondered if something besides the winter night lurked on the other side of the glass. There was always an element of danger, a thrill of the unknown, in drawing back the drapes in the middle of the night. Overcoming her hesitation, Grace pulled back the curtains. The light of the moon spilled into her room.

Through frosted panes Grace peered into the night. The smoke-grey sky revealed only the brightest of stars winking at her. As she studied their brilliance, a silent wind shivered through the trees. Down below in the frigid garden silver mounds of fresh snow lay frozen, fixed in time, a snapshot of stillness.

Grace wasn't quite sure what she thought she might see: a flying elephant, a white unicorn grazing at the edge of the garden, or even a fire-breathing dragon hungry for the blood of a young girl. The harder she looked, the less there was to see. Everything appeared in its rightful place; nothing extraordinary called for attention. Quite simply, the spectacle was just a typical winter scene in the middle of the night observed by a small face through a pane of glass.

Suddenly, the wind gathered pace. No longer a lingering breeze, it raced through the garden at alarming speeds. Gusts of bitter, cold air violently shook elms and maples, flailing branches about their trunks. Whipped into a glittering frenzy, snowflakes began to ascend from softly moulded beds, climbing higher and higher until they reached Grace's window. The flurry of flakes halted mid-air; Grace watched in astonishment as they blended together as if under the direction of some invisible snow-magician's wand.

At first an outline took shape. Turrets appeared atop towers. Arched windows opened in walls. A spire shot toward the moon. Wall-walks criss-crossed the sky and drum towers sprouted along the perimeter and at each corner of the keep.

Within moments, a castle of snow hung in the air, floating and shimmering in the moonlight. In awe, Grace stepped back and traced the shape of the castle with the tip of her finger. Gasping with delight, she rushed to the window and threw open the sash. A blast of chilled air slapped at her checks as she basked in the celestial structure's splendour.

"It's a castle," she whispered. "A castle made of snow." As the last of her words left her lips, the castle suddenly dropped from the sky scattering snowflakes back down to the garden floor. The wind died away and the trees again stood their posts; their branches made still by the forfeit of breeze. All at once, the garden settled as it had been.

Grace surveyed the landscape searching for remnants of what she had just witnessed, but found none. "Where did it go?" she asked the winter sky as she peered into the night searching for a sign — any sign — that would help her understand the strange apparition presented to her. The garden lay docile, silent and frozen, glistening in the moonlight. She scanned snow banks, tracing the mounds with her eyes along the edge of the garden to the back fence and around to the other side. She travelled up tree trunks through leafless branches to the tip of the tallest bough. Up and beyond, the night sky loomed dark and imposing, a vast ocean sprinkled with points of light.

Where Grace lived, December days are the shortest of the year. Light fades quickly in the afternoon, surrendering early to evening dusk. Silently, darkness spreads over the landscape, and with each passing hour, night takes its rightful place in the order of the day. On a clear night, even the most distant stars send their brilliance to brighten the sky, magically twinkling and winking, waiting to grant first-sighting wishes. Sometimes a star will appear one night, be gone the next, and return on the morrow. And sometimes a star if studiously watched will move mysteriously from place to place, then walk through the heavens at a snail's pace to return to its original spot. Stars may be a curious and playful lot, but rarely do they assemble together for a celestial dance.

The sky's smoky greyness suddenly dissolved: it was replaced by a canopy so black that even the most distant stars flickered brightly in the pitch dark. Grace cocked her head and studied the stars more closely. Some gathered in clusters sending to earth a misty brilliance; others stood alone piercing their mantle with a single spark. The longer Grace wandered the night sky, the more she could see. Stars appeared in places previously vacant. Singles doubled and then tripled. Clusters spread farther and wider. Every time Grace blinked, stars multiplied until finally she could see more light than night.

"What's happening?" Grace whispered as she leaned further into the windowsill. She watched the heavens transform as stars, graceful and silent, circled in a gentle whirlwind of light. One by one, each star fell into place just as the snowflakes had minutes before. Slowly the illustration took shape. The stars' shimmering tails soon became clear; like the focusing of a camera lens, what was once a blur now became sharp.

The castle was of gigantic proportions, filling the sky as far as Grace could see. Above her, turrets glistened and shimmered against the dark night, and with each brick and finial sketched in such detail, Grace marvelled at their construction.

"Another castle, why?" she asked the stars, "What does it mean?"

Again the stars began to dance, erasing the castle, and a new drawing emerged. With meticulous attention, each star took to its post, winking and blinking at Grace along the way. A long rectangular panel appeared. Two bold arms swept down from the centre sides of the panel and turned downward to form cabriole legs with claw-and-ball feet. From the centre came a second panel that lay flat between the arms. Embedded in the back of the chair, hundreds of stars clustered together to form a large, facetted diamond, and their combined brilliance caused Grace to shade her eyes.

"Is that a chair?" Grace said.

From the diamond cluster, a star stream escaped and drew a circular band with strands of glitter forming triangular peaks that zigzagged around its circumference. Finally, the circlet rested at the top-centre of the chair and waited for Grace's reaction.

"It's a crown of stars," she whispered. "Why put a crown above a chair?" Suddenly she knew, "because it's not just a chair," she said out loud, "it's a throne!"

As soon as Grace spoke, the illustration faded. Smoky greyness returned, seeping forward to once again dominate the heavens. Slowly the stars journeyed back to their original places in the sky, some winking out of sight. Grace caught her breath when she realized the show was over. She searched the night sky hoping for more clues to this magical mystery and found none. The message had been sent; now it was up to Grace to figure it all out.

She closed the window, rearranged her curtains and returned to her bed. "It's just the freakiest thing," she whispered to herself as she drew her knees up under her chin and hugged her legs. "It's like the snow and stars were sending me clues — only clues to what?"

Slowly her bedroom door opened, spilling in light from the hallway, and Grace's mother's face appeared in the doorway.

"Honey, why are you still up?" she asked as she walked into the room. "And why are you talking to yourself?'

"Mom!" Grace cried. "You should have seen it — the stars and the snow. They made a picture of a castle and then a royal throne with a diamond in it and a crown on top. Right outside in the sky."

"Snowflakes and stars made a picture of a castle and a throne? In the sky?" her mother repeated as she drew back the drape. She peered through Grace's window. "I don't see anything."

"Oh, it's gone now," Grace said matter-of-factly. "But it was really there. I saw it."

"Well, it sounds quite fascinating. You know, it's really time for you to go to sleep."

Grace crawled into bed and snuggled deeply under the covers as her mother drew up the bedclothes under her chin.

"You don't believe me, do you Mom?"

Her mother sat down on the bed and wrapped her arms around her daughter. "Well, I don't know what to believe. If you look hard enough you can draw pictures by joining stars. That's how constellations were made."

"It was more than that!" Grace insisted.

"Okay, okay, maybe it was, except now it's time to dream about castles and thrones," said her mother. She leaned forward and kissed Grace on the cheek. "It's time for sleep. I love you. Good night."

"Okay, Mom, good night." She gently yawned her words then closed her eyes.

In fact, Grace was more tired than she realized. When her mother softly padded out of her room, she rolled over in bed. For the second time that night, she allowed herself to drift away and again her dreams were filled with strange visions. A tiny voice inside her head consciously took notice. Twice in a row was unusual. Again she questioned the sudden frequency of these reoccurring intrusions. What bothered her most were the images she couldn't clearly see. Never could she grasp their meaning, nor could she define the curious apparitions that dodged in and out, their true form floating on the edges of her mind's sight.

Chapter Two

In a world away and set in the distant past, a royal heir was fraught with dilemma. Ice Princess Farren glared out the paned windows of the royal apartments at the frozen landscape below. She was seething with anger: fists clenched, lower lip furled, arms crossed defiantly. A lone snowflake caught her eye. As it tossed about in the gentle breeze wafting through the castle, she vehemently resented the freedom it obviously enjoyed. On the odd occasions she had ventured from the castle without permission, the king had sent Searchers out in pursuit to drag her back, and each time a lengthy lecture on royal responsibility ensued.

King Roarke was a stern man of medium build with jet-black hair and dark eyes set on a serious face that softened rarely. Oh, how infuriating he could be.

Never one to have willingly embraced her royal status or partake in the rituals of her position, she was consistently butting heads with the king. Princess Farren simply hated all the pomp and circumstance that went along with her station. She had had her fill of lavish balls and elegant soirées, tedious processions and endless receiving lines. She found it all so empty and felt she was somehow empty herself.

Many would say she was much like her mother who had long ago also rebelled against her father, but apparently under much different circumstances. What was it about the royal line of women that they just didn't seem to want to follow the rules? At least her mother's father had been her real father and not a stepfather as in Farren's case. When pressed for information regarding her true parent, answers came few and far between. It was something that caused her mother great distress and she simply refused to discuss it.

With each passing year, the princess's curiosity concerning her birth father's disappearance increasingly consumed her. Who was he? What had happened to him and where had he gone? She thought she was old enough to learn the truth, but the secrecy surrounding her birth was impenetrable. It was a topic not only barred from discussion, it was also barred from thought by anyone living in the castle. She had even approached Saithe, the Librarian, who recorded the kingdom's history and would know for certain said information. Yet, he was as tight-lipped as any, shooing her out of the library on the pretext of problems over shelving.

In his determination to reform the Ice Princess, King Roarke's latest behest was by far the most extreme. She dreaded the journey she was about to begin. It would be many days of exhausting travel before she and her guide would reach the finishing school her father (rather her stepfather) had demanded she attend. Just the thought of enduring week after week of endless royal etiquette lessons from stuffy old socialites and prissy debutantes was something she didn't think she could bear. But the king had insisted; it was time she knew her place and her role as future queen.

Protesting her fate to her mother was futile. "Why must I do as he demands? I am not of his blood. What rightful claim has he?" she lamented. Although Queen Isolte sympathized with her daughter's pleas, she sided with the king. The queen had long since submitted to her husband's wishes, just as she had years ago with her own father. King Roarke was after all, the only father figure Farren had ever known. She must learn to accept and respect that — much like the queen.

As the snowflake settled on a frozen mound, melding with its kin and lying in wait for future gusts of wind to carry it off, Princess Farren's anger turned to desperation. Once at school, there would be no escaping. She would be watched, confined and under constant scrutiny. Leaving the grounds would be foolhardy; its location was far too remote and she would need a mount and provisions for several days' journey. Perhaps she could steal away in transit; she would be alone with the guide and could possibly slip out under some guise, but to what destination? As the idea swirled in her head mimicking the snow outside the frosted panes, King Roarke burst into her room.

"Thou shalt take thy leave on the morrow. Pack thy valises and make ready." King Roarke announced. "We shall ride together. I'll not chance thy delivery to the school by any other."

Before she could respond, he turned on his heel and stormed out of the room, slamming the door behind him. Her plans now dashed, Princess Farren's heart sank. There would be no chance of evading the king — a guide perhaps — but not the king. His leash would be reined tightly and his sights set on her at all times. Had she been a boy, she would have been sent off as a squire to apprentice as a knight. Surely the virtues of valour, charity and aiding the helpless were far more intriguing than the finer details of petit point and the laws of court. Her younger stepbrother, Ice Prince Owyn, would surely have such an opportunity and she envied his fate.

"Such will be mine undoing," she whispered to herself as she paced the royal apartment. An unhitched window banged against its frame, interrupting her thoughts, and as she wrestled it back into position, she paused. The beauty of the landscape spread out before her in icy splendour. Beyond the gatehouse, tall mountains rose up from the frozen ground glistening in the white sunlight, their peaks piercing low-lying clouds. Farther off in the distance, a meadow of tall, white grass rhythmically swayed — each blade covered in ice waving to her, beckoning. It led to a thick forest of ice-covered trees, their branches heavy with freshly fallen snow. Such was the scene outside her window and she found she could not look away.

This was her world: it was a world so much bigger and offering so much more than a finishing school ever could. Here she would find her way, and in an instant she realized what she was looking for. If he were truly out there somewhere, she would find him. With resolve in her heart, she set out on her first task. She had to run away to find her real father, or at least discover his fate, and why he had been lost to her for so many years.

Aside from the royal family — the king, the queen, the princess and the prince — the castle in the Kingdom of Connacht was home to many who followed the orders of the king to the letter. This left Farren little hope in plotting her escape, for anyone aiding and abetting a runaway princess would certainly provoke King Roarke's wrath. She had to find someone she could trust, someone who was willing to take the risk, someone like herself who had nothing to loose — like Ice Witch Mayme. As a child, Princess Farren had befriended the younger of two sisters. When she and Mayme were left together, their mischievous ways almost always meant trouble.

Both resident Ice Witches, the sisters were very different from each other as were their positions in the castle. The older

Ice Witch Amity was revered among the people and the court. Wielding great magical powers, infinite wisdom and an imposing presence when called upon, she was steadfast in her charge of assuring the castle's security from dark and evil forces. Yet she was also endowed with a gentle manner and a kindness of heart.

The younger Ice Witch Mayme was the complete opposite. Of lesser powers and with a much more caustic demeanour, she was relegated to the more menial magical tasks around the castle. Her resentment over her standing and of Witch Amity were ever apparent. So it was only natural and rather befitting that Princess Farren seek out Witch Mayme to engage her in a devious ploy.

"What is my reward in return for this favour?" Ice Witch Mayme demanded.

Princess Farren had anticipated her query and had come prepared. "Always in thy sister's shadow, might thee not wish to be free of the station thee find so unsavoury? Journey with me that we might find our new callings. Might thee not have a quest of thine own? I know I have." Princess Farren cajoled, hoping the Ice Witch was buying into her scheme.

"A quest of my own? I just might, but it would not entail traipsing all over the Ice World with you on yours. And just what quest might that be?" the witch asked.

"The quest is to find mine kin," she answered.

"A quest for your kin," Witch Mayme said in a sarcastic tone.

"For mine true father, of course," she replied and when Witch Mayme burst out in laughter, Farren was taken aback. "I hardly find that amusing."

Still chortling, Witch Mayme took Farren's chin in her hand and shook it. "You silly little princess. You really have no idea.

They still haven't told you of your mother's sordid past, have they? I really shouldn't be all that surprised."

"Mine mother's what?" Princess Farren was appalled at such language and yanked her chin free. "What sordid past?" she demanded. "What dost thy know?"

"Perhaps it is not my place to tell you," Witch Mayme replied. "Should be the queen's place, shouldn't it?" Although she had tolerated the princess over the years, she found that of all the royals, the princess was the least obnoxious. She was probably the only one the witch could call friend, and even that was stretching the word. Yet, her poisonous side couldn't help but show; it was a rather enjoyable experience watching Farren squirm, knowing she had struck a sensitive nerve.

Beside herself, Princess Farren could not fathom how Witch Mayme had kept such vital information from her after all these years, especially since she knew what it would have meant to her. There had been countless times when the two had snuck off in hiding and indulged in private conversations and assorted disclosures of things they weren't supposed to know. It galled her that after everything they had been through together — all the pranks and follies, the breaking of rules and the suffering of consequences when ultimately caught — they could not share this confidence? Was she a true friend or not? she wondered. "Could she even be trusted?"

"I demand to know," she cringed at the words she was about to speak. "What is this 'sordid past' thou art referring to?"

"Just that your patriarch was not of royal blood. That, and a few other details I might add," Witch Mayme replied with a slight patronizing tone.

Princess Farren winced at first. "Not of royal blood . . . " her voice trailed away. If she was only half royalty perhaps that could explain away her reluctance for being at court.

"So now you shall be indebted to me on two fronts. One in helping you escape, and the other in revealing your mother's past. My, my, Princess. This is going to be costly on your part."

Princess Farren needed more information. She scrutinized her now questionable ally and wondered what she could possibly have to offer as suitable compensation.

"Name thy price," she said defiantly.

Circling Farren, Witch Mayme drummed her forefinger against her cheek. "Hmmm. Now what might be appropriate concerning such a revelation? I have been sworn to secrecy for so long and to betray that oath would surely come with consequences. But since your situation appears dire, perhaps I could comply."

Princess Farren rolled her eyes at the witch's overly dramatic verbosity and wished she would just get to the point.

"My desire is to be granted an elevated status in this castle and kingdom," the witch responded. "For too long my station here has been secondary, overshadowed by my sister, and my position relegated to menial tasks of inconsequence — duties which are beneath me."

"But thy powers are limited," Princess Farren answered. "There's naught I can do to change that."

"That's where you are mistaken," the witch answered back. "As a royal you have the power to grant me the permission to call upon a spirit who can increase my powers."

"What spirit? I know not of one," Princess Farren questioned.

"Of course you don't. You're a royal not a witch. Such knowledge does not concern you."

Princess Farren weighed her options. On the one hand, the witch could help her escape — she carried valuable information about Farren's father and where she might begin her search. What could it hurt if Witch Mayme gained more powers? Might it not benefit the castle? Would she be doing her people a favour? On the other hand, without the witch she was doomed to exile at finishing school.

"This quest for new-found powers will be used for the betterment of the kingdom, I presume." Although Princess Farren was keen to the witch's ill temperament at times, she really didn't believe the witch was bad, a tad rebellious perhaps, but a surge in powers might just be the cure.

"Why Princess Farren, I feel it as an affront that you might question my motives," Witch Mayme replied, her words dripping with artificial innocence, knowing she had the princess in her clutches.

"Thy wish is granted. What must I do for this task to be complete?" Farren asked.

"You have already done so, by making the wish," the witch replied.

Princess Farren understood: it was the way of the Ice World to have wishes granted when done so with good intentions. "And news of mine father," she pressed. "Pray tell?"

"There's no time to explain. I need to prepare." The witch reached into her cloak's pocket and withdrew an object, squeezed it in her hand, and whispered an incantation. "Don't fret, Princess, take this charm. Its powers will show you all you wish to know in the form of a dream," she lied as she handed the princess a dark crystal amulet set on a simple chain. Knowing it contained only a portion of the events that had occurred years ago, she thought the amulet was a convincing touch. Royals were always so impressed with enchanted trinkets. That it held far more powerful enchantments endowed by the witch was not something she chose to share with the girl.

"We must make haste. The time is nigh. Await another day and we are lost, for the king expects to leave on the morrow," said Princess Farren, urgency rising in her voice.

"Agreed. Make ready. I shall avert the attention of the castle when the time is right," Witch Mayme proposed, her eyes becoming dark slits as she devised her plan.

"With what means and by what signal?" questioned Princess Farren.

"The calling of the spirit will be the diversion needed to make your escape," she answered. "You will know when it is safe to flee. Slip out the gatehouse and head for the meadow and the forest beyond. The king will not suspect that you have departed and it will be many hours before your leave is noticed." Witch Mayme knew he would be furious with her, but that wasn't anything new. Besides, with what she had in store, King Roarke's temper really wouldn't matter at all. Just the thought of usurping her sister was reward enough.

"Now go! Go!"

Chapter Three

Returning to the royal apartments, Princess Farren began the tedious ritual of packing. Since the staff was privy to her journey and destination, her actions went without suspicion. She freely sought their assistance in accumulating the appropriate items for her travel and stay at the school. When the last trunk snapped shut and the chambermaids left her alone, she quickly reopened her bags. Selecting a few articles she deemed necessary, she stuffed them into a smaller satchel — one that could be carried on her back.

Downstairs in the kitchen, she requested provisions from the larder, a request perfectly natural for one about to embark on a journey. That she insisted on taking them with her to her room and not retrieve them at the onset of her trip the next day might have roused some suspicion, but didn't. Cass, the Mistress Baker was used to inexplicable eccentricities from the royals. What did get noticed was Farren's mood. She appeared nervous and jumped anxiously on approach. Again, the explanation could be attributed to her impending trip and being exiled to the school. Who wouldn't be apprehensive facing such an arrested future?

A knock on her door gave her a start. Was it the king checking up on her? Had she been found out? Instead, when she called "Enter," her younger stepbrother, Owyn appeared. Aside from her mother, he was the one she most regretted leaving. Deceiving him was even more torturous; she simply couldn't confide in him despite wanting to. Unlike his sister, the Ice Prince embraced the royal life and strove to achieve his father's approval. There was no point in having him caught up in her deception. It would serve no purpose and only enrage the king even more if he was a party to the scheme.

"Thou shalt be deeply missed," Prince Owyn said softly as he sat down beside her on the settee.

Tears welled up in Farren's eyes and she struggled to keep them in check. "Know this. We shall be together again. I know not when, but I pledge to thee a day will come when we will be reunited. I shall carry thee in mine thoughts always."

"Perchance I might visit, should father allow it," he said hopefully, causing her even more anguish, as she knew he could never reach her. This ruse stabbed her heart; she was mindful that her actions would also stab his.

"Perchance," she whispered softly as she embraced him. Liar; deceiver; sham. These were not labels she was proud of, since it would be Prince Owyn who would suffer most from knowing of her uncharitable attributes. Would he ever be able to trust her again after such a betrayal?

Shouts rose up from the courtyard and sailed through the open windows of the royal apartments. Startled out of their embrace, the Ice Prince and Princess rushed over to the window to see what commotion was taking place below at the far end of the courtyard. Castle folk and labourers left their posts to see what was causing such a stir.

"'Tis Ice Witch Mayme," said Prince Owyn leaning through the window. "I must advise the king. Come along."

"No, go on ahead. I shall catch up," resisted Princess Farren as she squeezed his hand one last time.

As Prince Owyn bolted out the door, Princess Farren snatched up her satchel, threw on a hooded white cloak and slipped out into the hallway. She headed for the turret stairwell that would lead down to the grounds outside the east wing. From there it was only a short distance to the gatehouse, and she stealthily dashed across the lawn to the arched doorway. Her heart was in her throat and her pulse raced. Beads of sweat surfaced on her skin and in the palms of her hands as she pressed on through the gatehouse's corridor and across the moat. Not once did she look back, not even for a momentary glimpse of what Witch Mayme was doing to cause this distraction. She bolted recklessly. Snow flew from under her churning footsteps. Her body braced against a hampering wind as she made her way from the castle and toward the meadow. Once amid tall grass she would be virtually undetectable from afar: her cloak served as camouflage in an ocean of white stalks.

Only after she had reached the forest beyond the meadow would she find shelter under the trees and rest. The canopy of woven branches offered protection, a place where she could feel safe enough to begin the journey to uncover the mystery of the past.

Many hours had passed, and she wondered how quickly her disappearance had been detected. Confident that the distance between where she hid and the castle was great enough, she took a well-needed break. Tucked under a copse of trees, Princess Farren decided to make camp. From the satchel she retrieved a thick slice of peasants' bread, and a chunk of cheese and ravenously fell on the meagre provisions. Afterwards, she curled up against the trunk of a tree and retrieved the amulet strung around her neck. She gripped it firmly, closed her eyes and fell under its spell.

A dream edged into her unconscious mind: Princess Farren stood in the middle of a wide valley under an enormous white sky which stretched so far and high that she felt terribly tiny, like a single flake in a blizzard of snow beneath it. A large white Glider appeared covered in ice-tipped feathers with a wingspan reaching double its size. As the magnificent bird sailed gracefully between mountain peaks, its call trailed behind. Softly within her dream she heard a voice, that of Ice Witch Mayme: *Follow the path of the Glider and you shall find clues to your quest within this valley. Look for the one known as the Guardian and for the creature he once watched over.*

Princess Farren studied the valley searching for signs of recognition that might aid her in finding this place. Although she had not travelled extensively, she had studied her world's terrain in great length and knew the placement of mountain ranges, valleys and seas. The Glider soared back into view and dipped its magnificent wings as it flew by. Slowly the image faded to black.

Farren's eyelids fluttered awake. She stared blankly at the amulet in her hand as if expecting it to speak. When it didn't, she angrily stuffed it back under her shirt. Thinking she had been played a fool, Farren chided herself for having trusted the witch. She could only imagine what her side of the bargain had allowed the witch to produce. However, what was done was done; nothing she could do would change that.

Armed with these few clues, her determination to find the valley and learn of her parentage had never been stronger. She gathered her things, crawled through the thicket and headed deeper into the forest, eager to distance herself farther from the castle.

Chapter Four

Few could remember a worse day in the history of the castle. It was troubling enough that the younger Ice Witch had conjured a catastrophe which plunged the Kingdom of Connacht into darkness. One of the royals was missing. It was feared that when Witch Mayme had suddenly vanished she might have taken Princess Farren along as hostage.

The king momentarily entertained such a thought, but he knew his stepdaughter well enough to suspect the timing was just a little too convenient, given it was the eve of her departure to finishing school, a place Princess Farren highly objected going to. He surmised that she had probably slipped away undetected during all of the commotion. It wouldn't have been the first time, he mused. She was a rebellious child who paid scant attention to her role as a royal and was always getting into some sort of trouble.

Farren in cahoots with the Ice Witch would come as no surprise to the king so he dispatched two Searchers to make chase and find her — just in case. With that taken care of, there were more pressing concerns to be addressed. King Roarke toured the castle with Ice Witch Amity assessing the damage, and chiding himself for not heeding the warning signs the Watchers had foreseen.

"There is no predicting how long this may last," Witch Amity said, gravely referring to the dark cloud hanging over the castle, blocking out the rays of the sun. "It's fortunate I was able to stop my sister from causing further damage but I have not the powers to disperse this cloud. The evil from which it came is too dark and must be allowed to recede on its own."

King Roarke looked at her with a puzzled expression, one that caused his eyebrows to rise and wrinkle his forehead. Enchantments and their consequences were not his strongest suit. Such matters were the witch's dominion and he looked to her for guidance.

"To meddle further may prove more catastrophic," she explained. "But I can contain it with a protective veil which will guard against further threat. Meanwhile . . . "

King Roarke nodded in agreement. The situation was grave and harsh measures were needed to insure his kingdom's survival. He had already met with council and advised his subjects on the next course of action.

"Send word to the Watchers. I trust they will be sympathetic and not penalize mine oversight. Dispatch Seekers upon their ready," said King Roarke. "A Guardian must be found. I must tend to the queen."

He turned and headed toward the royal apartments where Queen Isolte had taken to her bed, distraught with anxiety over the disappearance of her daughter, and the prospect of a loved one lost. If only she hadn't sided with her husband so often in dismissing her daughter's concerns. Farren was so much like she had been as a girl, cut with a rebellious slant, and the queen feared she might suffer gravely when left to her own devices. By allowing her husband to dispense disciplinary measures Isolte was relieved of having to chastise the girl, something she found very difficult to do.

"What news, my lord?" she asked, drying her eyes as he approached the bed. She had become a fragile creature of late;

her once formidable stature had fallen victim to past circumstances and although she still retained her beauty, its lustre had dulled.

"No word as yet," he answered taking her hand in his own. "Searchers have only just departed. It will take time." King Roarke loved his wife very much and it pained him to see her so distraught. Knowing what he was about to tell her would only add to her suffering, he hesitated briefly, searching for the right words.

"There lies no other choice. The kingdom is in peril," he said softly, "I have sent for a Guardian."

The mere mention of the title sent tears streaming down Isolte's face and she folded into her husband's arms, quietly weeping. All he could do was offer comfort and solace in her despair, holding her until she had cried herself to sleep.

Away from the castle and the extraordinary events of the day, Princess Farren was making progress. As she wove her way between ice-frosted trees, she played the dream over and over again in her head. "A Guardian, mine father was a Guardian?" She was keenly aware of what a Guardian was: centuries ago, at the dawn of the Ice World, the powerful white sun who nourished the land sent slips of light, Watchers, to other worlds to seek out them out. There, Watchers read souls and selected only those whose hearts were deemed pure of evil to serve — should ever a threat befall the Ice World. Once found, Watchers marked each Guardian with a talisman, one that appeared in many different forms depending on what they guarded. Over the years, many lay dormant (and many still do) until the time of their calling. Princess Farren had heard many stories heralding their cunning but had yet to meet one. Moreover, that her own father might have been one was truly baffling. It's no wonder her mother was so tight-lipped on the subject. Such a union would have indeed caused scandal among royal circles and would explain the absence of royal blood the witch had alluded to as something in "her mother's sordid past." The more she pieced it together, the more it made sense. Her mother's rebellion at a young age . . . the secrecy surrounding her birth . . . her own reluctance at being a royal . . . her stepfather's surly attitude and strict temperament toward her. "But a Guardian?" It was just so farfetched that it might just be true.

A break in the forest canopy offered Princess Farren an overhead view and, as she searched the sky to find her bearings, a Glider circled above her — its shrill cry announcing its arrival. Was it a mere coincidence that one had also appeared in her dream or had Witch Mayme made good on her promise by sending a guide? She wondered if she was so desperate that she would follow any sign, any clue that might point her in the right direction? In any event, she would need a better vantage point and headed for the crest of a hill a short distance away. Reaching the top, the vista stretched out before her without boundaries, a panorama of the Ice World as far as the eye could see showcasing snow-capped mountain peaks and valleys, frosted fields and meadows broken by frozen lakes and meandering ice-laden rivers. Somewhere within this vast landscape lay the valley from her dream. Never had she felt so small and insignificant or the quest she had chosen so dauntingly huge.

When the Glider called again, carried by the wind chasing over the landscape, she turned to answer. "Am I to follow?" Princess Farren shouted as it crested the hill and headed west. It tipped its wings, this time with such obvious exaggeration it confirmed her suspicion that coincidence was not at play here; the Glider must be a courier sent by the witch.

"I am to follow." Armed with the knowledge that at last she had a direction to follow, and judging that it would take a day's journey to reach the valley, her spirits lifted.

Trekking through fields thick with snow soon proved tiresome, and when she happened upon a road carved into the frozen ground, she welcomed the change of pace. Not knowing how often the road might be frequented, Princess Farren often glanced backward and strained to hear approaching travellers who might recognize her.

After a few miles, the road took a sharp turn and she rounded the corner heading toward a small inn tucked into a grove of trees. A group of horses, their reins tethered to a hitching post, restlessly stamped their hooves in the snow waiting for riders to return. From their numbers Princess Farren deduced that the inn was probably quite full. Not wanting to attract attention to herself, she pulled the hood of her cloak over her head to conceal her face and turned her shoulders away from the inn as she attempted to slip by. Suddenly, the heavy door of the entrance swung open and two men walked outside, both laden with heavy packs and stuffed satchels — obviously merchants selling their wares. Princess Farren quickly dodged out of sight and pinned herself against the side of the building breathlessly awaiting their leave.

"We'll have to turn back," she overheard one of the men say. "Word has it from the innkeeper that the castle to the east has suffered some sort of destruction."

"Just our bad luck, being stuck with all these stores," the other man replied. "I hoped we could have unloaded them there. But there's no getting in or out, the castle has been sealed by one of the witches' spells."

Princess Farren couldn't believe her ears. Her castle was to the east. Was that the castle they referred to? And one of the witches? She knew of few castles in the area that afforded two Ice Witches. One was the standard. A wave of dread washed over her as Farren's thoughts turned dark at the mention of the words "destruction and spells."

"We won't be back this way anytime soon," one merchant announced gruffly, heaving the packs onto the sides of a saddled horse. "It'll take years to rebuild — if that's even possible."

His companion nodded, untied the reins from the post and hoisted himself onto the back of his mount. With a swift kick to their flanks, both horses bolted past Princess Farren still glued to the wall, her presence remaining undetected.

A wave of dread crashed over her as she emerged from hiding, wishing the men had said more. Whatever Ice Witch Mayme had done was obviously quite grave and Princess Farren shuddered knowing that she was partly responsible. She desperately needed to uncover the fate of her people and the downfall of the castle. If the merchants were correct and the castle was under a spell barring entry, she couldn't very well turn back to find out. No, she would have to discover the truth on her own. Might she risk asking the innkeeper since it was apparently he who had broken the unsavoury news? But how could she explain her presence there? Although unusual, it wasn't completely uncommon for a girl her age to travel unaccompanied. However, her dress and speech would surely give her away and she chided herself for not having thought of such things before running away. Pinching a maid's cape would have been easy enough had it occurred to her at the time, but it hadn't and now she was without disguise.

Aside from the two merchants, no one else had quit the inn and it was still rather crowded from the looks of things. As she made her way to the back of the building, voices trailed through an open window and she inched up to peek inside. The common room was quite large and lined with long tables. Seated in heavy, mismatched chairs the inn's clientele was made up of merchants and a few travellers enjoying the simple fare offered up from the kitchen. Unable to make out conversations, Princess Farren eased over to the back door of the pantry and cautiously slipped inside, her heart pounding much as when she had fled the castle.

There was little fear of being heard — the common room was noisy enough — only of being seen. As she moved along the corridor she noticed a collection of cloaks hanging from wall pegs. The cloaks were simple in design and without ornament and far more suitable as a disguise considering her environment. She slipped the closest one off its hanger and replaced it with her own. At least now she would blend in a little better, and even though she hoped its owner would be pleased with the exchange, she couldn't help but add thief to her unbecoming resumé.

Fortunately the room was dimly lit and crowded with customers busy with one another. She managed to make her way to a chair in a darkened corner of the room unnoticed. She could barely see out from under the hood of her newfound cloak, but it didn't really matter since she was there to listen not to watch. Fragments of conversation drifted her way but none mentioned the subject of the castle and its demise. Fearing that she might have to adopt a bolder approach and risk her identity, the choice was suddenly made for her.

"It would appear you are attempting a particularly difficult feat," whispered a voice from out of the dim, startling her and causing her to turn to the source. "Invisibility is one of the toughest, you know. And you're not doing a very good job of it."

Still in shadow, the man speaking to her had yet to show his face and Princess Farren sensed he had not done so on purpose. Could this possibly be someone in a similar situation, someone who also pursued anonymity and could be trusted? Her experience with outsiders was limited and her first reaction was to flee, but the need to know the fate of her home was overwhelming and, naively, she took a chance.

"Mine lord, what tidings hast thee from the castle to the east?" She said, immediately aware of the mistake she had just made: speaking like a royal was a huge blunder.

"Ah, the Kingdom of Connacht. Most unfortunate," he answered in hushed tones. "Rumour has it a particularly rebellious royal has vanished around about the same time a particularly nefarious Ice Witch caused its demise."

"Pray tell, how and what damage was fraught?" There was no point in masquerading her dialect now, so she spoke freely.

"Not sure. The castle is sealed."

Princess Farren nodded remembering what the merchant outside had said.

"But Searchers have been spotted along the back roads looking for the missing royal."

Princess Farren cringed at his words.

Sensing her anxiety he leaned in closer and whispered, "Now what ransom might the king pay as reward for returning a lost princess?"

"Good sir, I beseech thee," she pleaded, instantly regretting the decision to engage this man. "Hold thy tongue and give me not away."

"Now that's where you're wrong. I am not a good man," he answered briskly. "I should like to line my purse with Roarke's silver."

Princess Farren bolted out of her chair and charged through the common room, jostling guests out of her way and anything else that barred her route to the front door. The man followed behind, but she was smaller and faster and able to weave her way without causing too much of a disturbance.

"Stop her, stop her," he shouted as he attempted to push through. However, his sheer bulk offended the customers already caught off guard, and they were not as accommodating when jostled a second time.

Princess Farren flew through the front door of the inn and, as she steered toward the road, she crossed into the path of two Searchers on horseback.

There was nowhere to run, nowhere to hide. Caught by surprise, both horses reared up on hind legs, their fore hooves dangerously pawing the air before crashing down to the frozen ground, narrowly missing her. Princess Farren fell backwards onto the road recoiling in fear at being trampled and angry she had been caught. Not that she was fearful of Searchers, they were honourable men who served their king well and would not harm her, but their stature and manner of dress was still rather menacing. Thick, heavy, white robes lay across their broad shoulders and billowed out behind revealing rough riding chaps and sturdy boots to the knee. Doublets made of coarse wool yielded to gauntlet gloves, and even the wide brims of the hats shading their faces seemed imposing.

One Searcher, his black hair pulled back and tied in a knot, exposed a dark, weathered face and hardened features. The other paled in comparison, with a long, dishevelled, white mane framing a softer expression; a façade made false by his piercing eyes. These were not men of finery or of the court, but they knew well the roads and terrain and the lay of the land and what was expected of them.

Princess Farren picked herself up and brushed the snow from her cloak as both Searchers dismounted and approached. Before they could exchange words, the Glider appeared out of nowhere — its cry distracting, before plunging downward, snatching her shoulders in its talons and carrying her away.

She wailed in terror, as she was lifted higher and higher, her legs dangling beneath her and her shoulders smarting from the pierce of the Glider's sharp claws. The Searchers stood helplessly below, bewilderment splashed across their faces as they watched their charge disappear from view. The king would not be pleased with their failure to contain the young princess and they expected their reputations to suffer as well.

Princess Farren soon discovered that she was securely anchored in the Glider's grip and would not fall. After a few harrowing moments, she managed to open her eyes and look down at the Searchers diminishing below. There was no question now of the Glider's commission and it certainly solved her travel dilemma, although it would have been much less disturbing had she been forewarned. The witch's voice in the dream had said to follow the Glider's path but there was no mention of a sudden abduction. What other surprises were attached to the witch's amulet, she wondered, grateful she had eluded capture. The Glider coasted effortlessly through rolling, white clouds in the direction of a distant valley nestled between two mountain peaks.

Chapter Five

Under the cover of darkness now shrouding the castle, the shadowy figure of a dark Stalker easily slipped in, out, and about the castle buildings. Her opaque form undetected, she eavesdropped on private conversations and snippets of gossip along the way. Such trivialities were not her mission — although they did prove rather entertaining. It was the exchange between Ice Witch Amity and King Roarke that the Stalker sought. Finally in range, she listened intently, committing each word to memory. When the two finally parted — their tête-à-tête complete — the Stalker abandoned the castle and headed back to her mistress.

On the other side of the mountain between two hills, a narrow opening offered a secret refuge, one that Ice Witch Mayme had frequented in order to practice spells that her sister had forbidden. The camouflage of the ice gorge had served her well — never once had she been discovered. She paced the frozen floor impatiently waiting for the Stalker to return with news. There was no doubt in her mind that King Roarke must be up to something and if she was going to get the upper hand, she had to know of his plans. She might not be able to stop him, but she could counter his measures in any number of ways.

The Stalker slid down across the wall of the gorge, her darkness rippling over the slippery slope and her shape gaining length as it crossed the rays of the sun before returning to her true height — that of her mistress.

"Well Snitch, what have you heard?" Witch Mayme demanded, her wits frayed and still smarting after her sister's interference.

"The castle is still in darkness," Snitch hissed. "Just the way I like it."

"I can do without your personal observations," Witch Mayme responded, imitating the Stalker's manner of speech.

Being intimately acquainted with the witch's true disposition, Snitch refrained from any further digression and began: "The king has sent out Searchers after the princess. The queen has taken to her chambers and the people of the castle are in upheaval."

"Yes, yes, that I could have surmised. What of the king's plans and my sister?" she interrupted impatiently.

"King Roarke has sent word to Watchers for a Guardian," Snitch answered. "Seekers will be sent to aid in the search." From the witch's expression, it looked as though she was about to explode. A thick vein popped out and throbbed on her forehead, while her eyes narrowed and chased from side to side in their sockets.

She pounded one hand with the other clenched fist.

"Sent for a Guardian, has he?" she fumed as she calculated her next move. "That will take time," her mood brightening at the notion. "Oh yes, that will take time and that works in our favour."

Witch Mayme reached for her satchel and retrieved a small pouch. "Follow the Seekers. Whoever they dust with their powder, do likewise with this," she said, handing it to Snitch. "Was there anything else of use that you heard?"

"Your sister has cast a protective veil over the castle," Snitch answered. "One not easily penetrated."

"Yes, I noticed. The passageway from the castle to this gorge has been sealed," she said angrily, "and I will have to find an alternative route. Anything else?"

"Just one small thing. Unimportant really," Snitch stalled. "King Roarke has renamed you."

"Renamed me?" She asked, wondering if she should be flattered or annoyed. "What's my new name?"

Snitch hesitated. The delay further agitated the witch. "Spit it out or I will douse you with so much light, you'll vanish forever."

The witch's threat was not lost on Snitch and she quickly complied. "The king has renamed you the Evil Ice Witch," she hissed, expecting the worst. Instead, the witch shrieked in laughter, her howls echoing off the gorge's walls and back.

"The Evil Ice Witch! How imaginative! So what's my sister's name? The Nice Ice Witch?" The epiphany sent her deep into hysterics and just when it seemed she might lapse into convulsions, she took a deep breath and her howls tapered to mere cackles. Snitch, befuddled, hovered in anticipation, unsure of whether to carry out her orders immediately or await further instructions. Evil Ice Witch Mayme's temperament was so unpredictable; there was just no telling what would set her off in any direction. Serving her was indeed a challenge.

Recovering from her bout of histrionics, Evil Ice Witch Mayme turned her concerns to other matters. She dismissed the Stalker, sending her off to follow Seekers and once alone, she began to formulate her next course of action. If she was ever to gain power over the Kingdom of Connacht she would have devise a more elaborate scheme. The Ice Princess was key.

Controlling Farren's wishing-powers would better the outcome; the witch would ultimately achieve her goals. Or so she thought.

Withdrawing an amulet from beneath her cloak — a twin to one she had given the girl — she said to herself, "Where are you, my Princess?" For the witch, a trance was unnecessary for the charm to work. Her powers of enchantment allowed her to see the secrets it possessed while fully alert. It revealed Princess Farren's progress to date: her flight from the castle, the encounter at the inn, the clash with Searchers and finally the Glider's timely rescue.

The Glider descended and released its grip before soaring back up into the clouds, its cry piercing the air once again. Princess Farren dropped gently to the ground amid ramshackle cabins and abandoned buildings that lay strewn in shambles, their inhabitants long gone and, from the look of things, not likely to return any time soon.

"What place is this?" she asked herself as she searched the deserted village for signs of life. She peered through broken windows at vacant rooms scattered with debris and broken furniture. Doorless entrances gaped at her and the walls that held them crumbled at her touch. Never had she seen such demolition. She was accustomed to the finery of the castle and wondered what circumstance might have caused this. It was apparent that this was once a flourishing hamlet — until catastrophe had struck.

"Not from around here, I'll chance?"

Startled, Princess Farren spun around at the sound of a rasping voice coming from behind her. A haggard woman withdrew from the shadows of a doorway and stood where she could see her.

"I beg thy pardon?" said Princess Farren politely. "Dost thou reside here?"

The woman nodded and limped over, depending on a weathered walking stick for support. Slightly bent forward, her measure proved small and feeble, hardly more than skin and bones. Deep wrinkles lining her face indicated a long life of worry, and under her eyes, their twinkle long faded, dark circles made her look all the more weary and spent.

"I am one of the last. All the others left years ago," she said brandishing a pointed forefinger as she spoke.

"The others?" Princess Farren pressed further, noting a peculiar odour as she drew near. "What happened to cause such a departure?"

"The wrath of an enemy once known as a friend," she barked, her voice thick with wheeze. "What brings a fine lady like yourself to this wretched place? The last one who ventured here ignited our downfall, so you can understand why I am mindful of strangers. I have had my fill of misfortune through the years through no fault of my own. It is a plague passed down from generation to generation."

"Fear not. I seek only answers and have been directed to this valley to find them," Princess Farren said, hoping to reassure the decrepit hag that her intentions were honourable.

"This valley has only one claim to fame and that died away ages ago." She spat out in between coughs. " It dates back to the time of the Guardian and . . . "

"Guardian?" Princess Farren blurted out. "It is of the Guardian that I seek tidings. Pray tell, if there is anything thou canst share with me, I would be most grateful."

The woman scrutinized the stranger. There was something familiar about the girl. With a flick of her stick, she motioned to the princess' satchel, prompting Farren to reveal the provisions within. Farren eagerly complied and hoped the offer might be exchanged for the information she sought.

"Bring your fare to my table and I will tell all that I know," she said as she shuffled back to her hovel, Princess in tow. "Fair warning. You might not like what you hear."

Back in the ice gorge, Evil Ice Witch Mayme harkened to hear what the haggard woman would share concerning the Guardian and the events of the past. Never having been privy to all the details surrounding Princess Farren's birth, only rumour and conjecture had gotten her this far; to learn first hand could only add to her store of ammunition against the royal family. What she hadn't expected to hear was the beginning to a gripping tale of a precious stone long lost. One that would ultimately become an obsession and a pursuit she would strive to complete.

"The Ice Princess wasn't mistaken," she said to herself. "It appears that I do have a quest of my own."

Chapter Six

The Kingdom of Connacht still lay shrouded in darkness and the constant gloom of the surroundings weighed heavily upon those who lived there. Cracks in the castle walls gave way to crumbling blocks. The courtyard gardens — once overflowing with foliage of all kinds — withered with the lack of nourishing white sunlight. Trees in the orchard stood bare, their branches leafless and fruitless. In the royal stables, stallions and mares restlessly paced their darkened stalls. Without the energizing rays of the Ice World's white sun, the kingdom quickly fell into ruin. King Roarke tried desperately to keep up appearances and buoy the spirits of his people, but it became increasingly difficult as time wore on.

Although Seeker after Seeker had failed to bring home news of finding a Guardian, one finally did return from a world away, and her discovery there brought hope. Little did the kingdom realize how profound this would prove, for not only had she found someone bearing a Watchers' mark, but one also linked to the kingdom's past. When Queen Isolte learned of the Guardian's mark, she fell further into despair and King Roarke felt certain she was lost to him.

"The burden of this secret is unbearable," she cried. "The past is haunting the present and I fear for the future."

King Roarke knew that to further the ruse would prove the queen's undoing. She had already suffered too long in silence and desperately needed the care and understanding of her people to lift the guilt and sorrow in her heart.

"I have not the power to grant thy salvation," King Roarke regretfully said to his wife. "But perchance I might ease thy anguish." He assembled a cast of those closest to the queen: Ice Witch Amity, Prince Owyn, and Librarian Saithe to record the history.

"With news of the Guardian found and by the mark made by Watchers, it would appear that this Guardian holds a station far more influential than first surmised," King Roarke began, the topic surprising all who were present.

"My lord," said Ice Witch Amity, breaking the silence that followed his shocking announcement. "What does this mean?"

"Quite simply, this Guardian has ties to the kingdom and the Royal Family," he replied. "If such is the case, it is even more pressing that we guide this Guardian to our kingdom without fail."

"Why pressing, Father?" Prince Owyn asked.

"Should Witch Mayme discover this connection, she will gain an advantage over the Guardian if they ever meet in combat," answered Witch Amity, aware of the tricks her sister would employ. "The reason Watchers choose Guardians off-world is because it ensures an element of surprise. The enemy knows not its opponent and cannot prepare an effective assault."

"We must ensure that this Guardian is fully prepared and when the time comes to make the calling, the Guardian must feel a genuine kinship for the kingdom and welcome the challenge to defend it," said King Roarke. "Witch Amity, what enchantments might be served?"

"A Seeker has dusted the Guardian with powder that grants the gift of extraordinary sight," answered the witch. "We shall reach the Guardian through dreams, and over time the images that we send will become deeply embedded and part of the Guardian's being."

"Should we not tell the Guardian of these ties?" asked Prince Owyn. "Would knowing of such a bond not prove to our advantage?"

"Nay," answered King Roarke. "Only Watchers may reveal such a truth to someone from another world. To meddle would upset the order Watchers have followed since the beginning of time. That we even know such information could be considered heresy."

"The knowledge will be passed on," said Witch Amity. "Timing is key. If the Guardian is called just prior to the Festival of the Crystal Ice Spirits, and Watchers deem the Guardian worthy, all truths can be revealed."

King Roarke nodded in agreement and dismissed his charges, save for Prince Owyn. There were private details he needed to impart to his son. Once done, he was anxious for the process to begin. There was much work ahead and he knew the sacrifices that would have to be made. It would be many years before the Guardian would reach the age to assume this role, and King Roarke was keenly aware of what such a lengthy wait would mean. But the first step had been taken and it was one of salvation. The Guardian had been found.

After many years of darkness, the sky finally began to lighten, giving the kingdom false hope that their predicament was less dire. Soon the sun was as bright and full as ever, and fuelled by the energy of its powerful rays, the kingdom slowly rebuilt itself. However, King Roarke knew better than to give in to such a false sense of security and conferred often with Ice Witch Amity.

"I shan't make the same mistake twice," he said gravely. "The sooner the Guardian is called, the better."

"There are cracks developing in the protective veil and I am unsure whether I can conjure another," she replied. "With this year's Festival fast approaching, I believe we must chance a beckoning, whether the Guardian is ready or not."

King Roarke sat on his throne, drumming his fingers on his cheek. Finally, he rose and turned to Witch Amity. "Make ready, I shall advise my son."

Witch Amity nodded and headed out of the Great Hall on her way to the Seekers' mound. After so many long years of preparing and sending images, now the most important message of all was about to be sent.

Chapter Seven

A new morning unlike any other awaited Grace. Gradually, the journey from dreamland back to reality brought Grace to her room, and her first vision of the day, on opening her eyes, was her mother's smiling face.

"Well, aren't you a sleepyhead. Were your dreams so adventurous that you didn't want to wake up?" asked her mother.

Grace smiled, "My dreams. I don't remember all my dreams but I do remember one. The one that keeps coming back to me," she replied with a yawn and a stretch.

"You're still having that dream," her mother commented.

"Yeah. It's so weird. Like someone's calling to me and sending me these strange pictures. They're always so fuzzy and I can't make them out. What do you think it means?"

"I don't know, honey," replied her mother. "Sometimes a person's imagination gets carried away. Especially yours. I wouldn't worry about it. It's only a dream," she remarked as she left Grace's room to make breakfast.

"I guess so. It's only a dream." Grace shrugged to herself. However, what wasn't a dream were the visions she saw outside her bedroom window; those were real. What disturbed her most was that she couldn't conceive of a plausible explanation, other than her eyes playing tricks on her and she knew that wasn't true. No, there had to be more to it. Perhaps visiting the garden might hold the answer or at least give meaning to what she thought were clues.

On an ordinary day, Grace would content herself with waffles and orange juice in the company of her favourite morning television shows. But today was not an ordinary day, just as the night before had not been an ordinary night. She wolfed down her breakfast, raced back to her room and within moments was fully dressed at the back door.

"I'm going outside," Grace announced to her mother.

With a knit brow and a puzzled smile, her mother was quite unsure what to make of her daughter's behaviour. Grace had long since given up playing in the snow and had shown scant interest in venturing outdoors in the cold, and yet this day she was determined.

"Okay, honey, are you sure? It's really rather cold outside, so you'll have to bundle up," her mother said, reaching for Grace's parka, gloves, hat, and the snowpants she hated to wear. Convinced she had outgrown the garment, Grace reluctantly pulled them on, knowing she would need their warmth. After all, it was only the backyard, where no one would see her in such a juvenile costume.

Grace stood at the threshold of the back door; a butterfly of excitement fluttered inside her as she stepped into the morning sunshine, her snowpants singing a swishing tune as her heavy boots strode through snow on the back porch. She glanced back at her mother, "Thanks, Mom. See you in a bit," she said offhandedly. Her mother blew her a kiss and closed the door, leaving Grace alone.

Snow crunched under her boots as she approached the steps of the veranda. Down six, snowy stairs, sinking ankle deep with each step, Grace arrived on the edge of the garden's winter scene. Before her lay the same mounds of snow, glittering and sparkling; the same leafless trees with ice-laden boughs and the same brisk, snow-swirling breeze Grace had seen from her second-floor bedroom window. Everything might seem the same to anyone passing by, and yet to Grace everything was very different.

With a smirk she whispered to the garden, "I know you have secrets. You can't hide them from me. I saw the castles and throne last night."

The garden remained silent as if avoiding Grace's suspicions and kept to the task of just being a garden. Grace knew better though, and she fully expected the garden to somehow reveal its secrets. It was just a matter of time.

Grace ploughed to the middle of the yard and hoisted herself onto a mound of hard-packed snow. Standing tall, she surveyed her surroundings, searching for telltale signs of the castle's remains. The garden lay idle, not offering to share its secrets nor professing it even had some. Wishing to shout with the full force of her voice, Grace held back. She knew if she did and anyone overheard, embarrassment would overtake her. So instead she whispered, "I wish to know the secrets of the garden, tell me them now."

Like the crack of a whip, the wind suddenly surged and just as the night before, snow swirled violently, tree branches thrashed and scattered icicles in every direction. No longer a spectator, Grace stood dead centre in a great whirlpool of blustery wind and flying snow. Her cheeks stung from the slap of cold air. Icy flakes spotted her eyelashes as she struggled to see the source of the turbulence. A gust of wind unkindly toppled her over and she was flung forward to her knees on the hard-packed snow.

Grace screamed, but her voice was immediately swallowed by the wind. Tears streaked across her face. She crouched into a ball, head towards her knees, arms wrapped around her head, shielding her face and protecting her shaking body. Eyes squeezed shut, she clasped her gloved hands to her ears trying to shut out the flurry around her.

"Grace," a whisper. "Grace." A singsong whisper.

Slowly she opened her eyes and uncovered her ears. She looked about. An uneasy feeling washed over her as she realized how familiar the scene was. It was just like her dreams the night before: a raging storm, a flurry of white and a voice calling her name. How was that possible? Though the garden was still caught in a swirl of ice, snow and wind, a tranquil cloak enveloped her body and she no longer felt the wrath of the elements. Within this pocket of calm, Grace strained to listen.

"Grace," softly the whisper beckoned, "Grace."

Grace cocked her head, "Who's there?" she meekly responded, while thinking this was bordering on weird.

"Grace, the secret, the secret, the secrets are in the castle, the secrets are in the castle, in the castle."

In a blink the turbulence fell away and the garden grew still. Wind blew itself out, snow settled on banks, and trees stood stationary. Bewildered, Grace stood up and searched the landscape. "Just like last night, just like my dream," she said out loud. "It left as quickly as it came."

Grace wiped the tears from her face and the snow from her lashes. This was all too impossible. Where had the voice come from and what did it mean by the secrets being in the castle? What castle? The castle from the night before? Which one? Both had disappeared. How could the secrets be in the castle if there was no castle? Would another be back that night? Or was the appearance of the castle simply meant as a clue? How could the garden know of her dream and reproduce it so exactly? Questions whirled in Grace's head much like the snow had swirled moments ago. The forces at large, whatever they were, originated in the garden, and that's where she'd ultimately find the answers she craved. Again she whispered, "I wish to know the secrets of the garden. Tell me them now."

A thin jet of snow swept up from frozen flowerbeds and circled the yard. Grace looked up and watched as it sailed above her aimlessly through the garden, trailing glittering ice flakes behind. Suddenly it dove down to encircle Grace as she stood in the snow. Thoroughly fascinated by the swirling force, Grace thought she could hear something more than the rustle of the wind through the trees.

"Grace," came the same singsong whisper, as the snow stream spiralled around her. "A wish, make a wish."

"What? Make a wish?" she repeated. "I just made a wish!"

"Make a wish," the whisper prodded. "Wish for a prince, wish for a prince."

The snow stream circling her grew thick with flakes and swirling white was all Grace could see. "What? What? A prince?" Grace questioned in disbelief. "Wish for a prince?"

In a sudden strong rush of wind, the snowstream abandoned her. With a gush it surged upwards, halting abruptly mid-air, and hovered above. As Grace looked up with wonder into the cloud of lingering snow, it started to fall —slowly at first, and then as a gentle sprinkle landing on her face and hair, melting the moment the snowflakes touched her warm skin. She blinked at the ones caught in her eyelashes and licked away those that kissed her lips.

"Where are you, where have you gone?" she asked her curious visitor.

Suddenly, the snow cloud dropped in one thick clump at her feet and at precisely the same moment Grace heard quite distinctly, "Wish for the Ice Prince."

Grace snapped out of the snow cloud's trance. "What?" she whispered, trying to clear her foggy head and remind herself she was still in the garden.

The wind died down, leaving only a slight breeze chasing through the trees. The sky was still cloudy white, exhausted from relieving its snowy loads all day long, and the chill in the air caused Grace to shiver.

"Did I hear that right, wish for a prince . . . ? No, wish for an ice prince. The 'Ice Prince', it said." Grace was perplexed. "Who the heck is the Ice Prince?" she asked the sky.

As she stood in the garden, her mind raced to comprehend why she would even want to wish for a prince, let alone an ice prince. Moreover, she'd wish for a sister or brother, given the choice. At crossroads, Grace knew in her heart she had been given a final clue and if she did not oblige, the secrets of the garden and the mystery of her dreams might remain unsolved forever. So she coupled the two — that of the mysterious voice's request and that of her own desire.

She straightened her back, held up her head, and closed her eyes. Clearing her thoughts, Grace brought forth the image of the crystal ice castle drawn by snowflakes outside her bedroom window. Slowly the castle shimmered and faded, replaced by the one sketched by stars. Finally she imaged the throne with its glistening crown and diamond-shaped brilliance, the mysterious whispers that had called to her, and the tremendous force of swirling snow and wind. Sounds echoed in her ears, and pictures whirled inside her head like a series of snapshots flipping from one to the next, overlapping until everything was a blur.

Grace took a deep breath and opened her eyes. " I can do this, yes I can. I wish for a sibling," she thought to herself. Heeding the whisperer's request in a gentle voice, neither too loud nor too soft, and with perfect diction, she calmly announced to the garden, "I wish for the Ice Prince."

Expecting an Ice Prince relative to suddenly appear was a little far-fetched, but Grace had to believe that one might. To her dismay one didn't. Instead, a tiny speck of light appeared in the distance, emerging from the fence at the back of the garden. As it travelled closer and closer, making its way over the freshly-laid snow towards her, it grew in size and lustre. Grace felt warmth on her cheeks as the light silently approached her and an icy, cold breeze tickled her nose. Now the size of a silver dollar, the light stopped just a few short feet away.

"You don't look like an Ice Prince." Grace said dryly as she stood up to face it. As though cued by her voice, the light began to move in a circular pattern; tiny at first, it grew wider and wider as it spiralled downward toward the garden floor and back up again. A tail of white light trailing behind created a swirling cyclone of brilliance that caused her to squint. Suddenly the cyclone exploded in a blinding flash, sending all of the light it contained through her and out over the garden. Grace felt the impact and stumbled back, raising her hand to shield her eyes.

"Greetings, young Grace."

Grace slowly looked up into the eyes of a boy a few years older than she. He was finely dressed from head to toe in white and wrapped in a hooded robe trimmed with white fur and glistening with crystal ice dust.

"I have awaited this encounter over many a year and it is with the greatest of pleasure that I make thy acquaintance," he proclaimed as he bowed lavishly before her.

Chapter Eight

There are places where few choose to venture: places too harsh, too unbearable to endure; places where the elements take charge and claim the landscape, hindering those who might dare to enter. Such a place was this. The ice field stretched league after league: a vast plain of thick, translucent snow hardened by the cold and hammered by the frozen wind. Far off in the distance, jagged glaciers pierced the sky; their steely cold ridges stabbed at the few low-lying clouds that drifted on cold currents. Sheets of ice grew from accumulated snow and froze into slippery avenues too perilous to cross. Calm days were few, when the breeze died down and the snow settled. More often than not, it was an unfriendly place fraught in the whims of bitter, cold wind and storms of ice mixed with snow. Any life existing in this land of abomination remained hidden, protected from the elements in attempts to survive. Crevasses riddled the glacial mountains offering a bleak refuge to the creatures that chose to reside there in self-inflicted exile and relish in their own miserable seclusion.

A lone figure arrived at the edge of the ice field. The wind ripped at the heavy cloak and thick grey hood hiding the Traveller's face. With a single step, the trek across the ice field began. Now, on the final leg of a journey begun long ago, the Traveller gained a second wind, knowing that soon the quest would be completed.

The glacier loomed forbiddingly. Standing at the foot of the great mountain of hardened ice, the Traveller peered upwards to the jagged peaks only to lose sight of their summits as they disappeared into the clouds of snow. The ascent would be arduous, even dangerous, but the Traveller was determined. Scaling the icy cliffs would demand agility and concentration. One slip, one ill-positioned grip, one uncertain toehold would hurl the climber to the ground in a spectacular death. Higher and higher the Traveller climbed, battling the ripping winds and blinding snow. Finally, the glacier offered a sturdy ledge; the Traveller hoisted across, and for a moment rested. Looking up, the Traveller faced a great, gaping hole punched into the side of the glacier. The mouth of a cave hungrily beckoned.

"Come in, come in," it silently urged, eager to devour anyone who entered. The Traveller walked into the opening and disappeared from sight.

Although without a clear source of light, the walls of white ice shone brilliantly and it took a few moments for the Traveller's eyes to adjust to the brightness of the cave. Scattered around the cavern lay icicles randomly strewn. From the roof of the cave, stalactites of tapering ice stretched downwards reaching to their stalagmite mates rising up from the ground. After centuries of longing some pairs had met creating hourglass columns of ice. Beyond count, they stood passively as a frozen forest inside the cave; the Traveller wended a way around and between them.

Deeper into the cave, away from the main chamber, a path chiselled its way through the mountain and brought the Traveller to the mouths of several tunnels dissecting the glacier. Only one opening was large enough to allow passage; its wide yawn could easily accommodate an elephant. The Traveller hesitated for a moment. The task ahead seemed daunting now that the challenge was near. With renewed determination the Traveller entered the passage.

The tunnel wound deep into the glacier and seemed to go on forever. Many twists and turns and roundabouts made the way long and repetitive. Finally, finally, the passage ended in a wide cavern in the heart of the great mountain. At this depth, sounds were left behind, the silence broken only by the Traveller's soft footfalls. The light was dimmer here and dark shadows cast their images against icy walls.

"Where are you, my treasure?" whispered the Traveller. "Show yourself to me."

Chapter Nine

Grace had seen a great many spectacular things in her twelve-year-old life, mostly in movies and on television, though nothing quite like this. Here was a boy, summoned by a simple wish, who had miraculously appeared out of nowhere in a flash of light. With raised eyebrows, she looked him up and down. He was unlike anyone she had ever encountered. Firstly, his dress was oddly foreign. Grace had never known a boy to wear tights or knee-high, white leather boots. His doublet was made of rich brocade garnished with silver trim, and the delicate linen shirt he wore puffed out between shoulder and elbow, tapering along his forearm to his wrist. All sorts of fancy buttons and ornate trims adorned his sleeves and the front of his shirt. Draped over his shoulders hung a thick, white velvet cape and Grace was tempted to stroke the soft, white fur of his collar. Atop his head sat a flared silver crown embedded with diamonds and pearls — it looked rather heavy to have to wear all day long. He looked as if he had been plucked from a medieval tale and dropped into the garden. He certainly did appear princely enough, so that part of the wish had come true, and she wondered whether the long-lost relative side of the wish might also.

"Who are you and how do you know my name?" Grace finally spoke as she picked herself up.

"I am Ice Prince Owyn and I have carried thy name in mine thoughts for quite some time," he answered. "Thy name is renowned in mine kingdom and among mine subjects."

"My name is renowned?" she asked sceptically. "And you have my name in subjects? You mean, like math and geometry?"

Prince Owyn laughed. "Although we do engage in formal education in mine land, mine subjects are the people I serve and rule." And then he bowed again.

"You certainly like to bow a lot, don't you? And you talk kind of funny. You know, like a grown-up or teacher or something."

"Let not the manner in which I speak concern thee, Fair Grace. Fear not, mine purpose here is one of friendship." He said with another bow.

"Yeah? How did you get here?" Grace demanded, noting that he said friendship and not kinship.

Prince Owyn reached for Grace's hand but she snatched it away. She didn't like to be touched by strangers, especially ones who appeared out of thin air.

"Thou hast summoned me with thy wish," he said. "There is much to learn but in time thou shalt gain all of the knowledge thee seek. I will answer all thy queries as best I can."

"I'm listening."

Prince Owyn peered deeply into Grace's blue eyes and smiled warmly. "Dear Grace, a well-told tale is indeed something to behold and yet, I do believe thou shouldst see it for thyself. Will thee journey back to the Ice World with me so that I may better tell mine story?"

Grace looked at him with a puzzled expression. "The Ice World?"

"Indeed."

"Listen, I really should be going in. My parents are waiting for me." Grace was suddenly quite suspicious of the prince and his motives for wanting her to go with him. Her mother had warned her about people she didn't know and often reminded her to be careful to whom she spoke.

"There is much at stake in both our worlds and thy presence is desperately required in mine." And then he bowed yet again.

Grace took a deep breath. "I don't know about going anywhere with you. I don't even know you. I mean is this something you do on a regular basis? Suddenly appear to people out of nowhere and expect them to go off with you to some, what, other world?"

"Thou must search thy heart and follow its lead, fair Grace," he replied. "Hast thou not had recurring apparitions of late in thy dreams?" he asked. "Ones that could not be explained away? Is there not a yearning for someone amiss in thy heart? The answers thou seek can be found in mine world."

Grace shook her head at his manner of speech. It all seemed so scrambled and foreign; she wished he would lose all of his pretence and start making some sense. "What do you know about my dreams?" she demanded. "And who is this someone, er, amiss in my heart?"

"I cannot say. Not here, not now. That is why it is imperative thou return with me," he answered.

"Okay, so if I go with you, how long would I be gone? I mean my parents will be wondering where I went," she asked nervously.

"'Tis truly the ways of enchantment, fair Grace, that when thee leave thy world to venture into mine, time does not follow. Thou may stay for as long as it pleases thee and upon thy return, it will be the precise moment thy left," he answered, relieved that the previous tension had been broken. Grace was just glad he didn't bow again.

"You mean like I'd never gone?" Grace asked.

"Indeed." This time he bowed.

Grace turned away from him and paced the mound trying to figure out what to do. It wasn't as though she could actually ask her parents: "Hey, Mom, Dad, the Ice Prince I wished for wants me to go back to his world with him. Can I go?" she imagined herself asking, rolling her eyes. "They would never believe me and would rush out to the garden in search of the maniac threatening to kidnap their daughter," she said to herself.

"If there was only a way I could see your world without actually leaving mine. Don't you have any pictures?" She stalled.

"I chanced thou might yearn for a glimpse and I am able to offer much more than an illustrated view of my home. Behold!"

Prince Owyn reached inside his doublet and pulled out a small silver mirror. He held the mirror out to Grace and she took it, turned it over, and inspected the fine carving etched on the back.

It's beautiful," she said. As she turned it over again, she saw her own reflection gazing out from the bevelled glass, "but what am I supposed to do with it?"

"Simply tell the mirror what sights thou wouldst like to see," Prince Owyn replied.

"I wouldst like to see the sights of thy world," she said, imitating his formal tone.

"Ask and thou shalt be answered. Ask through a wish."

"You're really big on wishes where you come from, aren't you?" she retorted. "Okay, Prince. Here goes. I wish to see the Ice World."

The glass of the mirror clouded over and Grace could no longer see her reflection. It happened so quickly that Grace almost let the fragile mirror slip from her fingers. She recovered and held the mirror firmly in both hands. At first there was nothing to see except a cloudy blur, but slowly it melted away to reveal a winter scene of tall, snow-clad mountains against a white sky.

"This is like watching a movie," Grace exclaimed in wonder. "This isn't a mirror, it's a movie mirror!"

"What, may I inquire, is a movie?" asked Prince Owyn.

"It's a . . . " Grace stumbled. How does one describe a feature film to a medieval Ice Prince? "Another time. I'll explain another time." Grace said, her focus of attention on the mirror. "I feel like a bird flying through the air," she remarked as she wended through a forest of white frozen trees, their branches and leaves all covered in ice. Leaving the forest, she burst out into a clearing where fields of white, frozen grass swayed in the wind. Something darted from one side to the other so quickly that Grace could not make out what it was.

"What was that?" she asked without looking up.

"Most likely a Seeker intent on some task," he answered. "They are a busy lot, they are."

"A what?"

The scene changed again and Grace let out a gasp. Inside the circle of glass was the image of a huge castle of ice. Its towers and turrets glimmered and glistened as an icy drawbridge lowered to allow her entrance. All sorts of activities were taking place on the grounds of the castle. Flying creatures darted about like hummingbirds and a team of large, white horses suited in silver tack cantered by pulling a clear, white carriage behind them. Lords and ladies lavishly dressed in silver and white strolled between topiaries of ice, occasionally stopping to share conversation and bowing before taking their leave. From the courtyard she entered the keep, flew into the Great Hall and toured the lavishly decorated throne room.

Grace looked up from the mirror. "This is your world? It's so, so, so, magnificent. And magical," she exclaimed as she handed the mirror back to the prince. It would have been wonderful to keep the image in the mirror forever.

Sensing her desire, Prince Owyn placed it back into her hands. "Please accept this as a gift, from mine world to thine," he said with another bow.

"No way!" she exclaimed. "Really? Thanks."

"Grace, now thou hast glimpsed mine kingdom and I am gladdened that thee find mine home so pleasing. There was a time when 'twas not so, when, alas, it was left in ruin. That is another tale," he said as he continued to implore her. "Won't thee kindly reconsider mine offer to journey to mine kingdom in the Ice World, now thou art assured that it is indeed a welcoming place?"

"I don't know. I mean it looks really cool," she hesitantly said. "But really, why should I?"

Prince Owyn's polite demeanour suddenly changed and he grabbed her arm a little more roughly than he had intended and pulled her toward him. "There are evil forces at work in mine world, ones that may have crossed over into thine." He said darkly. "Heed mine warning, to hesitate would change us both and our demise would be certain and final."

Grace pulled her arm free and stepped back. He was beginning to scare her and she chided herself for having been so flippant in trusting him. A long moment of silence hung heavily between them while her inner voice screamed for her to run back to her house. "I think you should leave now," she said quietly, knowing his departure would leave her questions unanswered, but she was willing to forgo that knowledge in return for her safety.

Prince Owyn acknowledged his blunder; he had succeeded in frightening her, something he had not intended to do. His initial strategy had been to offer the invitation to his world through friendly means in the hope that Grace would trust him and follow. Instead he had done the exact opposite by threatening her. He dreaded the return home empty-handed; it would not bode well with the king. Desperate, he attempted to salvage his mission and made the appeal once more. "Make the wish and return with me, Grace. Simply make the wish."

Grace cocked her head slightly puzzled, but still guarded, and then the realization of what he had asked her to do — to make a wish — brought an acute understanding of the power she now wielded. Instantly she knew what might be the perfect solution to her dilemma. She locked eyes with the Ice Prince, took a deep breath, and quickly whispered "I wish you back to your world."

In a flash of light and a thunderous clap, Prince Owyn vanished. Grace stumbled back on the mound fearing the light might hurt her in some way; it was so very bright and so very loud. Unharmed, Grace found she was trembling, not from the cold, but from the encounter with the prince. She ran as fast as she could back to the house.

"Are you all right?" her mother asked as Grace slammed the door behind her and locked it tightly. "Your face is all white. You look as if you've seen a ghost."

"Not exactly a ghost," she whispered under her breath, inaudible to her mother as she walked past her. "I'm just cold.

And I've got a headache." Under no condition was Grace about to tell her what happened in the garden. If her mother could barely handle her invisible sister obsession, learning about an Ice Prince from another world would certainly drive her over the edge.

Chapter Ten

King Roarke was not pleased when his son, Prince Owyn, returned from the Guardian's world earlier that day. His abrupt appearance in the Great Hall shocked the court. He was not expected back so soon and he had arrived alone, without the Guardian. After so many years of careful preparation with so many who had tirelessly laboured and wilfully sacrificed, it was devastating that all should be dashed by a single wish. No one took it harder than Prince Owyn. Failure was something he didn't want to admit and he pressed his father to allow him to try once more. Instead King Roarke declined his son's offer, stating that stiffer measures would be employed, and set off to meet with Ice Witch Amity.

Returning to the royal apartments, Prince Owyn found his mother curled up on the settee absorbed in a book, which she dropped in surprise when he announced his presence, Never quite back to her old self since Princess Farren had disappeared, and with still no news of her whereabouts aside from the Searchers initial sighting, the queen was prone to retreating to her chambers for days, even weeks, at a time, reading or sleeping — anything that would distract her from visiting the events of the past. Although most of the castle had recuperated from that fateful day, Queen Isolte remained a casualty; her wounds were deeper and took longer to heal.

"Back so soon," she said, startled, retrieving her book and holding it tightly to her chest. "What news of the Guardian?"

Prince Owyn joined her on the settee and proceeded to recount the details of his botched mission, including the regrets he felt over having failed. He feared that his father might not enlist his services again, nor offer any real responsibility in the near future. After he finished, Queen Isolte drew him near and offered the consolation only a mother's embrace could achieve.

"The Guardian," she asked. "Pray tell, is there a resemblance?"

When Prince Owyn nodded, she gasped with tears already forming in the corner of her eyes and quit the company of her son, favouring her bedchambers instead. He knew better than to engage her during such episodes and withdrew from the apartment in search of his father and Ice Witch Amity.

As he walked through the bustling courtyard, his future subjects traded whispers. He knew his unsuccessful assignment had to be the main topic of their hushed conversations. Ordinarily, he was perceived as a polite young man who carried himself with the poise and grace typical of royals, but without the pompous and superior attitude. His heart was true, and he rarely took to mischief or pranks and could be counted on doing the right and proper thing when called to the task.

Prince Owyn had been chosen to acquire the Guardian for reasons the king deemed wise. He hoped his son could better appeal to Grace, being closer in age and less threatening than King Roarke. Not wanting to overwhelm her, he had hoped that Prince Owyn could have aroused her curiosity so that she would see the adventure as a wonderful game. Right down to the last detail, every calculated move . . . the celestial drawings ... the dreams ... rehearsal of probable conversations ... even the mirror had been thought of as a convincing device. King Roarke had warned his son not to reveal anything remotely ominous that might scare her away. But the prince had panicked and done exactly that.

"It's obvious the dusting powder of extraordinary sight has been tampered with," Prince Owyn overheard the Ice Witch telling his father. "Seekers will be sent to apply the dust once again."

"Such harsh measures," said King Roarke sternly. "Will the bait be taken?"

Witch Amity crossed her arms and sighed. "There are no assurances, my lord. But we must trust that it will. We'll know soon enough when the Guardian's arrival is announced. Mind you, we will not be the only ones who will hear it. And there's no telling where she might appear."

King Roarke responded with a pained expression then nodded in agreement. "Send forth Searchers and Seekers, advise Watchers as well. She shouldn't be that hard to find."

"All will be taken care of," she answered.

"I would have preferred to handle this mineself," he replied. "The timing is poor but unavoidable. I must take mine leave with the queen."

"The welfare of Queen Isolte is as important as the welfare of the kingdom," said Witch Amity soothingly. "We shall contend with the Guardian and should there be need, we will send word."

Turning to his son, King Roarke motioned for him to join them. "The castle is now in thy keeping. Serve it well."

Prince Owyn's face lit up at his father's renewed confidence. "But ... I thought ... I failed," he stammered.

"A leader must make mistakes to learn better his station," King Roarke said as he clapped his son on the back. "Little has changed. The Guardian will come. When is uncertain, but we must be expectant.

Prince Owyn's spirits soared to new heights as he embraced his father in an affectionate hug. "I shall make thee proud," he announced with resolve. "May the Healers to the south have a cure for what ails mine mother."

King Roarke bowed to the Ice Witch and she curtsied in return as he set off through the courtyard toward the royal apartments. Finding his wife secluded in their bedchambers again, furthered his resolve to find an effective treatment for the melancholy that had consumed her for so many years. That the availability of the Healer coincided with the Guardian's arrival could not be avoided. He had two choices: either wait for the Guardian or seek help for his wife. He picked the latter. As long as the protective veil remained in place over the castle, he was willing to take the risk of leaving to travel south.

Chapter Eleven

A change in the weather occurred later in the day and reports of freezing rain mixed with snow showers blared out between newscasts on the radio. A storm in the winter was a usual occurrence and was even expected every few weeks. But this was different: within a few hours the city was paralyzed, the temperature had plummeted, the rain frozen and everything was covered with a layer of ice. Tree branches had fallen under the weight of accumulated ice, crashing down and damaging cars parked in the street and littering lawns and gardens with broken limbs. Pedestrians were warned not to venture outside — the danger of being struck too great. Power lines were down, their metal structures bent over like injured steel skeletons with wires strewn haphazardly about like tossed spaghetti. Lights went out all over the city, furnaces shut down and hot water tanks eventially cooled. Transistor radios, the only source of information, were retrieved from storage spaces and suited up with new batteries. Candles and flashlights flew off the shelves of the few shops still open as customers scrambled for every last one. Fires were stoked in every available fireplace and well-stocked woodpiles were rapidly depleting. The long-range forecast called for similar weather, and with no end in sight, the city braced itself against the worst storm of the century.

That night when sleep finally overcame her, Grace plunged into dreams clearer than ever before. So accustomed to the blurry visions of her past, this new clarity caught her by surprise and she felt wide awake. Grace was flying; how, she was unsure, but there was no mistaking that she was travelling through the air of her own accord. The view below was the same panorama the movie mirror had presented, except this time she wasn't just looking at the scene, she was actually in it. Gliding over the same forest of white frozen trees and banking above the clearing of waving ice grass, she embraced the beauty and grandeur of this magnificent world. Soon Prince Owyn's ice castle loomed into view nestled into the gentle slope of a great mountain. It towered before her. She hovered in awe, its icy splendour appearing even more magnificent up close than dwarfed in a small circle of glass.

A moat surrounded the castle and passage across was gained once the drawbridge in the gatehouse was lowered. Flanking the gatehouse, two rounded towers stood at attention guarding the entrance to the castle. Constructed of huge blocks of ice tightly stacked and topped by turrets with white banners flying from their pinnacles, the towers glistened in the white sunlight. The castle's outer wall, notched with crenels and merlons, wound its way around protecting the interior. Square, arched, and round, portal windows garnished the walls and any number of terraces and balconies jutted out from arched, double doorways.

The drawbridge sighed as it gently lowered to allow her to cross over the moat. Grace curbed over to the side, curious to see what she was actually flying over. The moat was encrusted with a frozen layer of crystal-clear ice. Beneath the ice, schools of silver fishes lazily swam, changing direction every few strokes as they meandered under the bridge and disappeared from sight, only to reappear on the other side.

As Grace approached, she heard the same soft sigh as the heavy silver gate of the portcullis rose above her and disappeared into the ceiling of the gatehouse. Crossing the threshold, she entered an arched corridor of solid ice walls and a glassy floor. Out through a doorway and into the courtyard, Grace realized she was flying into the scene she had viewed in Prince Owyn's movie mirror earlier that day. The same creatures flitted about — Seekers he had called them — the same horse-drawn carriage cantered by, the same lords and ladies casually strolled, but this time her presence was instantly noted. Seekers fluttered still, horses halted abruptly, lords and ladies paused, and all eyes looked up at Grace.

At first, a great hush fell over the crowd, soon broken by whispering and the pointing of fingers. An infectious applause erupted, building louder and louder, as one by one, spectators brought their hands together. The clapping gave way to cheers and hat flinging, pats on backs and handshakes all around. Grace wondered what prompted all this commotion, until she realized it was directed at her. Most likely, she assumed, it wasn't everyday a stranger appeared — a flying one no less. Whatever it was, she rather enjoyed all the attention.

As she flew over the crowd, those close enough reached out to touch her and many of the gentlemen — arms outstretched — attempted to shake her hand. Children waved to her and she happily waved back, revelling at the appearance of their smiling faces. Retreating from her admirers, she followed a wide, sculpted pathway towards the centre of the courtyard. The grounds on either side overflowed with landscaped gardens of flowers and bushes, all white and covered in glistening ice. To the right lay a long block of two-storey buildings, all fashioned with arched windows and doorways.

White, icy ivy curled and twisted as it gently spread its tendrils, climbing and covering the facade.

The pathway led directly to the largest building of the castle. Standing four storeys tall with all sorts of turrets, balconies and finely detailed finials, the keep looked as grand as any royal estate should. That it was created purely from ice made it even more spectacular. Grace drifted up a large ice staircase onto a terrace and through a large set of doors into a great hall. It was an enormous white room with an elaborately carved ceiling supported by massive ice columns sculpted with intricate patterns and designs. Hanging from the ceiling, dozens of crystal chandeliers spread clear, white light throughout the room giving the hall a luminescent effect. The walls were covered in frescos etched in fine detail, depicting assorted winter scenes. In large-paned windows — easily twice her size — hung lavish, white brocade drapes drawn to one side allowing the white sunshine to spill into the room.

Directly across from the door sat a throne of formidable size and for the first time in her dream, she paused. The throne appeared to be an exact copy of the one formed by the stars outside her bedroom window. Or perhaps this wasn't a copy, but rather the original. A twin to her celestial drawing, this chair appeared equally majestic in construction with fine details and carved turnings embedded with a large diamond in the back. A chill ran up her spine and she turned away from the throne as an uneasy feeling pushed her to return to her tour.

To the right of the door rose a solid ice staircase with carved banisters and chiselled posts. Up ten tall steps, the staircase split in two and continued to wind up to the second floor. On each side of the staircase, arched doorways led to other rooms of the keep behind the Great Hall, and Grace wondered what fanciful treasures she might find there. The floor of the Great Hall lay polished and gleaming, reminiscent of a perfectly flawless ice rink waiting for dancing and twirling skaters to take their turns.

Grace flew out the terrace doors and into the open air. Over gardens, between sculpted topiaries she glided effortlessly, basking in the brilliant light that bathed this world, but as she circled back to begin again, the scene drastically changed.

Chapter Twelve

Down in the courtyard, Grace spied a lone figure who flailed her arms and ranted incomprehensibly at a fragment of black ice twitching violently in the snow. Suddenly an earth-shattering explosion erupted and an ominous cloud billowed up from the ground. As it increased in size, denser and denser, the silhouette of a black demon began to take shape. Beady black eyes and a huge gaping mouth appeared on its face, slithering arms stretched out from its sides halting in paw-like groping hands. It hovered above the courtyard, leering and drooling, and sweating a foul stench.

The Ice World was plunged into darkness. A split second later, a flash of light exposed the castle again before being doused to black in a blink. Pulsing rhythmically, the shunts from light to night strobed images of chaos below.

Pandemonium ensued and with each flash of light, Grace watched as castle folk scattered hysterically and a solitary figure in a white-hooded cloak purposefully bolted through the gatehouse to escape the turmoil. "Why only the one?" Grace wondered. Screaming children ran frantically in terror and their piercing cries filled her ears. Mothers pressed their infants close to their hearts.

All of the beauty and splendour of this world was suddenly threatened, without warning, without apparent reason. Helplessness seeped into Grace's heart as she watched the mayhem unfold before her eyes. She moved closer, disregarding the danger that she might be exposed to, and without quite understanding why, her first concern was not for her own safety, but for those suffering below. They needed her; why else was she here? "What can I do?" she lamented as she hovered mid-air. "How can I help them?"

The light continued to strobe, pulsating and throbbing, each time revealing more hysteria as the black demon grew in size, until it consumed the sky. Then, as all hope of salvation seemed lost and destruction imminent, the cloud unexpectedly exploded.

The darkness remained. The force of the explosion threw Grace backwards and her ears rang from the force of the blast. Upon recovery, she surveyed the damage. The light still strobed, and even though the pace had slowed, the haunting images flashing in and out were as disturbing as the ones she had just witnessed.

The castle walls were crumbling. Huge blocks of ice plummeted to the ground shattering upon impact. Iced topiary trees split and fell. The once beautiful ice gardens were crushed and splinters of ice scattered.

Grace flew into the courtyard desperately looking for signs of life. A small child staggered forward, dirtied with black ice dust, and reached up — her tiny outstretched arms begging. Soon another child appeared, even more dishevelled than the first. Then another, and another, their pleading faces throbbed in the diminishing light.

"Grace, you must help us."

Blended with the chanting, the strobing light, and the children engulfing her, Grace began to spiral out of control. Sights and sounds melted together in one overwhelming blur and she was helpless to fight it. All the horror, all the destruction, all the terrible images of sorrow and despair swallowed her. Finally she gave in and opened her eyes to escape.

Chapter Thirteen

The question remained unanswered. Again the Traveller whispered, "Where are you, my treasure? Do not hide yourself from me." The Traveller slowly ventured further into the chamber, keeping to the walls, mindful of each step. Something underfoot skidded noisily across the floor of the cave. The Traveller froze momentarily, then slowly released a tight, pent-up breath and resumed the trek. The floor now crunched with each step. Emerging from the shadows into a large cavern, the Traveller looked down with a broad smile and stroked the rubble strewn on the floor.

"I have you now," the Traveller exulted, inspecting piles of glittering jewels littering the far end of the cave. "You are near, very near." Tossing the jewel back onto the heap, the Traveller straightened up and tiptoed carefully, following the jewelled trail to a second chamber gouged into the wall of the cave. Mounds of silver trinkets, hoards of diamonds and pearls, and crystals of all sizes and shapes filled the chamber waist deep.

The Traveller stood before the cache of treasure pleased with the find: nestled among the heaping fortune lay the long-coveted prize.

The dragon was asleep, curled up like a kitten in a basket. Its long body curved at the spine and its back legs tucked neatly under its flank. A huge, wedge-shaped head lay nestled upon two smaller forearms crossed in front, and its long, spiked tail wound around from the back and lay motionless, inches from its face. Two bat-like wings of gigantic proportions spread over it like a blanket. Covered from head to tip of tail, the dragon's tear-shaped scales shimmered as they neatly overlapped one another down its body.

Peaceful in the depths of sleep, the creature barely conjured the ferocious capabilities of legends. Yet the Traveller knew better than to be deceived by its gentle appearance in slumber. This was indeed a powerful beast with powerful magic, and persuading it to do one's bidding would take great cunning.

The Traveller circled the dragon, admiring its beauty. Pearlescent scales glistened as the beast's chest rose and fell with each rhythmic breath. Two long, sharp, twisted horns jutted out from either side of its forehead, both tipped in silver, as were the spikes at the end of its long, thick tail. A row of spiked ridges ran from the back of its head, down its spine to the middle of its tail, and long curved talons grew from four claws on each foot, ending in sharply pointed, silver tips. A shimmering frill spread around the back of its neck like a collar giving the dragon the appearance of being formally dressed.

Deep in dragon dreams, the dragon slept unaware of its observer and oblivious of what it would face once awake.

Reaching into a pocket, the Traveller withdrew a small vial. A thick, silver liquid swirled within the glass, coating the sides. Turning to the dragon, the Traveller unplugged the vial. Silver gel clung to the crystal stopper as the Traveller held it out to the dragon's face. Slowly the gel slid down the stopper and gathered at the tip briefly before it released and plunged toward the ground.

At precisely the moment the gel hit the floor, a fine mist filled the cavern. Soon the dragon was engulfed in a cloudy haze and the beast began to stir. Its great head slowly lifted off its forearms, its eyelids fluttered, and its long, spiked tail twitched where it lay. In a state between slumber and wakefulness, the dragon was now open to the Traveller's persuasion, but only for a short time, as the mist would soon clear.

The Traveller approached, leaned close, and whispered, "Dragon of ice, hear me now, for I am your salvation. I know your deepest passion and what your heart desires most. And only I possess the power and the knowledge to grant your eternal wish. Heed this message, for it will be offered but once. When finally we meet, bestow my request, so that what you cherish above any other, will be returned unto you."

The Traveller quietly backed away, relieved the message had been successfully delivered, and headed for the entrance of the dragon's cave. The mist had almost completely cleared, and the dragon settled back to resume its deep sleep. In the main chamber, the Traveller clung to the wall of the cave for a moment before returning back up through the glacier and beyond. It would be many hours before the dragon would wake, time well-needed for the message to seep into its being and become its own thought. And just long enough for a second visitor to make her arrival.

Chapter Fourteen

Dawn silently crept across the garden and spread over Grace's house on the boulevard. The first glints of light seeped through shadeless windows and gently nudged the weary to wake. A cloudy, white sky gloomily welcomed the slowly approaching day. The air hung dull and heavy, with thick remnants of the storm and offering the promise of continued bad, winter weather.

Grace had been awake for hours under the covers of her bed, her fingers tightly clutching the duvet under her nose as she searched the ceiling for a plausible explanation of her most recent dream, or more aptly, nightmare. Her head still throbbed, less pronounced than before — or perhaps she was just getting used to it. Nevertheless, Grace knew she was at a threshold and there was no going back. That her reoccurring dream, clouded and marred in the past, was now clear and concise, disturbed her tremendously. This dream, coupled with recent events — the visions and the prince — made all the difference. Dismissing it solved little; as much as she hated to admit, this burden was just too huge and she had to tell her parents.

Grace quietly rolled out of bed and stepped on to the floor, mindful of the old wooden planks and the creaks they might utter. It was still quite early and she hoped her stirrings would not wake her parents. She wanted a little time to herself to rehearse her story, knowing her parents would react as they typically did when faced with another of her quirky exploits.

It was cool in her room; the heat was still off, so she pulled on an extra sweatshirt, left her room and tiptoed down the staircase to the main floor. The clock in the kitchen read the same three o'clock of yesterday when the power had failed, so she checked her own watch to verify the time. Just half-past seven, still early, and because it was the winter holiday, it wasn't unusual for Grace's parents to still be asleep.

Grace looked outside. The scene remained unchanged from the day before. Ice covered everything: the trees, the garden, the lamp posts, even her parents' car parked in the driveway was sheathed in a layer of glistening film. The boulevard was empty of cars and buses, which was unusual for such a busy street — unquestionably due to the storm. She switched on the transistor radio hoping for news of the day, but it was dead — no doubt the batteries had drained. Toasted waffles in front of television were out of the question. Instead, she poured herself a bowl of cold cereal topped with milk from the fridge.

On the odd morning she liked to read the comics' page offered in the daily paper with breakfast, but when she went to retrieve it from outside the front door, it wasn't there. Again the power outage must be to blame. Printing presses couldn't operate without electricity and, as she closed the door empty-handed, she hardly gave it another thought.

By nine, her parents were still asleep and Grace wondered if she should wake them. That would be a turn of events. It was usually Grace who slept in late and needed to be roused. Today was different though; she had good reason to do so and returned back up the stairs.

Grace silently entered their bedroom. Of all the rooms in the house, she loved this one most. When she was little, Grace would sit in the middle of the huge brass bed surrounded by pillows of soft down upholstered in custom fabrics and trims, and watch as her mother made herself up and dressed in fine clothes, while imagining herself doing the same in years to come. This was where Grace had felt the safety of her mother's arms on nights when sleep was interrupted by bad dreams, and this was where early morning pillow fights took place — her father wrestling her beneath the covers to tickle her into giggling fits. This was one advantage she had as an only child: her parents were hers exclusively and never did she have to share their attentions with another.

"Mom, wake up," Grace whispered softly in her mother's ear, " I need to tell you something." Although she was known as a deep sleeper and had a history of sleepwalking, Grace's mother was usually an early riser, often the first to be up and rarely one to sleep late. When she did not respond, Grace gently nudged her shoulder. Still no response.

"Mom, wake up," Grace repeated louder. "MOM, WAKE UP!" she shouted, shaking her mother who still showed no sign of waking. So Grace crossed over to the other side of the bed, attempted the same with her father and was met with the same result.

"What's wrong with you?" Grace pleaded, fearing that her parents had somehow succumbed to some sort of illness during the night. They had seemed fine last evening when she went to bed.

Grace clamoured onto the middle of the bed and began jumping up and down as she had so often as a small child, hoping the bouncing would disturb her parents enough to jostle them out of their deep slumber. But to no avail; they were still breathing and felt warm to the touch so it wasn't like they were . . .

Grace didn't want to say or even think the dreadful word for fear of activating a jinx that might become true. Reaching for the telephone on her parents' bedside table, she pressed 911 before placing the receiver to her ear. Much to her surprise, she met with silence. The familiar ring on the line was not there and it was obvious the phone line was dead — or at least as non-responsive as her parents. She stared at the handset in disbelief, half expecting it to offer an explanation for its malfunction since power failures did not usually affect phone lines. As she put it back into its cradle, the wheels in Grace's mind began to churn and she decided to go elsewhere for help. Surely the neighbours would be up by now and wouldn't mind being disturbed.

Grace returned downstairs and reached for a jacket and boots. As she left the house she couldn't help notice how quiet it was, both inside and out. An eerie stillness weighed heavily in the air amidst the freezing rain and the foggy mist. Branches split from their trunks and crashed loudly down to the ground, piercing the silence with each fall. The street was still deserted as she made her way up the icy walk of a neighbour.

The neighbour's cars were parked in the driveway indicating that they should be home, and Grace knocked loudly on the front door — there was no point in ringing the bell — power failure at play. When no one answered, she headed to the next door and attempted the same.

Grace tried every house on the street, peeked through windows she could reach, and pounded every door as hard as she could. No one answered. How was that possible? There was no absence of parked cars — it was, after all, a holiday and early enough that everyone should be awake and sitting down to breakfast.

As she walked back toward her own house she was suddenly stopped in her tracks by the memory of the ominous words of Ice Prince Owyn

"There are evil forces at work in mine world, ones that may have crossed over into thine." He had said darkly. "Make no mistake, to hesitate would change us both and our demise would be certain and final."

Chapter Fifteen

Grace's knees went weak and buckled under her weight as she sank to the ground in the middle of the sidewalk. Her stomach rolled and she thought she might loose her breakfast. The notion that the Ice Prince and his world were responsible could be the only explanation for what was currently happening in hers. She had been warned and had foolishly dismissed the threat. By wishing him away, she had sealed the fate of her world, of her friends, and of her loved ones. Help was not coming; of that she was certain. The one and only person who could possibly correct all this mess was somewhere in a world away. Tears welled up and she sobbed quietly, wrapping her arms around her legs and clutching her knees. Her heart ached with guilt and her mind screamed over and over, "What have I done? What have I done?"

Grace sat on the curb in quiet contemplation before noticing how wet she was from being in the freezing rain. It was almost as though she had surrendered her will and joined the rest of the landscape as a permanent resident covered in ice. Finally she wiped away her tears and slowly trudged back to her house. Inside, she peeled off her wet clothes and padded back to her room to change. Along the way she stopped in her parents' room, gave her mother and father a kiss on the cheek and whispered, "I love you."

She dressed quickly (what did one wear in the Ice World?). Pulling on blue jeans and a white T-shirt, she tucked Prince Owyn's movie mirror into her pocket, thinking it might come in handy.

Grace reached for a dry set of outdoor clothing and reluctantly grabbed the black snowpants (how cold is it in the Ice World, really?) and slipped into her yellow parka. With gloves in hand, a hat on her head and a scarf wrapped around her neck, she made her way outside.

It was still rather dangerous in the backyard; the ground was slick and hard and strewn with branches. Although the temperature was not as cold as some days, she could still see her breath in the air as she trudged down the balcony steps. Grace headed for the mound where Prince Owyn had first appeared, with every intention of carrying out the plan she had plotted on the sidewalk a little less than an hour ago.

"Now I have to do exactly what I did yesterday for this to work," she said out loud. "Okay, here goes."

Grace stood on the same mound as the day before and in the same gentle voice, neither too loud nor too soft and with perfect diction, she calmly announced to the garden, "I wish to see the Ice Prince."

Grace waited for the tiny speck of light to emerge from the fence at the back of the garden. Yesterday, it took only a few seconds to appear after she had made the initial wish, but in the dawn of this day, the speck was taking its time.

"Maybe I didn't say it right," she surmised. "I'll try again. 'I wish to see the Ice Prince.'" Grace closed her eyes hoping and trusting that when she opened them, the speck would already be upon her, growing in size and lustre. But only glinting reflections bounced off the frozen snowdrifts and winked at her mockingly.

Rain splashed on her face and trickled down her neck causing shivers. Prince Owyn wasn't coming, that was apparent, and the realization was devastating. Frustrated, she stomped in the snow muttering under her breath, "Where is he? Why hasn't he come? What have I done wrong?" until finally she yelled, fists charging the air, "I MUST GET TO THE ICE WORLD! I WISH TO BE IN THE ICE WORLD!"

The garden disappeared; her house disappeared. Grace stood surrounded by blinding, white, swirling light. A wail of wind rushed the air, a wind Grace could hear but not feel. She dared not speak in case her words would somehow shatter the wish.

The cyclone of light swirled faster and brighter until Grace was so completely engulfed in bright, white light she could no longer see any part of her body. Suddenly, the light exploded in the same blinding flash in which Prince Owyn had appeared, only this time Grace was on the inside looking out. The force of the flash broke apart the great light, shattering it into tiny sprinkles. As the specks touched ground, their light faded and died.

A thunderous clap rippled across the Ice World, its blast so great and so widespread it reached across the landscape through mountain ranges, into gorges, across meadows and into the depths of glaciers; its announcement was clear to all concerned.

The noise distracted the Traveller and sparked Farren awake.

"She hath come!" exclaimed Prince Owyn.

"She's arrived," said Ice Witch Amity, relieved.

"She's here," hissed Snitch.

"The Guardian appears," spat Evil Ice Witch Mayme.

Momentary blindness prevented Grace from realizing her landing site. Finally when the light cleared and she looked beyond, she took a step back and gasped in astonishment. "This isn't it!" she exclaimed. "Where am I?" Grace expected to see Prince Owyn's fine castle laid out before her as it had in the dream. Instead, she saw quite the opposite.

Transported to the middle of what she perceived as nowhere, Grace found herself standing in a wide valley nestled between two mountain slopes. This was not a scene she had visited in the movie mirror, nor one from her dreams; this was an altogether new destination, albeit it was in the Ice World, she was sure of that. Everything was covered in ice and snow, a colourless world glimmering under a white sun set in a clear white sky. She couldn't understand why she was here and not in Prince Owyn's home kingdom and wondered if the phrasing of her wish was responsible. Whatever the reason, she knew it must be a good one.

Grace tugged nervously at her ear lobe under her hat as she surveyed the surroundings. Never part of her plan, she anxiously considered her options, few as they were. She could try wishing herself home, but that would serve little purpose and she wasn't even sure that was possible. Perhaps the castle was hidden somewhere off in the distance, just around a corner, and if she explored a bit, she might find a clue to its location. However, deciding on which direction to take would be a stab in the dark and could lead her farther away. She knew there had to be people somewhere in this place, so she decided to investigate what stood before her.

"What a dump," she said to herself, walking toward a collection of broken-down houses and dilapidated buildings littering the landscape. "It's like a ghost town," she commented as she scouted the abandoned village for signs of life.

"Hello! Is anybody there?" Grace called. " I need some help. Hello!"

Grace picked her way through fallen timbers and stepped over broken glass and discarded items that lay in her path. She repeated her call again and again. After searching the village from one end to the other without finding anyone, she sat down on a set of crumbling stairs in despair. She looked across the valley's expanse, all glimmering and glistening in the bright sun. Ice-covered trees with branches seemingly sheathed in clear cellophane laden with frosted leaves shimmered as they stood amidst fields of tall, white grass. On both sides, snow-tipped mountain peaks rose gently from the valley floor, their jagged pinnacles pointing to the clear white sky. There was no denying the beauty of the Ice World and its spectacular scenery, but as far as Grace was concerned, it served little purpose to admire its charms while she faced her particular dilemma.

Grace retrieved the movie mirror from her jacket pocket which, coupled with recollections of her dreams, she thought might serve as some sort of map. Completely absorbed in the images portrayed in the mirror, she stood up and walked away from the stoop without bothering to take notice of the person standing a short distance ahead of her.

"I see you have returned," said a rasping voice. Startled, Grace looked up and stared bewildered into the face of a haggard old woman.

"What? Where did you come from?" Grace asked.

"I have always been here. It is my lot in life that I am tied to this place," she answered. "And I choose carefully with whom I acquaint myself."

"Er, what does that mean?" Grace responded, taken aback. Was it the norm in the Ice World that everyone spoke in riddles, she wondered?

"I wanted to be sure that you were indeed the one who had sought my council so many years ago," the woman said.

"Only I've never been here before," Grace protested.

With the support of a cane, the woman hobbled towards Grace and eyed her from top to bottom. "I am mistaken," she apologized. "The resemblance is uncanny."

"Resemblance to what?" Grace said, wanting the woman to speak less cryptically.

"Not to what, to whom," she wheezed at Grace, spewing foul breath.

"I need to get to this castle, do you know the way?" Grace said holding the mirror out for the old woman to see. The image reflected the tour of the castle and when it revealed the Great Hall where the king's throne sat, the hag gasped and pushed it away.

"This castle houses an ancient relic," the woman hissed gravely. "It has been the bane of my existence, one lost for ages and should rightfully be returned. Might you be the one destined to take up the task I wonder?" she spat as she poked her nose in Grace's face.

"What task?" Grace stumbled back.

With the support of a cane, she hobbled. Suddenly she lunged at Grace, her bony fingers clawing at her clothes and pawing her person while frantically muttering, "There must be a sign; there's always a sign . . . " Grace tried her best to fend off the attack without causing injury, but it was only when her assailant had snatched off Grace's hat that she ceased the assault. The hag recoiled in fear and slapped both her hands to her face, awed by what she saw.

"What is the matter?" Grace demanded curtly as she recovered from the attack.

"You bear the mark of one who came long ago and caused the ruin of this place," the hag replied ominously. "And it is both a burden and an obligation for you to right that wrong."

"I just need to get to this castle." Grace snatched back her hat. "Can you help me or not?"

"It is indeed crucial that you find this castle, just not for the reasons you may think," she hissed. "I cannot tell you the way. I am bound by a curse that can only be broken after you, and only you, have followed its trail. Only then will you reap the rewards and set our worlds right." She wagged her walking stick in the direction of foothills in the distance and said, "I can point you to the first leg of your journey — for it is all that I know.

"Curse? Its trail? What's 'it'?" Grace asked tiring of the woman's vague banter.

The hag's withered frame straightened slightly; she appeared almost menacing for a moment before speaking. "'It', Guardian child, is the quest for the Diamond Heart. Sit and I will tell you its story."

Chapter Sixteen

After so many years, Farren was tired and weary from wandering the Ice World in search of the creature her father had once watched over. Too many times to count, she had been steered by vague recollections to dubious locations, each one failing in the outcome. So when she happened upon a fellow traveller, her expectations remained in check.

Farren passed through a gorge cut between two mountain peaks. Suddenly a gale swept through and she sought shelter in a deserted rest stop built against the mountainside. As the storm brewed outside, Farren took stock of another who sought refuge from the miserable weather. The Traveller's build was feeble and slight, and she was draped in a cloak far too large for her frame with an enormous hood drooping down over her face. Only after the Traveller lifted her shroud did Farren realize the woman was blind, and as she stumbled forward, Farren rushed to give aid.

"Not to worry, my dear, " said the Traveller. "My eyes may be faulty but that does not mean I am without sight."

"Oh, of course, I wasn't sure, is all," Farren responded, trying not to stare into the cloudy whites of the Traveller's eyes.

The Traveller reached out with both hands and searched the landscape of Farren's face before cradling it between her palms. "There is much that I see and much that I know," she said, so cryptically that Farren couldn't help from being intrigued. "And it would appear that you also carry a vision of what you seek. Not true?"

Farren was taken aback. By lucky chance had she found herself in the company of a Seer? "I do," she admitted before revealing her quest and the destination she sought.

When Farren finished her tale, the Traveller reached out and fingered the dark amulet strung around Farren's neck before squeezing it tightly and muttering something under her breath.

"You would do well to keep this charm close to your heart. Its enchantments may well prove your success or failure."

"And of what I seek?" Farren implored.

"Your journey is clear," said the Traveller confidently. "Cross over the plains in the north and enter a belly of ice. Patience will be measured and if served, will be rewarded."

Lasting the duration of the storm, the Traveller shared many of her visions and sights. As she drew on her cloak and retreated into its hood, she signalled the end of their exchange. Farren stared blankly for a few moments, and when the squall finally blew itself out, she left the shelter in search of the places the Traveller had seen.

The trek across the ice fields, and the journey down into what the Traveller had called a "belly of ice," had drained Farren of her strength and she fell asleep outside the dragon's lair. Suddenly a thunderclap jarred her awake, and she muttered softly. Her makeshift bed against the wall of the cave offered little comfort and she knew there was scant chance she might fall back asleep. Instead she sat up, massaged her stiff neck, and waited as the Traveller had instructed.

Upon arrival, she had taken a peek at the dragon sleeping in the chamber next door but did not dare to enter for fear of waking it. Hour after hour crept by, as the two unlikely bedfellows lay deep in the heart of the mountain of ice. Prior to the Traveller's arrival, the dragon had enjoyed the pleasures of tranquil repose. However, upon departure, each passing hour found the dragon grunting and mumbling, tossing and turning on its bed of jewels — once crying out, eyes opened wide, only to fall promptly back to sleep.

"OUCH!"

Farren was startled by the loud voice and sat frozen, listening to the rumbling and cursing coming from the nearby chamber. Jewels and crystals skipped through the entrance of the dragon's cave and skidded past her. After what seemed an eternity of stomping and thrashing, the commotion finally died down.

"Who goes there? Your presence is most bothersome," the dragon snapped.

Skirting the jewels strewn about the floor, Farren cautiously approached the opening to the dragon's cave and stopped at its threshold, awaiting a second invitation just to be sure.

"My time is precious," sniped the dragon. "Tell me what you want and then be gone."

In its sleeping state, the dragon appeared smaller, but awake and standing, it loomed over Farren's slight frame. Its eyes glistened silver; sharp teeth rimmed its mouth and gleamed like the crystal stalagmites in the chamber above. It moved about the cave in graceful strides, its long, spiked tail elegantly sweeping through the air as though following a mind of its own. The dragon's wings lay folded tightly to its body and one could only guess at their wingspan once fully extended.

"I trust I am not the cause of thy awakening," Farren politely observed.

"You are not. A spiked crystal pierced my scales as I shifted in my sleep," the dragon groaned, plucking a shard of glass from its tail.

"I have travelled a great distance," Farren began. "To seek thee out to make a request."

"Yes, yes, of this I already know. I've been expecting you. What I don't know, is what you want," retorted the dragon. "I am not in the habit of granting requests, however it seems you may have something to offer in return. So I am prepared to hear you out."

"I warn you, my tale is lengthy," Farren said apologetically. "I trust thou wilt grant me the time to tell it from beginning to end."

The dragon sighed, cleared away a heap of jewels and settled down on its haunches. "Begin."

She entered the cavern, closed the lid of a large silver chest overflowing with gems and sat down.

Farren began. "Some time ago, I learned of a tragic event and of an impenetrable veil that shrouded a castle dear to mine heart. Without means of entry, I chose to set on a quest to seek a way to return and offer salvation to those who reside imprisoned there. Along the way, I heard many tales of legends past. Whit by scantling whit, I was able to piece the story together until finally I had the complete tale. That is what I have come here to share with thee."

The dragon, already finding its guest tiresome, reluctantly nodded for Farren to continue.

"I speak of a union of creatures," she resumed. "Percival and Brynn of the Glenn who shared a deep love and passion.

The last of their kind and paired for life, they had lived many years and expected to share many more."

The dragon perked up from its reclining pose and gave Farren a quizzical look.

"The lovers sought only companionship and kept to themselves, shying away from the company of others. Word of their great love spread far and wide, and the kingdoms beyond the valley in which they resided took great pride in knowing such devotion existed. Suitors courting their intended claimed as much; many damsels swooned at such professions of admiration and commitment. Many travelled to the valley hoping to catch glimpses of the creatures and to discover the secret of their bond."

The dragon leaned in closer with an expression of great intensity as it listened.

"On occasion, farmers working the fields nearby would look up from their toil and watch as the creatures frolicked in the open skies, diving great depths and swooping upwards on great outstretched wings. Sunlight bounced from the creatures' scales, and glinted down long rows of silvery, spiked ridges and gleamed off the tips of their silver tails. The farmers, and for that matter anyone encountering the creatures, felt little fear. Being peaceful, they had never caused any harm. Sightings were considered omens of love and good fortune, and all who had been blessed with such a viewing left trinkets of silver and gemstones of fancy at the entrance to the valley in appreciation."

"I am familiar with this tale," the dragon interrupted. "It is one of long ago."

"Indeed it is," answered Farren.

"I am not sure I wish to hear the end of this story," said the dragon eyeing her apprehensively.

"But, the story has not yet ended, at least not the way thee might assume."

"I am not interested in your riddles, friend," the dragon said irritably as it shifted its weight. "I haven't the time or the patience."

"Time and patience art all thou possesseth. It would serve thee well to hear me out, to use thine own words."

The dragon glared at her. "All right, I gave you my word. You may continue."

Farren drew a breath and resumed. "As it is the world over, there was good in the valley and there was evil. Watchers knew all too well and took the appropriate action to preserve these last two creatures by summoning a Guardian to insure their survival."

The dragon cocked its head, puzzled, at the mention of that name. "Guardian? I had no knowledge a Guardian had been called."

"Indeed. Regrettably, there were those who regarded the creatures as a prize to be won. Many a hunter aspired to claim the creatures, hoping to bring back a trophy proving his skill. Fortunately, the Guardian was cunning and easily spoiled any attempt to bring about their demise. Years passed, many years, and talk of their slaying dwindled and the creatures were finally left in peace. Sightings were fewer and, although tales of their existence grew into legend and fable, the story of their undying love still captured those who made the pilgrimage to the valley. This proved well for the creatures; they were quite content to be left alone."

Farren paused for a moment before continuing. The dragon had become restless, picking up jewels and tossing them about, inspecting its talons and preening its scales — almost as if it were avoiding the story and trying not to listen.

"Finally, one fateful day a lone traveller much like myself happened to venture into the valley, but unlike myself, this traveller was of mean spirit and evil thoughts. A burly man, gruff and surly with selfish intentions, he came upon one of the creatures unseen. He eyed its treasure of trinkets and jewels, and smiled at his good fortune. Encumbered with many mouths to feed at home, this cache would surely ease his burden. Silently he approached the creature, drew a great broadsword out from under his cloak and raised it high above his head. The creature turned, with breast exposed and . . . "

"I will hear no more!" the dragon angrily cried as it began stomping and thrashing about the cave.

"But thou must!" shouted Farren back.

"And who are you to tell this tale" the dragon bellowed. "After all these years!"

"This story must be told after all these years. Years squandered in self-pity and agonizing regrets," she retorted. "Years of loneliness and solitude. Years of pain and sorrow."

The dragon careened to a halt and glared down at Farren.

"Years of love lost." Farren's voice softened to a gentler tone. "Years of reliving cherished moments, only to be burdened with a final devastating act of horror."

The dragon's eyes narrowed and its brow furrowed in contempt. It turned its back on her and marched over to a corner, its tail thrashing wildly behind. Farren slowly approached the angry beast.

"I have not come here to add to thy sorrow, neither to relive events past. Thou hast done that enough thyself over the years," said Farren, soothingly. "I have come here to offer a different ending to this story. One that will lift thy spirits and release thine heartache. Allow me to continue, as painful as it may be."

The dragon jerked its head around and stared at Farren, considering her request, and finally took a deep breath, "You may continue, but I warn you, I do not take kindly to those who upset me".

She nodded, " I understand, I will tread cautiously so as not to offend. As the story goes, the Guardian left his post, lured away by the charms of a fair maiden, leaving the creatures vulnerable and allowing an opportunity for the hunter to attack."

"Where is this Guardian now? I should like a word with him," seethed the dragon armed with this new knowledge.

"Vanished," Farren answered quickly, anxious to resume the tale. "The hunter plunged the sword deep into the creature's chest; the tip reached the heart and the creature fell. Far off in the distance, its mate had crested the valley, and to its horror, witnessed the falling of its beloved. Overpowered with rage, it raced across the valley, but the distance was too great, alas. The hunter withdrew his sword and instantly the creature's body shimmered with light as it rose from the ground, lingered for a moment, then shattered into thousands of crystals of ice.

As the crystals fell covering the floor of the valley, only one thing remained of the shattered body. The hunter grabbed it and quickly stole off into the woods and disappeared."

The dragon stood up and began pacing about the cave, scattering jewels about with each step.

"The surviving mate . . . "

"And what do you know of the 'surviving mate'?" the dragon harshly interrupted. "You speak with knowledge gained only from gossip and hearsay. Only I know what did, in fact, occur and only I can recount the truth." The dragon stopped pacing and sat down.

Farren withdrew, knowing better than to challenge the dragon further. A satisfied smile spread across her hooded face. Her quarry had reached the emotional state she had hoped for. Perhaps now with its guard down, the dragon would be prepared to participate in the telling of the story. And that would be to Farren's advantage.

Chapter Seventeen

Grace listened intently as the wearisome woman recounted her story. Had she not seen for herself some of the magical creatures this world offered, she might not have believed that dragons existed. As descendants of the hunter who had slain the dragon's mate, the woman's family history read tragically and she was now one of the last members to suffer the same fate. Vague about Grace's connection to the Guardian, she kept insisting that Grace was the singular one who could break the curse cast years ago.

"Know this," the woman warned. "You'll not see your home world till your quest is complete." She then rambled on about crystal spirits called Watchers and vows that could not be broken. Watchers, Seekers, Guardians . . . it was all very foreign to Grace. Whatever they called themselves really didn't matter much; all she was interested in was finding the castle. That she had to follow the trail of a precious stone along the way seemed somewhat inconvenient but as it served as a means to an end, she accepted the challenge.

The hag sent Grace off with a few scraps of food stuffed into a well-worn sack and she nibbled from it as she walked out of the valley. The hag knew only the first leg of the Diamond Heart's journey, and armed with directions to this new destination, Grace hoped that her own journey would not be a lengthy one — she was anxious to get back home.

"My beloved Brynn was gone," the dragon Percival wailed, succumbing to Farren's tale, overwhelmed by the events of the past while admitting his true identity. "Gone, all gone. I gathered all of the ice crystals hoping somehow I could bring my love back. Sadly, it was all for naught. In my anger I tore through the forest searching for the killer, day after day, fuelled only by my drive to seek vengeance. I terrorized villages, sending simple, ordinary folk screaming and begging for mercy. My quest for revenge consumed me. I lashed out at everything and everyone who crossed my path. Alas, it was all in vain. The slayer had cleverly eluded me and I could not find him."

Percival dropped his head in despair. "In time, my anger turned to agonizing grief. I fled, seeking escape from that wretched world and I brought myself here, where I have been ever since."

"Yes, here. In this mountain of ice," said Farren. "Surrounded by the jewels and trinkets gathered from the valley."

"It is all that remains of the love I once shared. These baubles and bijoux hold great memories and are more precious to me than anything. This is why I have hidden away, lest even these be taken from me."

"I assure thee, I have no desire to rob thy precious jewels. 'Tis not what I seek," Farren responded.

"And just what do you seek?" Percival demanded. "You have gone out of your way to repeat my history, as painful as it was. Why? I ask again as I did before, what is it that you want?"

"Although thou hast finished thy story thyself, 'tis not this ending I was about to tell," Farren replied. "'Tis true, thy mate was slain and thy revenge was never sought. Thy retreat to this prison of ice has kept thee from the ways of the world and the events of late. Things have changed in the great world beyond thy cavern."

Percival sighed. This game was getting tiresome, yet a lingering premonition nagged at him and he was inclined to allow Farren to continue.

"The death of an Ice Dragon is a spectacular occurrence as thou canst attest. A direct stab to the heart is the only means by which one may be slain. Upon the moment when its life is extinguished, the body is turned back into the ice from whence it came and scattered over the landscape — all except the heart."

Percival flinched. "You need not remind me. In death, the heart of an Ice Dragon transforms from a living, beating organ to the clearest, purest diamond. It is prized among my kind and cherished almost as much as the dragon it gave life to. I would gladly honour my beloved's Diamond Heart, if it hadn't been taken from me."

"Indeed. The hunter not only took the life of thy mate Brynn, he snatched the Diamond Heart as well," Farren said. "And although he did indeed elude thee, the treasure he carried turned out to be more of an unwanted burden than a coveted prize. Word of thy pursuit spread far and wide — and news of thy rampages as well. The hunter soon discovered that no one even dared to look at the Diamond Heart, let alone acquire it. Many villages had caught the wrath of thy fury and townsfolk everywhere feared for their lives. The hunter was shunned by all and finally, realizing the jewel was worthless, tossed it away."

"Tossed it away!" Percival shouted. "Cast away like a piece of rubbish? This is your ending of my story, with my beloved's diamond heart tossed away?"

"Hardly," she answered, desperately. "The journey of the Diamond Heart is a story unto itself. It only commences with the slayer's thievery. Eager to be free of the stone he cast it into a small glacial sea."

"The slayer threw my love's Diamond Heart into a sea? What sea?" he demanded.

"An icy sea. Where silver sea serpents chanced to live," she replied.

"And what, pray tell, would a sea serpent want with a Diamond Heart?" he agonized.

"Nothing. Nothing, except perhaps as a toy for its young to toss about."

"It's a disgrace and a dishonour to my beloved," said Percival in quiet fury. "What of these sea serpents and of the Diamond Heart?"

Farren sat back down on the chest. Rendering the tale was taking longer than expected, and she began to tire. But there was much too much at stake, and by telling the story she hoped to gain the dragon's trust. As long as she kept him entertained with tales of the heart — even if some proved untrue — success was surely guaranteed and he would comply with her requests.

Chapter Eighteen

Grace encountered few travellers along the way, and those she did sent her strange looks and offhand glances. She wasn't that surprised. After all, she was a stranger here and nothing made that fact more pronounced than her clothes — her yellow jacket and jet-black pants shouted in this world of white. As horse-drawn carts rambled down the road, Grace thought of sticking out her thumb to catch a ride, but decided against it. Hitchhiking might prove dangerous and, presently, she didn't need any more drama in her day.

However, when a young man drove past her, stopped and called her way, she paused.

"Oye! Yeh there," he said with a thick accent. "Ne'd a ride?"

At first, Grace looked back thinking he was calling to someone behind her. With no one there, she turned and put her hand to her chest in a gesture of "Who me?"

"Ya, yeh. C'mon, hop in."

Mindful of strangers, she initially hesitated. But she knew she would have to trust someone eventually in order to get the information she needed to find the castle, so she tossed her sack on the seat of the cart and jumped aboard.

"Thanks, I could use a lift."

"Wher' yeh frum?" he asked her. "Wher'yeh goin'?"

"Let's just say I'm not from around here. I'm just visiting." Grace replied, hoping her answer would be accepted without further explanation. "I'm looking for this castle," showing the mirror to her driver.

He whistled in admiration at the image of the castle reflected in the glass. "Can't help yeh with tha'."

"Oh," Grace responded. "Well, then maybe you can tell me how far away is the sea? I was told it was this way."

"Tha sea's jus' beyon' tha' hill."

Grace was overjoyed with her good fortune; finally something was going her way and she smiled at the young man in appreciation. She bounced in her seat as the cart rambled along the bumpy road. As they crested the hill, the charming vista below surprised her. Seemingly plucked straight from a picture postcard, the sea went on for miles, its crystal water lapping at the shore and sparkling in the sunshine. A large fishing village stretched along the shore and Grace couldn't help thinking how quaint and picturesque the buildings all looked, with their thatched, white roofs and clapboard walls. Boats in the harbour bobbed in the surf as each wave rippled to shore, their decks laden with silver nets filled with the catch of the day. It was a busy port — stalls and booths were piled high with fish of all shapes and sizes and the air was filled with fishmongers' cries as they flung their wares back and forth. The cart lumbered into the village and stopped in front of a large shop where Grace stepped down from her seat.

"Is there someone who can tell me about a diamond that was found here a long time ago?" Grace asked politely of her ride.

The young man eyed her with a touch of suspicion. "Bin a long time anybody bin askin' 'bout tha'. Yeh sure yeh want t' go diggin in anc'ent histry, Miss?"

Grace nodded, noting his change in demeanour from happy-go-lucky to sombre and she wasn't sure she liked his tone. "I'm sure," she said almost reluctantly.

"Best ta go find Ormann, the Master Fisherman," he said. "He'll tell yeh straight. I'll show yeh wher' he is."

Grace followed the young man to a long dock at the far end of the harbour where a large fishing vessel lay moored in its slip. After introductions, and her request offered up, the Master Fisherman left his nets and guided Grace down to the end of the dock, away from the bustle of his boat.

"Now, why would such a young thing be wanting to know about the Diamond Heart?" he asked, his accent less pronounced than that of the young man's.

"It's really important." Grace implored him. "If you can tell me anything, anything at all."

Ormann, a man of many experienced years, knew better than to question a young girl bent on the truth; he had daughters of his own who could attest to that.

Grace told him what she knew of the hunter — but that was as much as she knew and where the lead went cold. Ormann was unaware of the hunter's role and picked up the story as it had been passed down to him.

"If you look yonder at the far end of the bay, there lies a secluded inlet, home only to sea serpents. This part of the sea is quite unwelcoming and, although the meat of their young is considered flavourful fare, it is a sea where few dare try their luck at fishing. The serpents are reputed to be a vicious lot. They are rarely caught and are known to strike swiftly at any who threaten their brood, going to great lengths to protect their pups.

"As always, there are those who hazard the risk," Ormann continued. "A daring young fisherman and his youngest son set out to capture a sea serpent pup. The sea was unusually calm and the air was still. The father and son launched their vessel and were soon sailing smoothly through the icy waters toward their catch. Off in the distance, the serpents and their young glided on the surface of the water, their glistening scales catching bright sunlight and their silver manes slicing the sea. Beauty and grace were hardly what the fisherman had expected of these beasts, and when he caught sight of the serpents' watery dance, he was taken aback in awe. He turned to his son and thought to himself, *Who am I to take such a life when I, too, would protect my young?*

"He brought his vessel about, dropped his sails to drift back with the wind in the current, and watch the serpents frolic and play. As the boat bobbed into view, the serpents ceased their antics, rallied their young, and prepared to fight. When they saw the fisherman lay down his weapon, they cautiously approached. Never had a friendly encounter occurred between man and beast — this was a first for both. The fisherman's son laughed with delight as the pups circled the boat, playfully diving and splashing about as he tossed bits of bait overboard. The elder sea serpents eyed the man with distrust, but the actions of their young, playing together without fear or threat, caused the elders to withdraw.

"Many times afterward, the fisherman and his son sailed the icy waters just to watch and play with the sea serpent pups. Should other fishing vessels approach, the father and son intervened. In time, with trust, respect and even a sense of kinship earned, the elder serpents embraced the visits from the man and boy. So much so, that the pair was offered a gift of friendship."

"A gift of friendship? What sort of gift?" asked Grace.

"The eldest serpent swam out to the boat and emerged from the water, his flattened, snakelike head looming over the bow. Clenched in his teeth was an object of considerable size and he dropped it on the deck at the father's feet. The man was awestruck. It was the largest, purest diamond he had ever seen."

Chapter Nineteen

After such a lengthy dramatisation, Farren opted for a more theatrical ending. "It was Dragon Brynn's Diamond Heart."

Percival shook its head in anguish, "So, a fisherman now treasures my beloved's heart?"

"As I have said," she answered. "The history of the Diamond Heart is a story unto itself. Over the course of many long years, it has changed hands many times, commencing with the fisherman. Suffice it to say, those who gained it through goodwill were blessed with good fortune and those who acquired the Diamond Heart with ill intent suffered grave consequences. The tale is lengthy and I choose not to burden thee with such a longwinded account."

"Fine. Save your tedious tale for another time. I am growing impatient. Say what you have come here to say and be gone," sighed Percival.

"Only I know of its whereabouts," she said.

"Pray tell," Percival said mockingly, through clenched teeth.

"'Tis a secret. A secret I may choose to share with thee," she replied defiantly. "If thou wouldst grant mine one request."

Percival rushed at Farren and grabbed at her cloaked neck with his taloned claws. He lifted her off the ground and pinned her against the frozen wall of the cavern.

"You dare to toy with me," he hissed, his icy breath showering Farren's grimacing face. "I am not amused."

She clutched at the dragon's claws, gasping for breath. "Please . . . I, I, beg thee . . . "

"Ah, begging, now are you?" Percival snarled with a grin. "I like begging. It puts one in one's place."

"I . . . only . . . ask . . . a simple deed," she struggled. "A deed so simple, 'tis hardly a strain for one so powerful as thyself."

"So, you seek the use of my powers in exchange for the location of the Diamond Heart," he taunted. "I am unaccustomed to bartering with the likes of you, yet something tells me I should make an exception. Speak." Percival released his grip and Farren crashed to the floor, scattering jewels every which way upon landing.

"A kingdom, as I have recounted, is shrouded in an impenetrable veil," she croaked. "Journey back with me and break the veil, so I may enter."

"And then you will reveal the Diamond Heart?"

"Indeed. Once thou art reunited, the kingdom will again prosper."

"And what makes you so sure I can complete this task?" Percival asked, enjoying her discomfort. "Even if I was so inclined?"

Farren stood up brushing flakes of ice off the heavy fabric of her long robes. "I have heard tell of the power of thy vapours. One breath delivers a cone of frost so mighty it rivals even the harshest wind. The other releases flames of silver so extreme in intensity that great glacial mountains have been known to vanish with a single exhale of thy lungs. Surely such powers could accomplish this small task."

Percival circled Farren rubbing his chin with a talon. "Perhaps, if you revealed the site of the Diamond Heart, I would consider your request."

"Dost thou take me for a fool?" she exclaimed. "I have not come from afar only to be used for mine knowledge and then cast aside!"

The dragon halted abruptly, impressed by Farren's staunch insistence. "You are a courageous one and your devotion to your quest is admirable. You must truly love and honour those of that kingdom to take such risks," he said, his voice softening. "Just as I would have to save my own beloved. And now, the one thing in all the worlds that is still denied to me you offer in fair trade. Although the life of my love is lost, I take great comfort in knowing I may still cherish her Diamond Heart and remember with great joy the times of our life together." Percival stepped forward to face her. "Your request is granted. Our journey begins in good time. For now I wish to rest, as you should likewise. We will depart once I am refreshed." Percival retreated to a corner of the cavern and resumed the same sleeping position in which Farren had first found him. Backing out of the cave, Farren breathed a sigh of relief. Step one of the quest had been fulfilled.

Chapter Twenty

"Wow!" was all Grace could muster after hearing the tale. First dragons, now sea serpents, what would be next? "What happened to the Diamond Heart after that?"

"For many years the fisherman guarded the Diamond Heart," Ormann answered. "He could not bear to part with its beauty and brilliance. It was not just a stone, but also a symbol of friendship and good will, and he felt that to sell it would taint his good fortune. And good fortune was exactly what the fisherman enjoyed during the years he spent with the Diamond Heart. As age crept upon him and his death drew near, he relinquished it to his son who promised never to surrender the stone. He knew and understood the value of the jewel and did indeed fulfil his father's wishes. The Diamond Heart remained in the fisherman's family, passing from one generation to another, until a time when the family's fortune had grown so great that owning the stone seemed selfish and humbling. Other families had not prospered as well, and the fisherman's family felt the need to share the stone with those less fortunate."

"And . . . " prompted Grace.

"In the village square," Ormann continued, "there stood a great fountain, one that jetted clear, fresh water from many tiers splashing to a pool below where children would often play. The fisherman's family proposed to set the stone atop the fountain so that all in the village could enjoy its beauty and benefit from its powers of prosperity."

"But it's not there anymore," said Grace. "What happened to it?"

"It was stolen many years ago."

"Stolen? Do you know who stole it?" Grace asked, fearing a dead end in the story.

"There was rumour of a knight gone astray, one who must have recognized the true value of the heart and hankered to possess it, but the village never made chase. With our continued good fortune, we soon discovered that we did not need the actual diamond. Its power remained and has blessed us to this very day."

His words brought a smile to Grace's face. "Do you know where I can find this knight?" she asked.

"There lies a Kingdom of Knights not far to the north," he replied. "It's doubtful he is still alive, although there might be someone there who can continue the story."

Grace and Ormann returned to his boat where he offered her a bowl of thick chowder. The meagre scraps from the hag had staved off her hunger for a while. Now they were gone and her hunger was back. While she ate, Ormann drew a map to the castle of the Kingdom of Knights. Grateful for his time and attention as well as for the meal and the map, Grace wished him well and set off on her journey again. As she left the village, the young man waved a friendly goodbye, cementing the notion that there were indeed trustworthy folks who she could count on for help.

Chapter Twenty-One

After too many hours to count, Farren was beginning to feel restless. The dragon had not moved since lying down to rest and didn't appear to be planning to wake anytime soon. True, Percival had indicated a need to refresh before beginning their journey, but as each hour dragged on, Farren wondered just how much time the dragon really needed. An hour, five hours, a day, two weeks? Perhaps he needed a wake-up call of sorts, like a soft whisper and a gentle nudge. Or did he require a more direct approach, such as a loud noise or a splash of water to his face? Would it be prudent to rouse the sleeping beast or would that cause more calamity and vexation than allowing him to awaken on his own? Thus embroiled in deciding on a course of action, Farren barely noticed the tip of the dragon's spiked, silver tail slide by.

"Well, it's now or never, my travelling friend," bellowed Percival as the startled girl jumped up to retrieve her satchel and other belongings.

"Coming," she called to his departing back as she skittered over icicles trying to catch up. "Couldn't have chanced a bit of a warning?" she muttered indignantly.

Farren crossed the open cavern far less cautiously than when she had entered it and, since Percival had set such a brisk pace, toiling up the tunnel proved far more exhausting than the downward route. Ahead, the slither of the dragon's tail wending through the twists and turns of the passageway was all she could see.

Reaching the exit, Percival flattened his silver wings tightly against his body, and proving the Traveller's elephant theory true, squeezed through the opening. Farren followed and they were soon making their way up the cave's chiselled path. As they wove their way through the forest of hourglass ice, the dragon casually snapped a stalactite from the roof of the cave. He crunched it between his crystal teeth, much like a child enjoying an iced treat from the corner store.

"Well, this is where our journey begins," said Percival, fragments of ice dribbling down his chin as they stood at the mouth of the cave and looked out onto the stretch of ice field below. Swept by a persistent wind from the north, a layer of snow skimmed the ice like the ripple of waves lapping to shore.

"Shall we get started?" asked Percival. Farren nodded, then adjusted the hood of her cloak to block the wind and secured her satchel.

"See you on the other side!" shouted Percival as he suddenly unfolded his great silver wings and launched into the air.

"W-wait!" exclaimed Farren with a start, but the wind whisked her words away — the dragon was already too far away to hear them.

Angry at being left to trek across the icefield alone, Farren muttered unkind sentiments under her breath. With determination she began the descent of the glacier, slowly and carefully, and reached the bottom unscathed. The icefield lay ahead. Bowing her head, she braced against the pounding wind and began the crossing.

At the halfway mark, a large grey shadow crept up from behind, lingered momentarily above before darkening her path, then disappeared off ahead. Paying it no mind, Farren pushed on. Nevertheless, when the shadow returned over and over again, she could not help but wonder what it was. Farren strained to look through the blowing snow to discover its source but failed to catch sight of it, thus denying her suspicions that it was Percival. "Oh, how bothersome he can be," she thought to herself. The journey across the icefield was enough of a challenge; being stalked along the way for no reason was simply annoying.

As the edge of the icefield drew near, Farren could make out the treeline of the forest that lay beyond. The shelter of trees would bring relief from her vulnerability to exposure on the icefield, and put an end to Percival's antics.

She entered, pushing aside frozen branches with both hands, and followed a path that led to a large pile of icy boulders stacked randomly on top of each other. There, leaning against a particularly smooth slab, the dragon preened his scales and brushed snow from his wings.

"Pleasant trip?" inquired Percival sarcastically. "It took you quite a long time, mind you. Flying is much faster."

Farren glared at him. "Could thou hast offered me passage?"

"What? How?" asked Percival.

"On thy back," she answered.

"On my back!" he exclaimed. "What do you think I am? A beast of burden?!"

"No, although it mightn't have hurt. 'Twas arduous enough making the journey. Abandoning me to fend alone was simply reckless, as someone was following me," she said accusingly.

"Really? Who?"

"I have my suspicions," she scowled. "Alas, I never chanced a sighting."

"Were you fearful? Were you afraid?" Percival taunted.

"No, actually I was quite bothered that someone needed to resort to childish pranks to get mine attention."

"Oh," said Percival sheepishly, "I just thought I'd check your progress to see how long it would take you. For one of your size, you are rather sprightly, in spite of all that wind and blowing snow."

"How darest thee to make mockery of me?" she demanded. "Have I not proven mine worth? Must I continue to do so over and over again?"

"You will have proven your worth once I hold my beloved's heart next to mine," offered Percival. "Until then, I may do as I please, whether you like it or not."

Farren and the dragon locked eyes, neither willing to stand down. The silence between them roared as loudly as the howling winds across the ice field. An eternity seemed to pass until finally she spoke.

"The journey we face is lengthy and perilous. Arguments and bickering will surely be our failing. We must stand side by side, joined as one in our task. Might we not abide by some sort of truce?" She implored. "We have an agreement, have we not?"

Percival eyed her with resentment at being berated like a misbehaving child. "We do indeed," he surrendered.

"So, honour it, as I will in return," she responded.

In time, after tempers had cooled and egos felt less bruised, the pair set off through the forest. Without a clearly marked path to follow, Farren and the dragon pressed on through dense thickets, overgrown brush and tall, ice-laden trees. Farren easily slipped in and out of tight spaces, but the dragon's size forced him to stomp his way through, crushing and flattening whatever lay in his path. Finally they reached a clearing and stopped to rest.

"A ways beyond lies a well-travelled road," said Farren, breaking their silence. "We must be mindful not to be seen."

"Are you worried that we might attract attention?" remarked Percival. "Surely dragons and hooded travellers are seen together almost everyday in these parts."

"Thy sarcasm is most annoying," she said dryly. "Surely, the sight of a dragon after so many years would cause quite a stir and perhaps rouse the ambitions of certain unscrupulous people. Wouldst thou be willing to share the fate of thy beloved?"

"I would not," answered Percival. "It is clear why I must conceal myself, but it is not clear why you must. What is it that you have to hide?"

Farren reached into her satchel, withdrew a flask and took a long drink, seemingly to avoid the dragon's question.

"Well?" He pursued.

"My concern is for thy safety."

"Bah! My safety! I assure you that I am quite capable of taking care of myself!" Percival retorted. "That's not it. Now tell me what you are hiding from, or rather whom?"

Farren tucked the flask back into the satchel. "Very well, if thou must know. I am avoiding those who have been commissioned to retrieve me. Searchers who would prevent the completion of mine quest, and unsavoury souls who would hold me for ransom.

"So, there is a bounty on your head," Percival gloated. "And who might pay such a ransom?"

"It is none of thy concern."

"But it is!" He objected. "I demand to know what dangers we may face or I'll not take one step further."

"As long as we travel unnoticed there will be no danger," said Farren. "Place thy trust in my judgement. Now, we must push on. Time is wasting."

Farren stood up and walked out into the clearing. Percival reluctantly followed, muttering under his breath, "Place thy trust in my judgement, place thy . . . "

Chapter Twenty-Two

By day's end, Farren and the dragon had covered a greater distance than expected and with little incident. The occasional appearance of fellow travellers along the way forced them to take cover — a feat not easily accomplished considering Percival's size. With the bickering and arguing at bay, they plodded on making good time. Tucked away in a small valley surrounded by fields of tall ice-grass, an abandoned stable served as accommodation and they settled down for a simple meal and much needed rest.

"You may continue your tale," Percival said.

"And what tale might that be?" asked Farren between bites.

"That of the Diamond Heart," He replied. "You said that it changed hands many times. I would like to hear its history and to whom it was passed on."

"The journey has sapped much of mine strength, hence I have none to continue the tale at this time," she answered. "Allow me the comfort of sleep, and once refreshed I will abide by thy request."

"Humph," sighed Percival gruffly. "Suit yourself, which seems to be so often the case."

"I have little interest in quarrelling now. It would serve thee well to do as I." And with that said, she got up and walked over to the far end of the barn.

Leftover bales of silver hay sat piled one atop the other and Farren struggled to pull some away from the heap. Having freed a few, she arranged the bales end to end, meticulously packing and stuffing the dry hay into place. Once arranged to her satisfaction, she lay down on top. With her satchel as a makeshift pillow, Farren stretched out quite comfortably on the improvised bed and promptly fell asleep.

In a corner Percival grumbled under his breath, indignant at being ignored and left alone. He sat back on his haunches, arms crossed on his chest as small puffs of white mist drifted from his nostrils — an indication of just how piqued he was. When Farren's rhythmic snoring grew louder and deeper, further aggravating his irritation, the dragon stormed out of the barn and onto the field.

After so many years of seclusion, the open sky and long stretch of field between two mountaintops seemed huge to Percival. He had wallowed in misery for so long that loneliness and despair were his constant companions. Now, with Farren's intrusion and her unexpected request, he realized he was due for change. Percival drew a breath, inhaling the surroundings and embracing the valley's splendour. With these delightful sensations, his displeasure with Farren quickly faded, replaced by feelings of renewal and a restored sense of purpose. The quest for the Diamond Heart was a quest for freedom, and Percival hoped to find peace and closure. The icy cave he had once called home felt a million leagues away and he vowed never to return. Somehow, somewhere, Percival would find his rightful place in the Ice World and begin his life anew.

Dismissing the thought that Farren might object, Percival unfolded his silver wings to their fullest span and took off in flight up toward low-lying clouds dotting the horizon. With each downward snap of his powerful wings he soared higher and higher, above the clouds, until he was beyond view. The pleasure and thrill of flight, denied for so long, cemented his resolve. When he began his descent after circling the valley and rounding the mountain peaks, the dragon felt something he hadn't felt in a very long time. He felt alive.

As Percival passed through the cloud cover, he noticed a figure far below on the ground outside the barn. The figure was flailing its arms and shouting loudly, and Percival wondered whether Farren had been detected, thus drawing attention to the dragon himself. Closer and closer he flew until the figure's identity was made clear. It was no stranger. It was Farren, fully awake and fully enraged.

"Art thou mad?" she shrieked as Percival landed. "Hast thee lost thy senses?"

Percival folded his wings back against his body as he approached. He knew the risk he had taken by making this flight and fully expected a less than approving reaction if discovered. He didn't care.

"I was just stretching my wings," said Percival nonchalantly. "Did you sleep well?"

"Sleep well? Sleep well?" she said incredulously.

"I'll assume so, considering the racket you were making by snoring. I couldn't abide by the noise, so I thought I'd take some air."

"Take some air? Thou didst more than just simply take some air. Thou wast *in* the air!" she shouted.

"Oh, be still. I was not seen, if that's what concerns you. I flew above the clouds where no one could see me from the ground," answered Percival as he brushed by her and entered the barn.

"Well, well, above the clouds. How artful, how cunning, how wily thou art to consider concealing thyself," she said sarcastically, following behind. "Didst thee consider that perchance, thou might be glimpsed on the way up and on the way down en route to thy place of concealment? What good is camouflage if one is sighted getting there and getting back?"

Percival turned to face her. "I am quite sure that no one saw me and if someone did, well someone did. It's most likely he thought his eyes were playing tricks on him. After all, a dragon hasn't been seen in these parts in years. Who would believe it? In any case, there's nought we can do about it now."

Farren began to protest, but stopped short. "Indeed, there is little chance of repairing any damage done. I beseech thee, reconsider any future ventures lest thee be sighted."

Percival reluctantly nodded and retreated to the corner of the barn, curled up on the floor, and closed his eyes. Satisfied at having had the last word, Farren returned to her makeshift bed and did the same.

Bathed in white, the terrain of the Ice World stretched out for leagues, gleaming and glistening. High overhead the sun shone brightly, sending rays of light throughout. Sunbeams spilled through open windows, danced between tree branches, seeped into cracks and crevices, and blanketed the landscape, leaving nothing untouched. Sunlight sent by the Ice World's sun took many forms, as rays or beams or licks of light, as it travelled down to spread its everlasting brilliance. So when a single sliver of light slipped away from the sun and playfully spiralled downward, it was not at all surprising that the two unlikely companions quarrelling far below did not catch sight of it swirling above. Had they been more vigilant, constantly scouring their surroundings for the possibility of detection, they might have had cause for alarm. But in their agitated state, airing their differences outside the stable, they overlooked the threat from above.

Chapter Twenty-Three

There was even less traffic on the road Grace followed. Although Ormann had estimated it would take only a few hours of travel by foot, Grace hoped another cart might come along and give her a ride. She checked her watch, more out of habit than to find the time; it read the same as it had back home. She shook her wrist and tapped on its face hoping to jar it back into working order, but the digital read did not budge and stayed permanently fixed at nine forty-five. Prince Owyn had explained that time would not change in her world while she was in his, and she wondered if devices from home might not operate here either. Grace kept her eyes open for the place marked on the map directing her to leave the road and enter the forest.

Soon enough, she came upon a break in the trees and found a path carved into the woods leading to the Kingdom of Knights — if the map was correct. Cut wide with dense forest on both sides, the pathway could easily accommodate a large squadron of knights riding through on horseback. It was very bright in the forest. Trees glistened under their coats of ice, and the opening above allowed the sun to shine directly upon her.

Away from the bustle of the village and amid the sparse traffic of the road, Grace was feeling very small and alone among the tall trees. Singing to herself along the way helped keep her occupied, but now in the quiet of the forest, her thoughts turned to her parents. Their sleeping faces came to mind and she studied their features as never before, imprinting their images in her mind lest she ever forget what they looked like. It was painful to imagine never seeing them again and she held fast to Prince Owyn's promise that she could return. But that promise had been made under very different circumstances and Grace had no idea whether it would still hold true. That the hag had told her that she couldn't go home until she had completed this quest nagged at her and she hoped that a Prince had more leverage than an old woman. For the time being, she banished such dreadful thoughts. She had to stay positive; she had a job to do, and nothing and no one was going to get in her way from doing it.

With a fresh resolve, Grace jump-started her pace. Her stride increased twofold once spires appeared above the treeline not far in the distance.

The Kingdom of Knights was a very different kingdom than that of the prince's. Whereas Owyn's castle was beautiful and majestic, this was a military establishment with a forbidding, baleful face. The main tower and the wall that surrounded it were not pristine white and did not sparkle in the sunlight. Instead grey ice formed the structure, almost as if soiled water had been frozen into blocks. Sharp metal spires shot into the sky as the grilled grate of the portcullis slid down within the entrance of the gatehouse. Arrow slits dotted the battlement and hoarding at the top of the tower afforded the castle additional defences. This was a stronghold; a fortress home to established knights as well as youths of noble blood who apprenticed as squires.

Grace wondered how she was going to approach such an intimidating place. Unlike the fishing village there was no one here to make introductions. Knocking on the door or ringing the doorbell was out of the question since there was neither. Instead she faced a drawbridge, a secure portcullis and a sizeable moat.

"Hello! Excuse me, anybody there?" She tried calling, waving her arms as she stood at the edge of the moat. Her voice was too tiny to breach the thick walls of the castle and her size was so dwarfed by the massive structure that someone on the other side would probably need a spyglass to see her.

"Maybe I should try wishing myself inside," she wondered, but quickly dismissed it. She just couldn't trust that the wish would take her precisely where she wanted to go and that she might end up in a Kingdom of Trolls. If she did have a wish that would actually come true, she would have to reserve it for getting home. So she continued to shout and wave over and over again, and just when her arms tired and her voice grew hoarse, she heard the gears of the gatehouse begin to grind. The drawbridge slowly lowered as the portcullis simultaneously rose in the entrance and she was sure she must have finally been seen or heard. Far off down the pathway a rumbling sound grew louder and louder as something quickly approached.

Turning, Grace found herself caught in the path of a squadron of armoured knights on horseback charging toward the castle. The drawbridge had not completely descended and without choice of another escape, Grace dove beneath it just before it touched the ground. She clung to the moat's bank as the riders thundered over the bridge, the sound deafening and causing her to scream at its tremendous force. When the last of the knights crossed, the gears began to grind again and Grace knew she had been given an opportunity.

She scrambled up from the side of the moat, hoisted herself over onto the rising bridge and hung from the edge. Easily five times her size, a drop from the top of the bridge would surely result in a sprained ankle, if not a break. As the angle of the bridge slowly increased, she scooted like a spider until she could step onto the floor. The portcullis gate lowered as the bridge rose and she rolled under it narrowly avoiding its spear-like tips that could have easily impaled her. She picked herself up and inched down the corridor following the knights' trail. Cautiously she poked her head through the opening at the other end.

The castle grounds bustled. Squires practised diligently in the tiltyard, jousting on horseback with lances and shields, while pages tended to their armour and their chargers' tack. In one corner a smithy pounded the blade of a broadsword, his hammer ringing with each strike cast. Upon inspection, he plunged the great sword into a barrel of water which hissed and steamed. Stable boys mucked out stalls and threw bushels of grey straw to the floor before leading horses to their water and feed. Carts and wagons carried stores and supplies to various stations and once relieved of their loads, lumbered back again. The knights who had ridden in ahead of Grace dismounted from their chargers, handing the reins over to attentive squires eager to serve. They clanged in their armour as they gathered in groups, jostling each another in camaraderie.

From her place at the entrance, the whole spectacle appeared intimidating and Grace wondered what sort of reaction they would have once she made her presence known. Fear that they might view her as some sort of enemy or spy quickly dissolved. She was hardly a threat in her yellow jacket and black pants — different yes, but certainly no menace. If she could discreetly attract someone's attention, she might be able avoid causing too much of a stir.

A stable boy about her size passed nearby carrying a bucket of water in each hand. Grace grabbed his shirt and yanked him into the corridor, causing the water to slosh over the rims and splash to the floor. She clapped her hand to his mouth to muffle his utterance of surprise and put her finger to her lips to signal silence. "It's okay. I'm a friend," she said.

Caught so completely off guard, the boy hadn't the sense to drop his buckets in defence, and stared wide-eyed at his captor. Finally, he nodded and Grace withdrew her hand.

"Where did you come from?" he asked incredulously, catching his breath. "And how did you get in here?"

"I can explain all that, " she answered. "But first I need your help."

"Help, you need help?" he asked.

"Yes, I need help from one of your knights," she answered.

"You need help from one of our knights?"

"Yes!' Grace said in exasperation. "What's a girl got to do to get some help around here?"

"You're a girl?"

"Of course I'm a girl," she protested indignantly.

"So you're a girl who needs help from a knight," said the boy.

"Exactly." Grace answered, relieved that she was finally getting through.

Suddenly the boy tossed away the buckets, pulled Grace by the hand, and ran onto the castle grounds, waving his arms and shouting. "Oye! We've got a damsel in distress!"

In unison, the Brotherhood of Knights cast aside their labours and snapped into action, brandishing swords and banding together to defend her honour. Grace stumbled forward and found herself surrounded by knights, and the focus of everyone's attention.

"What did you have to go and do that for?' she chided the boy. "Sheesh!" Without an apparent threat, the knights stood down. The sound of metal against metal pierced the air as they sheathed their swords in unison. One especially large, noble knight stepped forward, went down on one knee and bowed before Grace.

"How may we be of service, m'lady?" he asked politely.

Grace fumbled nervously. Blush rose in her cheeks as she stepped over to the knight and tapped him on the shoulder. "You don't have to do that. Please get up." The knight complied. He was used to taking orders.

Grace launched into her story and explained why she was there and how she needed their help. After she finished, hushed murmurs swept through the ranks and the knight who had stepped forward spoke for them all.

"There was indeed a knight, Sir Kenard, from long ago who brought such a jewel to this castle," he told her. "Alas, he has since fallen, but his tale remains and it is our duty to honour his memory by telling it. Follow me and I shall introduce the Master Chronicler."

Chapter Twenty-Four

Percival woke up stiff and sore all over. The wing muscles in his chest ached to the core from flying. His leg muscles were tight and inflexible — he had done too much too soon, and he deeply regretted not pacing himself. Flying now was out of the question, whether or not he would allow Farren to ride on his back. Even walking was going to be a struggle, but he was not about to let on that he was disabled. His pride ruled out such an admission.

Finally, Farren rose from her makeshift straw bed and was eager to leave.

"Don't rush me," Percival snapped as he heaved himself up trying to hide his discomfort. "You take the lead, I'll follow behind."

Farren and the dragon set off, leaving the stable and the valley behind. Fortunately, the terrain was rather flat and Percival was relieved there would be little climbing to endure. Nevertheless, Farren noticed just how far back he was lagging and waited to confront him.

"Might I remind thee that we are not out for a leisurely stroll," she said once Percival had caught up.

"This pace suits me fine," he retorted. "I'm enjoying the fine scenery lost to me for so long." He was keenly aware that even his tail smarted as it dragged along the ground.

"Sightseeing is not on the agenda, now hurry up" she quipped and stormed on ahead.

They crested a hill and arrived at the edge of an ice-covered forest. Passage through the thick forest seemed impossible, especially for the dragon. Heavy, gnarled branches with intertwining limbs wove a twisted and tangled canopy that very little light could filter through, making the forest dark and ominous. The wall of crowded trees stood taller than the dragon and stretched long and wide, covering the countryside and rising up along the slope of a mountain for as far as the eye could see.

Without a means to enter, Farren drew a long, sharp blade and began to hack through the overgrown brush. After what seemed an eternity of chopping and slashing, she fell back panting from exhaustion. Not a chip of ice or a noticeable dent had been made in the wood and she dropped the blade in frustration.

"There . . . must . . . be . . . another . . . way," she said between breaths. "Perhaps a way around."

"But how did you get through this forest on your way to my lair?" asked Percival, secretly welcoming this obstacle for a chance to rest.

"'Twas not here when I first passed through," she answered.

"Not here?" Percival said, rubbing his shoulder trying to work out a knot. "How is that possible? For a forest to grow in such a short time."

"I know not," Farren said dryly, pacing up and down in front of the barrier of trees, her attention directed away from the dragon.

"Well then, there's only one explanation," responded Percival.

"And what might that be?" she asked, stopping in mid-stride.

"It's enchanted, of course."

"Enchanted?" she cried. "By whom? By what and why?"

"Oh, now that is the mystery. It could be any number of things. Could be tree spirits, or dryads or even the wood itself could be bewitched. Could be an evil enchantment, could be a good enchantment. Why, it could be a mixture of good and evil enchantments. It could be an enchantment directed at only one thing and not at another. It could be —"

"Enough!" she interrupted. "Whatever the enchantment, how may the spell be broken so we may resume our journey?"

"Well, it might not be a spell necessarily," Percival countered, "It might be a charm or a hex of some sort. Or . . . " He paused.

"Or what?" she demanded.

The dragon reached out and stroked a twisted branch. "Or," he continued rather mysteriously, "this forest could be a living wood of Elder Trees."

"Elder Trees?"

"Elder Trees," Percival confirmed. "Very rare and even more rare to come across. For the forests of Elder Trees never stay in one spot. The trees take root in one place to be nourished by the soil and the rays of the sun. But once the soil has released all of its growing powers, the trees up root and slowly fade away, only to reappear somewhere else. The tangled branches keep the trees tightly together so that they move as one. Otherwise a sapling or two might be lost. That may be why this forest was not here when you first passed through, or you came by another route."

"Canst thee be certain that it is indeed a forest of Elder Trees?" Farren asked.

"If memory serves it bears the same characteristics of ones I have encountered in the past," Percival answered.

"Is there a way of telling when it might take its leave?" She pursued.

"None that I know of. Could be hours, or days, or weeks. Could be years," shrugged Percival, instantly regretting doing so, his shoulders were so stiff.

"Alas! Pray tell, what are we to do?" moaned Farren in frustration.

The dragon, on the other hand, was perfectly content to stay put for the moment. As he stretched his wings to work out their kinks, he inadvertently offered her a solution to their dilemma.

"We could fly over it," Farren coaxed, knowing it was an option Percival would not readily embrace. "I could ride on thy back, since I have no desire to find myself dangling from thy clutches.

"On my back? I have told you, I am not a horse!" Percival blasted. He was aware that the suggestion was the most logical answer, but knowing he was not fit to fly, he had to protest. Even if he could manage to launch, there was no telling how long he could sustain flight. The forest of trees blocking their path stretched so very far and wide he was unsure that he could cover the distance. Crashing in mid-flight would result in certain injury — death by tree impalement the most probable outcome.

"Swallow thy pride, obstinate ancient beast!" she snapped. "Thou couldst easily carry three of me."

"No!" bellowed Percival, indignant as ever, preferring Farren to believe him stubborn rather than weak. "There must be another way."

The dragon sat back on his haunches and considered their predicament. Meanwhile, Farren continued to fume, pacing back and forth in front of the trees "Well?"

"Well," Percival snidely mimicked. "We might just ask for passage through. It might be as simple as that," he said, his defensiveness waning as she shot him a questioning glare.

"Within each and every Elder Tree lives a spirit. She is the essence of the forest and keeper of the wood. The trees would perish without her magic. I have come across a few back in the valley. Perhaps we could convince her to allow us passage through."

"Are these spirits good or evil?" Farren prodded. "Are they spirits of charity and kindness? Or spirits of cruelty and malevolence?"

"They are not known to bother travellers, preferring to keep to themselves and to the tending of the wood. Little is known of their true character," Percival answered. "A polite and tactful approach might be best."

Farren paused for a moment to collect her thoughts. Finally, with open arms she faced the copse of trees and mustered an endearing voice. "Oh, Great Forest of Elder Trees and thy Spirits within, woodland of strength and beauty, we stand before thee, two travellers on two noble quests. We humbly seek passage and if thou wouldst grant our request, we may resume our journey unhindered." She finished with a lavish bow and waited.

Impressed with her stellar performance, Percival felt obliged to follow suit and, although bowing does not come naturally to dragons, attempted the same. Initially nothing happened; both remained frozen, poised awkwardly in a lavish bow to the grove of trees. To a passer-by, it would have looked ridiculous. But within moments, a gust of wind rippled through the trees causing the branches and leaves to rustle and whisper as though announcing someone's imminent arrival.

Then, on one tree, about halfway up its trunk, ridges of bark began to ripple awake. Slowly, sheaths of bark peeled back in every direction, their paper-thin layers tightly curling under and, as they retreated, a face emerged — a long slender face, almost gaunt, with hollow cheeks and a narrow chin.

"Who calls for Shae, the spirit of Elder Trees?" whispered the Spirit, drawing out each word like rustling wind.

Farren and the dragon slowly straightened up, faced the Spirit and wondered if it was wise to address her directly or to wait for further instructions. They motioned to each other to take up the task until finally, after egging each other on, the dragon stepped forward.

"It has been many a long year since I have flown above a great forest of Elder Trees in your keeping, Majesty," said Percival. "I am honoured by your presence."

"Dragon of lore, of time gone by," rustled Shae's voice. "Your kind is always welcome above my boughs. How does it come to pass that you seek me at my roots?"

"I am on a journey and have chosen not to call attention to myself by taking flight," Percival answered. "And my companion is of the land and not of the skies." He motioned toward Farren. "That is why I stand before you now."

"And what of your companion?" asked Shae. "The one who attacked my wood?"

"My apologies, Spirit," Percival said, eyeing Farren. "We did not know it was you and your Elder Trees that stood before us. Please forgive the actions of my companion. No harm was meant."

"Elders could never be harmed, not while my spirit lives within these trees," whispered Shae. "I am what protects and keeps them. But your companion has insulted the Elder Trees and must make amends."

Farren nervously glanced from the Spirit to the dragon, not knowing what to expect.

"Again, I apologize," said Percival quickly. "She has offended you. What measures might she employ to make restitution?"

The branches of Elder Trees began to quiver and the wind rustled through their leaves like a thousand whistling voices all speaking at once. Tree trunks swayed back and forth, and Shae closed her eyes as if caught in a trance. Suddenly, a large branch from Shae's tree reached out, grabbed Farren by the waist and pulled her toward the dense wood. Caught off guard, she struggled to break free without success; the force and strength of the branch was too great.

"Perce! Help me!" She wailed desperately. "Help!" Farren and her cries disappeared into the wood and the dragon was left alone.

The Elder Trees became still and the wind died down as the Spirit opened her eyes once more. "Your companion requested passage and it is granted," announced Shae. "Perhaps this will serve as a lesson for one who would attempt to abuse the wood of Elder Trees. You need not worry, your friend is unharmed, but will have to find a way through the trees in order to get to the other side. You, ancient dragon, may choose to soar over the forest as you once did, or I will make a path and you may walk through with me as your guide.

Percival bowed his head respectfully, grateful for having been given a choice and said, "I am honoured by your offer and accept. It has been too long since I have enjoyed the company of friends from long ago."

Shae smiled and stepped out of the trunk, her tall figure much like a tree itself draped in a sheath of crystal ice leaves with long limbs for arms and legs. Percival offered an arm, which she took and they turned toward the forest. At the wave of her willowy hand, the tangled and twisted branches slithered as intertwined limbs slowly unravelled and fell away. Tree trunks separated, creating an aisle in the forest for the dragon and the Spirit. Once they passed through, the trees moved back into place, weaving their branches together again and closing up the path.

The gentle pace Shae set allowed Percival to walk off the stiffness and stretch his muscles. It took the better part of the day for the dragon and the Spirit to reach the other side of the forest and, when they emerged, Farren was nowhere to be seen.

"Shae," Percival began, "although I have enjoyed our leisurely walk through the Elder Trees and the charms of your company, I am concerned for my companion."

She patted the dragon's talon, turned and walked back into an Elder Tree, where as before, only her slender face could be seen. She closed her eyes once more and again the rustle of voices whispered through the trees.

Suddenly Farren burst from the woods, thrown by a branch clutching her waist. Abruptly the branch released its hold and she crashed to the ground.

Percival stepped back and waited for her to recover. She stood up, muttering and brushing away ice dust from her rumpled robe. Stomping toward them, she glared first at the dragon and then at Shae's face revealed in the bark.

"May I never encounter another Elder Tree for the rest of mine life," she seethed.

"And Elder Trees share the same sentiment," returned Shae serenely. "I trust our paths may never cross again. In any case, I am certain that your experience among my trees has taught you a lesson you will carry forever. Never again will you attack a forest of Elder Trees."

The Spirit addressed the dragon. "As for you, my old friend, I hope our paths do cross again. May the rest of your journey be without further delay or peril."

Chapter Twenty-Five

L ater, crossing the open field Percival cautiously ventured to ask, "What happened inside the forest?"

Farren sat down on an ice-covered rock and took a deep breath. "'Twas terrible. I was thrust into the forest where trees grew so close to each other there was barely room to move. Branches scraped at mine face and tore at mine attire. I stumbled and fell over thick roots that sprang from the ground as I squeezed my way through that horrible tangle of trees and brush. And the voices! Droning on and on. The whispering and whistling pounded inside mine head. I thought it would never cease."

"The Spirit was very angry with you for chopping away at the wood," Percival remarked. "I guess she wanted to teach you a lesson."

"And a lesson was learned," Farren retorted. "Never again shall I approach such a forest of trees without questioning its true character. She may think she has instilled a sense of respect for all trees. She has only taught me to be more careful and more wary of things that might not be what they appear."

Percival sighed. "So your pride has been tarnished."

"Mine pride, I assure thee, is quite untarnished," Farren said defensively. "Now, enough time has been wasted. 'Tis time to push on."

Standing up, she surveyed the landscape to determine their bearings, and after a few turns, raised her arm and pointed,

"'Tis this way," and marched off. Percival shook his head and followed.

Wading waist-deep through heavy snow, Farren laboured with every step and soon fell behind while the dragon arduously ploughed ahead, forging a path. Halfway across a wide valley, a loud *whoomph* suddenly shook the still air, sounding much like a heavy book landing on a desk. Farren and the dragon stopped dead in their tracks and looked up the lee slope of the mountain. Breaking free along a fracture line, a huge plate of snow began its descent.

"Avalanche!" hollered Percival.

Ahead of the avalanche's distinctive crown, a cloud of powder snow mixed with air produced an aerosol effect that whirled wildly as it slid down the track, its speed gaining along the way. This was no mild, little sluff of snow. Instead, a full-scale slab avalanche — the most dangerous and unpredictable — hurtled their way.

Outrunning the mass of charging snow was out of the question — Farren and the dragon were trapped in its path, with only seconds to act.

"Come to me, come to me," shouted Percival as he turned around, back to the avalanche and ran toward her.

"Perce! Perce!" was all she could muster while struggling through the deep snow.

The avalanche continued down the track. Its glide increased foot by foot, as it headed to level ground where it would ultimately peter out and settle well past where Farren and the dragon were stranded. Percival reached for her, wrapping his great wings around her as a shield and braced for impact.

Seconds later, the rush of snow rumbled over them. Despite the pounding, the dragon stood fast, pelted repeatedly by the travelling snow-pack. Finally, after what seemed a lifetime, the avalanche wore itself out and the last flakes of snow came to a halt.

Buried up to his midsection, Percival thrashed frantically to shovel the snow. Once he had cleared enough away, he opened his wings to discover Farren's fate. Although his wings had offered some protection, Farren had still been buried alive and the rush of snow had knocked her unconscious. Percival brushed off her robes and checked for further injuries. When he found none, he sat back on his haunches in agony and exhaustion. On top of stiff and sore muscles, he now suffered a bruised back from the slamming force of the avalanche; he didn't think he could possibly feel any worse.

Suddenly, a second *whoomph*ing signalled another cascade of snow, confirming that the surrounding area was terribly unstable. Not wanting to relive the experience, Percival reached inside to muster his last thread of strength, picked Farren up in his arms and launched into the sky. Fortunately, cradling her was hardly a burden; his passenger weighed little in comparison to his own bulk. However, each flap of his wings sent sharp pains across his chest and back, and he struggled to stay airborne as he searched for refuge.

Finally, Percival passed above a slope of stone. Its smooth, even face clung to the side of the mountain, but on it was a ledge. Circling back, he arduously returned to the slope, straining to control his glide toward the opening in the stone's wall, then clumsily landed on the ledge — the entrance to a cave. Percival deposited Farren on the floor of the cave and collapsed, grateful to be back on solid ground.

Hours passed as the two companions attempted to heal in the sanctuary of the cave. Upon awakening, the ache in Farren's head was dull and throbbing. "Dragon," she said weakly as she nudged the beast. "What hath happened? Where art we?"

Percival stirred. "Leave me alone," he grumbled. "I am quite spent."

Farren stood up with her head in her hands and stumbled to the opening of the cave. Outside, the skies were clear and the sun shone brightly, sending soothing rays to the figure on the ledge.

Impatient to take stock of their predicament, Farren pressed Percival further. "I recall the rush of snow, but after that, all is lost. How is it that we have come to this place?"

Percival rolled over, resigned to address her persistence, and said, "I did my best to shield you from the avalanche, and when another seemed imminent there was no other choice except to flee."

"To flee?" She questioned. "And just how didst we flee?"

"By flight," answered Percival. "I picked you up and flew you away. Satisfied? You finally got your wish to be a passenger."

"What? Dangling from thy talons?"

"Oh, it would be so gratifying to tell you so," scoffed Percival. "No, I cradled you like a helpless babe in a mother's arms. Does that paint a better picture for you?"

Farren fell silent, humbled that Percival had saved her life, and turned away unsure of how to react. On the one hand, a display of gratitude was in order; on the other, she resented being in the dragon's debt.

Not bothering to wait for her show of appreciation — he knew it wasn't coming — Percival heaved himself up and walked stiffly toward the cave entrance. He looked across the frozen landscape and beyond to the mountain range that stretched far into the distance. Jagged peaks tipped with silver ice glistened in the sunlight and deep crevasses lurked with dark shadows cut into their slopes.

"How lengthy is this journey? We have already travelled a great distance and I see no veiled kingdom."

"The kingdom is but three days hence by foot," she answered quietly. "Of course there is a faster way . . . "

Percival turned and eyed her with a keen understanding of what she was suggesting. He rolled his shoulders and arched his back, testing whether the long rest in the cave had soothed their aching muscles.

"Dragon, what ails thee?" She asked with a quizzical expression.

There was little point in Percival continuing the ruse; the only possible way down from the cave was by flight — the cliff was simply too steep for a descent by foot.

"I fear I am not fit to fly," he admitted finally and explained how his muscles had ached after the first day of travel.

A wide grin spread across Farren's face as she instantly recognized an opportunity to take back the upper hand. Rummaging inside her satchel, she produced a vial filled with an elixir — one that had been included with her stores taken from the castle.

"This potion will ease thy suffering. For one of thy size 'tis best to drink it all. In return thou wilt allow me to ride on thy back."

Percival resisted at first but, in the end, snatched the vial and emptied its contents into his great, gaping mouth wincing at the taste. "Fine. I will allow you to ride between my wings," Percival agreed, already feeling the effects of the potion. "Just as long as you don't hold on too tightly. I will not be strangulated in mid-air."

Farren was delighted. Certainly flying would cut their travel time by more than half and without obstacles like a forest of Elder Trees or an unexpected avalanche to impede their way. Of course there was the risk of being seen, but they would be long gone before observers could take action.

As their launch approached, the one aspect she had overlooked was the actual mechanics involved. Farren stared at the dragon's spiked ridges running down his spine and contemplated the level of comfort she might enjoy while sitting astride his scaly back and between such powerful wings.

"Might I confess to a fear of heights?" she said nervously, recalling the Glider's rescue.

"Just don't look down. Keep your eyes closed if that helps," Percival replied, kneeling. "Now get on."

Placing one foot on the dragon's wing, Farren swung the other leg over his back and sat down, mindful to avoid the ridge of spikes. Fortunately they were evenly spaced and she easily fit between two.

"Much like a horse," said Farren, pleased.

"I am not a horse!"

In a display of grace and beauty, the dragon and passenger soared toward snow-covered mountain peaks in the distance and were soon out of view.

Percival flew for many hours and many leagues fell behind them. Both were exhilarated by this leg of their journey — Percival by the freedom of the skies; Farren by the shortened travel time — and both were in very good spirits as they approached their destination.

Chapter Twenty-Five

Even with the potion's healing powers, Percival began to tire and he knew he needed to find a place to rest. An overhang of rocks jutting from the side of a steep cliff offered protection in the space beneath and Percival landed gently on the ledge. He would have preferred the comforting walls of another cave, but this would have to suffice in the meantime.

"We must pause for a bit of respite," said Percival as he knelt down for his passenger to disembark. "We will be sheltered well enough here should a storm blow through."

Farren nodded and disappeared into the shadows at the far end of the overhang, leaving Percival to inspect their new haven.

"Might thee hanker for a bite to eat?" Farren said as she unpacked the satchel and shared the provisions within. A flagon of water and some ice fruits gathered the day before served as their meal. They ate in silence, both content with the company of their own thoughts.

"The fisherman kept the Diamond Heart for quite some time," Farren said offhandedly.

"What?" Percival declared with surprise.

"The Diamond Heart. Thou hast requested on many occasions that I continue the tale," she answered. "'Tis still thy wish?"

"Why, yes. Indeed," said Percival with much anticipation. "Please, do go on."

"For many years the fisherman guarded the Diamond Heart," she began.

Percival listened intently as Farren spun the yarn acquainting him with the progress of his beloved stone.

"So, that's where it is. It's in the village fountain," said Percival excitedly. "And I thought you weren't going to tell me."

Farren paused for a moment, carefully choosing an appropriate answer. "Sadly, no, the Diamond Heart no longer remains ensconced in the fountain of the fisherman's village."

"Aaghh!" Percival exclaimed as he pounded his fist on the ledge floor, sending ice chips scuttling.

"Might I continue?" she asked.

Percival nodded and settled down.

"A knight from a faraway kingdom chanced upon the village one day and spied the Diamond Heart. He was, of course, on a quest. Not the usual quest of rescuing damsels in distress. This was much more formidable, one thee might be familiar with: in many kingdoms to the south, a knight's quest was to slay a dragon."

"Only there were none left to slay, aside from myself. And I was hidden away in my glacier lair," said Percival.

"Indeed. Thou canst imagine the frustration the knight endured at being unable to fulfil his quest," she continued. "For he could not return to his kingdom without a trophy to offer to his king," Farren paused. "Now, knights are renowned for their valour, honour and purity of heart in their pursuit of noble deeds. But this knight was weary. Away from his kingdom for so long, he tired of such a futile quest and longed to return home to once again enjoy the company of the ladies and his fellows. So when he came across the stone, he instantly recognized it for what it truly was: the Diamond Heart of a slain dragon. Asking the villagers to give up the stone proved pointless for he could see how much they treasured it. So great was his desire to covet the stone, he cast aside his knightly vows and stole it away with the villagers unaware."

"Stole it away. Just like that. Right from under the villagers' noses!" exclaimed Percival.

Farren sighed. "I'm quite sure the robbery was far more complicated. But this story is not about the cunning of a knight gone astray; it is about the whereabouts of the Diamond Heart. Might thee be content with the simple fact that the knight stole it and let that be that?"

"Fine," replied Percival. "Do go on."

"Exhilarated with the prospect of presenting his king with such an extraordinary treasure, the knight raced homewards. Upon entering the throne room he offered up the stone for all to see. The Diamond Heart glowed brilliantly, sending streaks of radiant light out in all directions, its beauty and magnificence overwhelming all — including the king.

"So, is the diamond heart still there?" asked Percival warily.

Farren shook her head. "No, it is not."

"No, of course not. That would be too easy." Percival scoffed. "Why did I even ask?!"

"The stone was set atop the royal sceptre and the king carried it with him at all times," she continued. "Over time, the brilliance of the stone began to fade. And at the same time, the kingdom began to encounter more and more unfortunate events. Sickness spread among the people, horses grew lame, women remained childless. The king grew weary of struggling under the weight of the staff and the once-celebrated knight fell into despair. Finally, the stone grew cold and lifeless, its light completely extinguished with no indication of ever returning. So angered at his kingdom's demise, the king summoned the knight and cast him out, along with the stone, with orders never to return."

"The will of the stone," nodded Percival pensively. "The knight acquired the Diamond Heart through thievery and deception. No good comes to those with ill intentions. And all in his association would suffer the same fate."

"Indeed," Farren agreed. "Disgraced, the knight left the castle. Without a quest and without a kingdom, the knight was lost. He wandered the forests of the land for a time and travelled the back roads between villages offering his services to anyone in need. But a dishonoured knight, clad in rusted armour, astride a ragged old horse, is neither trusted nor welcomed. Villagers shied away behind locked doors, hiding their children, fearful of what he might do. Shunned, he retreated into the woods to begin a life alone."

Chapter Twenty-Six

"What happened to the knight and the Diamond Heart?" asked Grace. She was comfortably lounging on a settee accompanied by Orrell, the Chronicler, along with a handful of knights in the Great Hall of the Kingdom of Knights.

"Try as he might, he could never free himself of the Diamond Heart," answered Orrell. "It had brought him power and glory as well as ruin. Suffering greatly, Sir Kenard deeply regretted having stolen from the villagers and deceiving his own kingdom. Ever hopeful, he remained convinced that some day the Diamond Heart would regain its brilliance and help him restore his good name."

"And did it?" Grace asked.

"Not for many years," Orrell replied. "A time came when Sir Kenard journeyed deeper into the ice forest and came across a Seekers' mound." He paused at Grace's puzzled face.

"What exactly is a Seeker? I saw one in the prince's mirror," she said showing the image in the glass to Orrell who nodded, confirming her observation.

"In the past, Sir Kenard had never kept company with enchanted creatures, preferring instead to remain true to his quest." He continued without missing a beat. "Being lost, he paused, and hidden out of sight, watched with great fascination as delicate Seekers went about their ways. Time after time, the knight would venture back to the mound to catch glimpses of their glittering shapes and fluttering silver wings, but always from afar. Never did he dare approach; the fear of rejection would have surely caused him great pain."

"Great pain? What kind of pain?" asked Grace.

"Sir Kenard had grown quite fond of Seekers," said Orrell. "And although they had never made acquaintances, the Seekers' beauty and grace had touched his heart. Of his own accord, he proclaimed himself their unseen guardian and protector and found great comfort in finding purpose once again."

"And the Seekers knew nothing of the knight's presence?" asked Grace.

"'It's not known for certain," he answered. "But since Seekers do possess a special sense, it is unlikely Sir Kenard's presence went unnoticed. Perhaps they sensed his reluctance to reveal himself and respected this."

"That's awfully nice of them," Grace offered. She was beginning to like these Seeker creatures and hoped she would get to meet one. "What happened next?"

"It was a fateful day," said Orrell gravely. "As Sir Kenard stood watch, an evil force charged through the forest."

"An evil force?" Grace echoed in a hushed tone.

"That of a band of renegade Chasers. Spiteful tricksters, whose sole intent was to wreak havoc on any they might encounter, especially Seekers. Caught by surprise, the Seeker mound was soon overrun and the Seeker Queen taken captive."

"What did Sir Kenard do?" Grace asked.

"What any proper knight should do," said Orrell. "Damsels in distress needed to be rescued and so he did. Chasers stood little chance against a charging knight and quickly abandoned the Seeker mound, fleeing into the forest, yelping and howling along the way.

"Upon her release, the Seeker Queen glided up to face the man who had so bravely defended their honour. Overwhelmed by her beauty, as are all mortal men, Sir Kenard knelt down on one knee and bowed his head. With her tiny hands she lifted his chin and delicately kissed him on the cheek. From the moment her lips touched his face, a glistening wave of clear light washed over him and briefly he shimmered and glowed in his armour from helmet to toecap."

"Oh, how sweet," sighed Grace. "What did they do next?'

"Ah. This is the best part of this tale," said the Chronicler smiling. "Through this selfless act of gallantry, Sir Kenard had cleansed his heart and redeemed himself in the eyes of all. Again a true knight, he had fulfilled his quest and could now return triumphantly back to his kingdom to join his Brotherhood of Knights."

"Meaning here. Back to this castle." Grace said. "But didn't he still have the Diamond Heart?"

"Indeed. With his burden lifted, Sir Kenard retrieved the stone from his saddlebags. Much to his surprise the Diamond Heart glowed brilliantly again. Miraculously his tarnished armour regained its lustre and his steed stood majestically awaiting his mount. No longer bound to the stone, he presented the Diamond Heart to the Seeker Queen with hopes that its extraordinary powers would protect her and her people from further harm. He bid his farewells and was gone."

"That's so romantic," Grace cooed, caught up in the story's charm. "What happened to Sir Kenard after that?"

"He lived out his days regaling his tale to pages and squires hoping they would learn valuable lessons from his own experience," Orrell answered. "Many a good knight owes him much gratitude for reminding them of their vows and oaths to the Brotherhood."

"Excellent," she quipped. "So I guess I have to go find this, uh, Seekers' mound. Does anyone know where it is?"

The Chronicler and the circle of knights exchanged glances and silence fell over the group.

"What? What's the matter?" Grace groaned when faced with their reticence to answer. She had not come this far to leave empty-handed. If they were hiding something from her, she would have to convince them to reveal it. Thus far, the knights had been so candid with her; she couldn't imagine why they were reluctant to tell her. "Is it a secret that you can't tell me?"

Urged on by his brothers, a dark-haired knight named Sir Rodyne took charge of the forum. "'Tis not a secret, m'lady. We are honourable men who value honesty and truth and would never hold it from one in need." He explained. "But Seekers are known to move from place to place until they find their true home — truth be told, we know not where it is."

"Well, can't I at least try to find it?" Grace said determined. "Just tell me where it was and I'll figure it out on my own, somehow."

Again, a hush fell among the knights.

Chapter Twenty-Seven

"Wonderful," exclaimed Percival. "What a wonderfully, enchanting story. So we must find this Seeker mound and appeal to the queen to relinquish the stone. Once she becomes aware of my plight, she is certain to be sympathetic. Seekers and dragons share a very good rapport from centuries past — perhaps from the beginning of our kind. Perchance because of the magic we share and the shared power of flight."

Farren did not answer.

"Well, speak up," urged Percival. "Now's not the time to hold back."

She remained silent.

Percival glared at her in disbelief. "It's not there either, is it?"

Farren's head shook no.

With heartfelt disappointment, Percival sighed deeply and said, "Is there no end to this tale?"

Somewhere between the tale of a lost maiden in the woods and a mountaineer buried in a sudden avalanche, the dragon had grown drowsy from Farren's endless stories of the Diamond Heart and had fallen asleep. With less than a day's journey to reach the kingdom, Farren, too, had taken a nap, but now was up and anxious to be off.

"Awaken, Perce," she whispered in the dragon's ear and gently nudged his scaly shoulder.

Grumbling loudly, Percival slowly raised his head from his pillow of crossed arms and lingered for a moment, eyes still shut. Suddenly his mouth opened wide as he erupted into a huge yawn. Sucking in air with such force, Percival's gaping mouth with row upon row of sharply chiselled teeth and forked, silver tongue, startled Farren. And when he finally exhaled, the thundering force of his breath knocked her back against the wall of the overhang. Refreshed, Percival opened his eyes to find Farren sprawled before him wearing a look of astonishment.

"One must be mindful when attempting to rouse a dragon. There are consequences, you know," said Percival offhandedly as he began to preen himself and wipe the sleep from his eyes.

"In-deed," she stammered. "Mindful, indeed."

Standing up, Percival stretched, scratched his belly and wandered out to the ledge of the mountain. Farren followed.

"I suppose you'll want to be off," said Percival. "But as you can see, the journey will not be easy."

The sun was completely covered with huge, billowy clouds, which were dropping loads of heavy snow. A wall of snowflakes the size of large buttons fell so quickly and so thickly it was impossible to see much beyond the overhang. Gusting winds stirred up the drifts, sent snow swirling in all directions, and swept it onto the ledge.

"No!" exclaimed Farren. "'Tis not yet the season!"

"'Tis always the season!" exclaimed Percival. "There is nothing unusual about a blizzard at any time in the Ice World. Surely you know that?"

"No!" she remarked stomping back into the shelter. "Something has gone awry. Something is trying to block our path. First a forest that is not a forest, then an unexpected avalanche, and now a blizzard when a blizzard should not be, at a time when skies should be clear. Some force is at work to prevent me from completing mine quest."

"Force? What force?" questioned Percival.

"I know not," she seethed. "But I shall not be deterred. Perce, art thou fit to fly?"

"Through this?" Percival demanded.

"Though this!"

"Well, I never did fancy flying through a blizzard. Still, there have been times . . . " Percival's voice trailed off.

"Good," she confirmed while picking up her satchel and packing it with the last of their provisions.

"Mightn't we wait a while?" asked Percival hesitantly. "Just briefly. To see whether the storm will abate?"

Farren glared at Percival. Drawing her cloak's hood and tightening her belt, she made ready to mount the dragon without further discussion. Reluctantly, Percival offered his wing.

Together they plunged blindly into the storm, Farren shouting directions into the dragon's ear. Wind slapped at their faces and snow stung their flesh. Farren's robes flapped violently about and Percival's wings were soon encrusted with ice. Up over boulders and down under cliffs, he narrowly dodged obscured obstacles in his path. He clipped the tips of trees when a downward gust of wind forced him closer to the ground and then slung him forward.

The blizzard lasted for hours, pelting Farren and the dragon relentlessly with the full force of the elements, with little indication of letting up. On and on they flew, heads bent into the wind, the swirling snow blinding their path as they streaked over the landscape.

Many leagues away, beyond the reaches of the storm, a single sliver of light shot through the air in hot pursuit.

Chapter Twenty-Eight

Grace had finally managed to convince the knights to reveal the last known location of the Seekers' mound. She was eager to be off, but they insisted on giving her a full tour of the castle as well as show off their skills. She winced each time their lances struck and unseated their opponents, baffled at why they called jousting a sport. She smiled politely during one-on-one combat — two knights brandishing broadswords, hacking at each other in a great clangour of armour. Later she found herself blushing as one knight serenaded her with his lute.

They treated her with the utmost courtesy, acting as perfect gentlemen and hosts, and she reacted in kind. One thing was certain — made obvious by such lavish treatment — these knights were bored. Without dragons to slay and fewer and fewer damsels to rescue, they were desperate to honour their vows and prove their gallantry at any opportunity — even with a twelve-year-old girl dressed in yellow and black.

When departure seemed imminent she made one last request. "Do you think I could borrow a horse?" she asked optimistically. "I'll get it back to you, I promise." Grace had taken many lessons back home and was an accomplished rider. But the knights had been one step ahead of her. A squire with two saddled mounts walked out of the stables and handed her reins to the smaller of the two. Her escort, Sir Rodyne, would accompany her for the duration of her journey, and she welcomed the offer of companionship.

Whistling gears announced the rising portcullis and the lowering drawbridge as Grace and her escort rode through the gatehouse and over the moat. The pathway she had taken en route to the kingdom would not take her in the right direction; she needed to head east through the forest where there was not the luxury of a road.

Riding through the forest was arduous at first; the dense wood forced the pair to pick between the trees. But when a clearing appeared, they travelled at full gallop — something Grace hadn't done in a while. Although it was good to be back on a horse, she could feel her muscles beginning to smart. Once back under the cover of trees, Sir Rodyne rode ahead, hacked away branches marring their path and steered away from the more rocky terrain. They crossed meandering streams, through stretches of meadow and back into the woods, until finally Sir Rodyne stopped short of a very large, very dense, circular thicket and dismounted.

"Within this circle once lay the Seekers' mound befriended by the lost knight." He said. "Should they still reside here, breaking the seal of this protective circle may be perceived as an attack."

Grace dismounted her horse and joined him. "But if what the Chronicler said is true — that Seekers have a special sense — they'll know we don't mean them any harm. We have to take a shot, there's no other way."

Sir Rodyne accepted the order as any loyal knight might and began hacking at the thick barrier with his broadsword. Branches and twigs flew with each strike of his sword. Soon he had breached the perimeter — a single limb barring entry. As he raised his sword in one final fell, the branch began to glow and suddenly the whole thicket was ablaze in white light. His strike interrupted, he turned, threw Grace away from the thicket and shielded her body with his. As they hit the ground, the thicket exploded.

Grace heard the knight cry out in pain. After the last branches fell, he rolled off her, clutching his leg. From the force of the explosion, a thick spike of wood had pierced the flesh on the back of his thigh, and as he bravely yanked it out, blood gushed from the wound. Grace quickly removed her scarf and wrapped it around his leg hoping the tourniquet would stop the bleeding. She helped him sit against a tree trunk and applied as much pressure as she could on the wound. The first-aid training she had endured at summer camp popped into her head and she was glad that she had paid some attention in class.

"Are you okay?" Grace asked, immediately aware of how stupid a question it was, considering the man had just pulled a tree branch from his leg.

"'Tis only . . . a wound of the flesh," he grimaced. "Art thou hurt, m'lady?" He asked, his gallantry overriding concerns for himself.

"I'm fine. Just a bit shaken," she said as she brushed twigs and leaves from her jacket. "What just happened?"

"Seekers must have installed an enchantment. 'Tis an omen m'lady. Seekers must have been slain here long ago. To enter would break the sanctity of the tomb." He said hoping she would heed his warning.

"You think this is a grave, a Seekers' grave?" Grace asked.

"Do not dare to trespass any farther. It is uncertain what lies within."

Grace was touched by his concern for her safety and knew he would have bravely forged ahead had he not been injured.

Unnerving as it was visiting the dead, Grace had been to many cemeteries and although a tad uncomfortable, had never been afraid.

But this was the Ice World, and if what she had just witnessed was any indication of future danger, fear was something she would have to overcome. If she had learned only one lesson during her stint at the Kingdom of Knights, it was the lesson of not waiving and staying true to her course. "Thanks. I'll take my chances. Stay and rest. I'm going to look inside."

When Sir Rodyne protested again, she raised one eyebrow in defiance and he soon fell silent, knowing he could not change her mind. A ghostly, white fog hovered where the thicket had stood. She reached for Sir Rodyne's fallen broadsword but it proved too heavy and she dropped it in favour of a thick branch.

Grace stepped carefully through the fog. With arms outstretched, branch in hand, she prodded the emptiness for invisible obstacles. Deeper and deeper she advanced through the white mist that tingled her skin.

Finally, the fog cleared and lingered only around the perimeter. Grace found herself enclosed in a circle of white. In the middle stood the abandoned mound. Making one final sweep of the circle with her branch and finding no contest, she dropped it and ran to the mound.

Overgrown with iced weeds and gangly ice vines, it was apparent the mound had not been recently visited. It was about the size of a doormat and easily twice as thick. Grace knelt down along side and ran her gloved hand over the surface before picking at the overgrowth and tearing it away. A glint of silver caught her eye and she gardened even more furiously to uncover the source.

After she cleared away all of the debris, ten tiny, silver plaques the size of playing cards stared back at her, each with a message — an inscription — carved into their faces. An inscription in a language Grace could not read. The letters were foreign and oddly shaped. The more she studied the symbols, the stranger they appeared.

Grace took off her glove and traced one plaque with the tip of her finger, following the raised edges of each letter until she reached the last one. When she released her touch, each letter reacted by changing shape and redesigning itself. Slowly, each one formed into letters and words she could read.

Spirits of Seekers at peace, mourned by kindred spirits to the east.

Grace couldn't believe her eyes, couldn't believe what she was reading and wondered if each plaque held a different message. She traced the letters of another and read the same inscription, and when she tried a third, she realized they were all the same. But it didn't matter, Grace had been given a clue and empowered by it she flew away from the shrine, out of the circle and back to the knight.

"Seekers have left a clue!" Grace said excitedly as she wrapped her arms around the startled knight in a bear hug. "It's to the east. Seekers have taken the Diamond Heart east of here. That's where the castle must be. Now which way is east? We were already going east, weren't we? So if we just keep on going in this direction we'll run right into the castle." Her chatter caused Sir Rodyne to smile amidst his pain and he admired her zeal and devotion to her quest. She would have made a good knight.

"M'lady," he interrupted her banter. "I fear I am unable to travel on thy journey. Mine leg needs the services of a surgeon."

Grace was so caught up in her own excitement, she had completely forgotten about his injuries. "Of course, Sir Rodyne. How thoughtless of me. We'll go back to your castle and get help."

"Nay, m'lady. Do not delay thy quest because of me. Mine steed knows the way and is able to make the journey alone," he replied as she helped him to his feet. Grace found him a suitable walking stick and he limped over to his mount. Reaching into one of his saddlebags, Sir Rodyne retrieved a small compass and placed it in Grace's hand.

"May thee stay the course due east without peril," he cautioned. "And may we cross paths again soon." Then he bowed respectfully, although rather awkwardly with his injured leg. He would have knelt on one knee as any true knight should, but he feared embarrassing himself by toppling over.

Grace bowed in return and, with compass in hand, she straddled her horse, dug in her heels and trotted into the forest alone.

Finally reaching the edge of the forest, Grace broke through the treeline and cantered out into an open meadow of tall, white grass. She was tired and sore from riding through the woods; the ground had been uneven and rocky in places, and the strain of keeping her horse from stumbling had taken its toll. Swinging her leg over the saddle she dropped to the ground, deciding to lead her pony as she set off on foot. The grass was much taller than expected and blocked her view. Up in the saddle she had been able to see for miles; down on the ground she was blind. She considered resuming on horseback, but changed her mind. It felt good to stretch her legs and give her muscles a rest. She allowed the compass to be her guide.

As long as the needle pointed east she knew she was heading in the right direction.

Wading through grass with nothing to distract her, she allowed her mind to wander as she had on the pathway to the Kingdom of Knights. Up until then, she had managed to push away a nagging thought, and now, she decided to face it. After everything she had encountered to reach her final destination — the castle — Grace thought she would feel more elated. Instead, she felt nervous about seeing Prince Owyn again and was unsure how he might react to her arrival.

A mixture of emotions boiled in her blood when she tried to pinpoint exactly how she felt about him. Anger: "it was all his fault." Sadness: "it was all her fault." Desperation: "okay, let's not lay blame, it's nobody's fault, but could you please save my world." Joy: "I made it, I'm so happy to be here! Could you please save my world?" It was terribly confusing. Would she be at his mercy or would he be at hers? Prince Owyn's desperate plea to return with him could only mean she possessed something he wanted very badly.

The compass needle remained pointed east, and after shaking off her deliberations, Grace decided to remount her horse to get her bearings. When she looked ahead, Prince Owyn's castle stood a gallop away. As it glistened in the sunlight under a shimmering curtain, Grace gasped, overwhelmed by its size and spectacular beauty. She couldn't help thinking how the knights' castle paled in comparison. A twinge of apprehension fluttered inside her and she faltered for a moment, collecting her wits, then spurred on her horse and charged ahead.

Suddenly, a black wall sprouted in the meadow, blocking her path and spooking her horse into rearing up on hind legs. Grace lost hold of the reins and fell out of her saddle, crashing down to the meadow floor. Darkness surrounded her. She could see nothing but pitch and she waved her arms frantically, clawing at the void, trying to rip it away. Desperate, Grace cried out at her unknown assailant and lashed out blindly.

"Welcome to the castle," Snitch hissed as she wrapped her shadow around Grace and squeezed tightly, stifling her flails and subduing her cries. Grace felt a trickling of dust fall into her eyes that caused her to swoon. The Stalker, easily three times Snitch's normal size, embraced Grace into her mantle. With her captive vanquished and firmly secured, she flew back to the ice gorge.

Chapter Twenty-Nine

Seekers and Searchers had reported back with their findings, all of which proved fruitless; Grace was simply nowhere to be found. There had been sightings of her yellow and black garb — colours unfamiliar to the inhabitants of the Ice World — in the fishing village, but Ormann, the Master Fisherman had long set sail and was unavailable to provide her next destination.

Inside the Great Hall, Prince Owyn paced, his patience wearing thin; he felt all the more helpless with nothing to do. That Grace was stranded somewhere alone and without direction emphasized the guilt he felt. Not that he could predict any danger that might befall her — the Ice World was generally a peaceful place with mostly gentle folk — but there was still the off-chance that she might fall into the wrong hands. Just the manner of her dress caused concern; clearly, she was not of this world. What bothered him most was that time was wasting.

Startled by a loud crash from outside the Great Hall, Owyn turned to its source. From under the sweeping grand staircase, a panel of wall concealing a door shattered open, sending splinters of ice skittering as a figure burst out and landed sprawling on the floor. Caught by surprise, Prince Owyn bolted across the Great Hall not only to confront the intruder, but also to demand explanation for the deliberate demolition of the castle's interior. His outrage quickly faded when he discovered the identity of his unexpected guest.

"Could you have made it any harder for me to get in here?" Grace groaned as she picked herself up, rubbing a sore shoulder.

"Grace!" Prince Owyn exclaimed, rushing to her side and taking her arm. "'Tis thee, 'tis truly thee!"

"Yes, Prince, 'tis me, all right," she said snatching her arm from his grasp and glaring him in the face. "I'm not too terribly pleased with you at the moment, so you'll have to give me some space."

"Of course," he said backing off slightly, allowing her a chance to breathe. He was just so relieved to see her that he couldn't help fawning all over her. "'Tis such a relief . . . have waited so long . . . and now that thou art here . . . "

"Zip it, Prince." Grace cut him off abruptly. "You've got a lot of explaining to do. Like what's happening in my world. Know anything about that?"

"Well, ah, I know of certain measures taken . . . " he stammered.

"Don't play all innocent with me," she jabbed at his chest. "'There are evil forces at work in mine world, ones that may have crossed over into thine,'" she repeated verbatim. "Sound familiar? I don't remember the rest exactly, only that there was a 'final demise' thrown in there too."

"Believe me, Grace, I have no knowledge of what has transpired in thy world. I do know who might shed light to appease thy concerns. Trust that I will find the answers thee seek." He said sincerely, adding a bow in a show of good faith.

"Look Prince, no amount of bowing is going to get you out of this one," she retorted. "My world is a mess and it's all your fault and I want you to fix it so that I can go home. Do you realize what I've been through?"

"I can only imagine . . . " Prince Owyn answered before Grace cut him off again. She launched into a random re-enactment of the events of her day, embellishing the highlights with language that made Prince Owyn wince. "Everything's bloody frozen . . . no freaking power . . . can't wake my parents . . . wish sends me to some decrepit old bag . . . a curse, a quest, a dragon . . . trudging for miles . . . almost trampled by charging knights . . . blown up by Seekers . . . kidnapped by a Stalker and . . . "

"Grace . . . Grace . . . GRACE!" Shouted Prince Owyn as he grabbed her shoulders and shook her out of her tirade. "Halt thy ravings and heed mine words."

Grace locked eyes with him and a moment steeped with tension hung thick between them, neither one willing to concede.

"This is thy doing as well as mine," he accused. "Had thee returned with me at mine request, none of this would have occurred."

Spent by emotional turmoil, Grace dropped her gaze. She took a deep breath. There was really no point in berating the prince. He was right. She was at fault as much as he was, but it still stung to be reminded. Although it had felt good to rant, now was the time for compromise and she slipped her anger into a mental drawer and closed it shut "Okay. Where do we go from here?" she asked, her tone lowered by an octave or two.

"Allow me the time to explain, which was always mine first intention," he said cautiously.

Grace nodded in quiet agreement. She felt the playing fields begin to even out.

"A simple question before we begin. Might thee explain the manner of thine entry?" He said while inspecting the damage done to the wall under the stairs by opening and closing the door no longer concealed within.

"It's a passageway. Leads from some gorge outside the castle," Grace answered offhandedly as if such passage was a common occurrence in one's day. She was tired and needed to sit down and took little notice of where she was until she observed the room's grandeur.

"This looks just like in my dream," Grace whispered, her words falling away as she wandered deeper, leaving Prince Owyn behind. She stepped over the threshold, walked across the glassy floor and approached the throne.

"It's exactly the same," she gasped as she stroked the carved arms of the chair and the back where the jewel was embedded. "Down to the last detail," she mused running her touch over the smooth stone, relieved to be finally in its presence after all she had endured.

"'Tis known as the Diamond Heart jewel," said Prince Owyn. "It has adorned this throne for a very long time," he continued. "Now about that gorge?"

"Really?" Grace feigned, ignoring his question and wondering if he knew what he had in his possession. "Where did it come from?" she prodded.

"'Twas a gift offered many years ago," he answered. "From a flock of Seekers in return for refuge at a time when the wilderness was unkind."

"Interesting," Grace said dryly. She wasn't about to let on what she knew until she figured out her role with this stone. That Prince Owyn wasn't aware of its true origin just might work in her favour. "It makes the throne appear very royal."

"Indeed. The royal throne has seated many good kings and queens over time," Prince Owyn answered. " My father, King Roarke, is especially fond of his throne. He has been known to drift off on whilst entertaining guests."

"You're kidding? You mean he falls asleep and takes naps while people are here visiting?" Grace said incredulously.

"Regrettably so. Yet mine mother, Queen Isolte, usually brings him 'round before any notice is taken," he replied, sharing in Grace's amusement.

"Where are your parents — I mean, King Ro-arke and Queen I-solte?" asked Grace, stumbling over the foreign names.

"Travelling to distant lands in the south. Mine mother is ill and seeks a Healer there. The kingdom is now in mine keeping."

"That's a lot of responsibility," Grace said. "For someone so young."

"Mine father has entrusted me and I shall serve him well."

"All by yourself?"

"Alas, I am all alone here. All members of mine family have departed and I sorely miss their presence. One especially, I miss most of all, and I know not when she might return or if, in fact, she will." He said, sadness in his voice as he turned away.

It was an awkward moment, the second of the day. "I'm sorry," she said softly. "It must be lonely. You know, being here without your family." She pictured her parents' sleeping faces in her mind's eye.

At first Prince Owyn did not answer, but finally turned back. "Thy condolences are welcome, fair Grace. In mine heart I hope one day we will all be reunited once again," he said, forcing a smile to his face. Suddenly, he remembered what he had wanted to ask her. "What gorge has a secret passageway leading into the castle? I know of none."

"Just because you don't know about it doesn't mean it's not there," Grace answered. "What difference does it make?"

"The castle has been sealed for a very long time and to learn that it might have been breached is of great concern," he told her, serious again. "How is it that thou came there?"

"Well, if you must know," Grace began, shrugging her shoulders. "I was on my way to the castle when this big dark thing grabbed me and knocked me out. The next thing I knew, I was waking up in between two slabs of ice on the side of the mountain."

"Who was thy captor?" he asked gravely. "And how didst thou escape?"

"It was this shadow-like figure calling herself a Stalker who kept hissing at me about her mistress and how she was going to get me," Grace explained.

"A Stalker?" Prince Owen said gravely. "Those kind have not been seen in these parts for many a year. Who is her mistress?"

"No idea. Anyway, I really wasn't in the mood and just wanted to get out of there, so I made her disappear."

Hanging on her every word as if all life depended on the outcome, Prince Owen dropped his jaw in an expression that asked how.

Grace picked up on his query and continued her story. "It was no big deal, really. Getting rid of shadows is easy with a bit of light, anybody knows that." At the time, she had thought a wish might do the trick, but she wasn't about to take any chances until she knew more. Instead, she relied on her resourcefulness. "I used the mirror you gave me and reflected the sun at the Stalker. Poof, she was gone. That's when I discovered a doorway that led to the passageway. When I got to the end, I couldn't open the door. So I crashed through instead."

"The presence of a Stalker is most disconcerting. I will have to bring this to the attention of others here in the castle. Didst thou perchance happen upon a barrier of some kind along the way?"

"As a matter of fact I did. It was like a shimmering curtain, the same kind that was all around the castle," Grace answered, and saw Prince Owyn sigh with relief. "Does that mean something?"

"Only that the protective veil is still in place," said Prince Owyn. "It was altered to allow thy entry."

"Well I certainly gained entry, only it might have been a lot less painful going through the front door." Grace said before she turned serious. "Why am I here, Prince Owyn? I need to know."

"The purpose of thy presence here must be thoroughly explained and 'tis not I who is the most qualified for such a task. Accompany me to the library and meet the librarian."

"The librarian? Fine," she said anxious to get going.

Prince Owyn politely offered his arm. Compelled, Grace consented. They walked out the Great Hall and mounted the winding staircase to the second floor.

Chapter Thirty

"I must warn thee, the librarian is rather a unique soul. Tread gently, for he is known to take offence at any slight," said Prince Owyn as he steered her down a long hallway. At the end of the hall, they stopped in front of a thick white door set into the side of a rounded turret. Corridors continued to the right and left, lined with arched doorways that led to other rooms in the castle.

"What's in those rooms?" Grace asked.

"These are the royal apartments. The west wing accommodates the king and queen's chambers, and their attendants' quarters," he said, gesturing to the left. "And the east wing is where the royal family resides and any guests who may be visiting," he continued, pointing to the right. Prince Owyn reached out and grasped the handle of the white door and it slid open with a hiss. Inside, a spiral staircase wound around the turret, seemingly endless in both directions.

"Are we going up or down?" asked Grace.

"The library is on the uppermost floor of the Great Tower," he replied.

Grace entered the turret and began to climb the thick white stairs, gripping the banister for added support. After twenty complete turns around the turret, Grace sat down on a step.

"How much further?" she asked, out of breath.

"Five more circles of steps and we will have arrived," answered Prince Owyn.

Grace groaned at his response as she picked herself up and began to mount the stairs once again, convinced that she'd already had her share of exercise that day. Finally, with the last stair behind her, Grace stood on a small landing leading to an arched corridor with windows on each side looking out onto the grounds. Grace paused for a moment to take in the view.

"What's that over there?" She asked pointing out one of the windows.

"At the back of the keep lie the royal stables, beyond the stables lie the orchards, and beyond the orchard live Seekers and the Ice Witch," he replied.

"The Ice Witch?" Grace gasped. "Is she old and ugly with warts on her nose? Is she . . . ?"

"Grace! The librarian will answer everything," Prince Owyn interrupted. "We must continue across the bridge to the Great Tower so we may enter the library."

"We're on a bridge?" Grace leaned over the side. They were crossing a bridge that spanned from the top of the turret to a very tall, very large tower. "We are on a bridge," she said dryly.

Upon reaching the other side, Prince Owyn pulled open yet another heavy door, held it for Grace to pass through, then followed behind.

"Wow!" Grace quietly mouthed. After all, she was in a library and knew better than to make any loud noises.

The library sprawled before her — one great, circular room filled from floor to ceiling with rows of shelving, neatly stacked with books of all sizes. Ladders strung along railings every few feet offered access to books on the higher shelves. At the centre, stood a huge round desk cluttered with books and stationery. The desk sat on a raised platform reached by four steep steps and was circled by rows of long tables with chairs neatly pushed in. Rays of white sunlight spilled in through skylights set into the peaked roof above, and low hanging fixtures offered additional light to those who chose to peruse the stacks.

"Where's the librarian?" Grace whispered as she surveyed the deserted room.

"I am uncertain as to the librarian's whereabouts," Prince Owyn whispered back. "Patience, fair Grace. I am sure he will join us in good time."

Grace wandered over to one of the bookracks and ran her finger over the titles as she read aloud. "*Seeker Lore and Customs, A Complete Guide. Seeker Legends and Fables. Seeker Memorabilia, A Collectors' Handbook. Seeker . . .* "

"Are you looking for something in particular, my dear?"

"Oh!" Grace blurted out as she turned with a start. "You scared me!"

"That's what happens when you nose around and get caught," the librarian scolded.

"I wasn't being nosy," Grace protested. "Are you the — ?"

" . . . librarian?" He leaned forward almost nose to nose with Grace. "Yes. My name is Saithe, and who are you?"

"Master Librarian," Prince Owyn interrupted, stepping between the two. "May I present Grace."

Saithe took a step back. He stroked his chin with his hand as if pondering a huge mathematical equation. "Mmph. Well then, we've got a lot to do, so we better get started." He turned and shuffled away, leaving Grace and Prince Owyn puzzled at his sudden departure.

Grace shrugged her shoulders at the prince and followed Saithe to his desk. Now huddled over a number of opened books, he ignored the pair as they approached.

He was a much older man, probably about the same age as Grace's grandfather. Not very tall, and rather portly, he sported a balding head, bulging eyes and a double chin. His long robes hung loosely on his rounded, slumped shoulders and covered the bulge of his belly. He mumbled and grumbled under his breath as he busied himself with his books and papers.

"Now, my dear, it is time to tell you why you are here. Are you ready for a very long story?" Saithe asked.

"Sure, as long as I don't have to go anywhere to hear it," she replied, looking forward to staying put for a while.

Saithe left his desk and marched over to a row of books. "Give me a hand here, Prince," he called back. "It's the big one on the second shelf."

Prince Owyn reached for the book, took it from the shelf and placed it into the librarian's open arms. Saithe heaved the massive book onto the desk. It landed with a loud thud. "This is the history of the Kingdom of Connacht. It contains all the stories of our people, our kings and queens, our triumphs and failures. Everything in this book is the truth, nothing made up, only the truth. The part where you come in is toward the end. Now, let me find the right chapter." He leafed through the pages.

"Ah, here it is," he sighed contentedly. "'Chapter Eighty-six, The Dark Years'. I despised those years, as did everyone in the kingdom. It was our bleakest era."

"Are you going to read it out loud," Grace wanted to know.

"Grace, this is no ordinary book. Yes, of course, I could read it to you like any other, but the beauty of this book is its magic. This is a book that will read to you. Just simply ask it through a wish."

Again with the wishes, Grace thought to herself, noting that perhaps permission was required for one to come true. "Okay,

I wish to be read the story of 'Chapter Eighty-six, The Dark Years'."

"Chapter eighty-six, The Dark Years." A clear, friendly, female voice emanated from the book to tell Grace of the incredible turn of events in the kingdom: the story of how a Guardian came to be chosen and why one was so desperately needed.

" . . . and the Guardian child's name was Grace," the chapter concluded.

Chapter Thirty-One

Despite prevailing winds and walls of thick snow, Farren and the dragon managed to cover a considerable distance as they approached their destination. Although still falling heavily, the snow was more of a nuisance than a deterrent. Numerous times, Percival was forced to shake the accumulation from his wings and brush the ice gathering between his scales. Still unable to see more than a few feet ahead, the dragon was forced to pay careful attention to avoid the towering trees and jagged mountain peaks that careened into his limited view. When the wall of white suddenly turned dark, Farren and Percival knew danger approached.

Black clouds of rain replaced snow clouds, but not with the gentle drumming of an afternoon shower; instead, they unleashed a torrential downpour. Visibility was further compromised and when the rain became sleet, Farren and the dragon felt each painful sting as they were repeatedly pelted with frozen drops the size of grapes.

Blinded by precipitation, Percival hollered back to his rider, "I think we should seek shelter." Farren nodded, agreeing that this kind of storm was not one easily travelled. Over an ice-covered lake, Percival headed toward the closest shore in hopes of finding refuge from the battering ice-stones. Each blow struck hard and fast as he struggled to remain airborne, forcing him toward the surface of the frozen lake.

On his back, Farren clung for life, and when a random ice-stone crashed into the dragon's temple knocking him senseless, both rider and mount plummeted like a duck felled by a hunter's good aim.

The force of the impact threw Farren from the dragon's back to land bruised and battered, but not seriously hurt. Percival, on the other hand, had not fared as well and lay motionless on his belly, wings sprawled wide with his head stretched out on the ice. The hail-like stones still pelted mercilessly, bouncing all around them and, as Farren crawled over to assess the dragon's condition, a loud crack tore over the pounding storm. She froze as she watched a fissure in the ice snake jaggedly from the tip of the dragon's spiked tail to his pointed snout, then back around to the other side.

"Perce!" Farren yelled over the din, afraid to venture closer should more cracks develop and also put her in danger. The ice-stones had turned into liquid, and now a drizzling rain made the frozen lake slick, filling the uneven surface with puddles. "Wake up! The ice is breaking!"

Heaving under the dragon's weight, the ice began to fold causing fractures to open and water to seep through. Farren watched as the ice separated, isolating Percival on a floe. Gravity eventually prevailed, and the island listed to one side, tipping the unconscious dragon into the water.

"NO!" Farren screamed, as she knelt with outstretched arms while the dragon disappeared beneath the ice into the lake. Disposed of its cargo, the ice floe splashed back in place and bobbed in the water.

Shocked by the spectacle and distraught with the loss of her valued companion, Farren pounded the ice with clenched fists that bruised from the force of her blows. But she felt little pain aside from that of broken dreams. Any hope to complete her quest was now dashed, sent to the bottom of the lake in a moment that felt like eternity.

Chapter Thirty-Two

"What?" Grace exclaimed incredulously. "What?

"'Tis true, fair Grace," Prince Owyn soothingly responded.

"What are you saying?" Grace questioned as she backed away from the book. "That I'm supposed to be your Guardian?"

"Grace . . . " Saithe intervened.

"No, no, no, no, NO!" Grace said shaking her head and waving her hands at the prince and the librarian. "No way, uh-uh, you've got the wrong Grace."

"I assure you, Grace, we are not mistaken," Saithe said firmly.

Grace began to pace the library, weaving between tables and chairs and along the stacks. A look of complete bewilderment adorned her face.

"You guys are trying to tell me that some little Seeker flew into my room when I was a baby and threw dust on me 'cause she thought I was your Guardian?" Grace spewed. "Are you nuts or something?"

"Nuts? How curious," Prince Owyn reflected. " I assure thee I was not born of a shell."

"Prince, it's just an expression," Grace said in an exasperated tone.

Saithe caught up to her just as she was about to circle the room a fourth time, and steered her back to the desk. He placed his hands lightly on her shoulders and pushed her gently down into her chair.

"Grace, now calm down. I know it may sound quite remarkable, but it's all true," he claimed. "I know you have doubts, so allow us to explain."

"Master Librarian," Grace began. "How can I be your Guardian? I'm just a kid. I don't have magical or special powers. And I certainly have no idea how to fight your Evil Ice Witch, and even if I did, I'm pretty sure I don't want to! What I do want to do is fix my world and go home."

Saithe shot Prince Owyn a look, "There have been minor complications," said Prince Owyn.

"Minor complications — I'll say!" Grace objected.

Saithe walked over to his desk and closed the talking book. "Allow me to finish the story myself and you may interrupt me at any time with your questions, all right?"

"But . . . " Grace began to protest. She knew it was futile, she was stuck there whether she liked it or not.

"Over the years we sent pictures and memories hoping to help you embrace our world and influence your decision to come here," explained Saithe. "By rejecting Prince Owyn and the wish he wanted to grant, we knew that your dreams had been tampered with."

"Tampered with?" Grace asked. "By who?"

"That we are unsure of," answered Prince Owyn gravely.

Grace stared incredulously, disturbed by his words and his tone. "What? You think your Evil Ice Witch is out to get me? Is that who the Stalker was taking about?"

"At this time we have no way of knowing," the prince replied, lightening his tone and chiding himself for frightening her yet again.

"Let me go back to where the book left off," Saithe proposed. He quickly brought Grace up to date.

"Sounds awfully complicated," Grace said, trying to sort it all out. "But what I really can't help wondering is why I'm supposed to be your Guardian.

"Grace, why you are is because of who you are," insisted Saithe. "It is not our purpose to question how things come to be, or why certain events lead to others. We must trust in whatever presents itself and accept the consequences; age is of no issue, Grace. Whatever powers you possess will be revealed in good time. You just might surprise yourself. I think you've heard enough for now. I'm sure we've given you lots to think about and it will take a while for it all to sink in. Why not take a tour of the castle and get to know the kingdom. I know Seekers and Witch Amity are anxious to meet you," Saithe concluded.

"Indeed," spoke Prince Owyn. "Master Librarian, I am grateful for thy time and thy company. Grace, let us take our leave and allow Saithe to return to his duties." Prince Owyn bowed as Grace rose from the chair.

"I'm not saying I believe any of this and I still have a lot of questions," Grace reminded her host, knowing that to press further would fall on deaf ears. "I hope I'll see you again and you can tell me more."

"Of course, my child, you are always welcome in my library. Come anytime it pleases you," replied the old man.

Chapter Thirty-Three

Saithe escorted the pair to the door and ushered them onto the bridge. Grace and Prince Owyn crossed over and entered the turret's spiral staircase.

"Well, at least we're going down, this time," Grace muttered as she began the descent. "Where to now, Prince?" she asked dryly when they reached the bottom.

"This way, fair Grace. The route to the Seekers and Ice Witch Amity is past the stables and through the orchard," he said as he gestured forward.

They walked through an arched passageway on the main floor of the east wing and into an open area in back of the keep. Pathways wound through the courtyard dotted with elaborate topiary ice sculptures and lined with icy, white hedges. An awning of ice stretched out from the Great Hall shading a large oval terrace and, as they passed by, Grace imagined all sorts of fancy parties the terrace might host.

The path Prince Owyn chose led to the stables where a great barn of ice stood gleaming in the sunlight. On one side, a paddock held a number of grazing white horses and on the other sat an equestrian ring complete with jumps and gates of varying heights. Attached to the barn stood the tack room, where rows of silver and white saddles sat on pegs awaiting riders. Bridles, halters and riding crops hung from wall pegs, and brushes of all sizes lay neatly arranged on a shelf. Inside the barn, stable hands raked silver straw from empty stalls while horses whinnied and stamped their hooves, disturbing the quiet peace of the barn.

"I did some riding on the way to the castle," Grace said. "I know how to ride, you know." Grace was quite proud of her skill as a rider — blue ribbons tacked on the bulletin board in her room offered proof.

"I would like to hear of thy journey and of the places thee toured," he answered.

Leaving the stables behind, they followed a winding path to the edge of the orchard. For as far as Grace could see, rows of ice-covered trees grew in perfect formation, one after the other, their trunks thick, their branches dense and full of ice-frosted fruits of different shapes and sizes. When Grace reached up to pick a fruit from the closest branch, Prince Owyn rushed over to stop her.

"Only the Pickers may pluck the fruit from the trees," he chided, "and only when 'tis the season." Grace withdrew her hand, feeling somewhat embarrassed that she hadn't asked for permission.

Grace and Prince Owyn continued and soon the castle was no longer in view. All around were white, iced trees and Grace envisioned travelling from one ice umbrella to another. Lost in the beauty and splendour of the setting, she momentarily forgot why she was there and what was expected of her.

"Shall we pause for a rest?" said Prince Owyn, interrupting her reverie.

"What?" Grace stammered, "Oh . . . Sure."

Prince Owyn indicated a bench at the side of the path and the two sat at opposite ends.

"Thy silence is curious, fair Grace. Would thou like to share thy thoughts with me?" He asked.

"I wasn't really thinking about anything — which felt good for a change. Just enjoying the orchard. It's so beautiful," she answered.

Grace squirmed in her snowpants until she found a comfortable position on the bench and turned to him. "Owyn . . . oh, am I allowed to call you that?" He nodded. "Thanks, you know there's a good friend in my grade whose name is Owen," she remarked. "You even kind of look like him." Her comment bolstered his ego a notch, flattered that he reminded her of someone she cared for. "Anyways, you must think I'm really being a pain and all, you know, with everything that's happened so far."

"Not so, fair Grace," he responded kindly. " Any thoughts that might be considered shortcomings are far outweighed by those that are not. Why, even thy attire is impressive, such that I have never seen before in mine world."

Grace looked down at herself and considered his compliment. Grace's mother liked to colour-coordinate all of her outfits, and this was no exception. Aside from her bright, yellow jacket and black snowpants, her boots and gloves were both black and yellow, as was her matching hat.

Grace laughed out loud, "I must really stick out like a sore thumb!"

"Are you injured, Grace?" said Prince Owyn, concerned.

"No, no, it's another expression. It means that I stand out, as if I had a big bandage on my thumb that everyone would notice. I know I stand out here in your world because I'm wearing colours your people have never seen before. One big yellow and black bumblebee walking around the Ice World." She doubled over in laughter.

Prince Owyn was unsure how to react to Grace's outburst but when she slapped him on the back and said, "C'mon

Owyn, don't you think it's funny?" he let down his guard and joined her, starting with a slow grin and then erupting into hilarity. For a full five minutes, every time they exchanged glances, their laughter exploded anew.

Finally both took deep breaths and wiping the tears from her eyes Grace said, "Oh that felt good. I needed a good laugh. C'mon, let's go find your Seekers and the Ice Witch."

Walking down the path, Prince Owyn turned to Grace, and asked, "What's a bumblebee?"

Chapter Thirty-Four

A fine, white circle of mist hung in the air, rising from the ground and clouding the view of what lay beyond. Sunbeams danced from droplet to droplet causing the mist to glimmer and glow, and tingle the skin of any who passed through the sparkling curtain. Within the circle, atop a large snowy mound, sat a miniature castle. Tall, slender buildings made of ice on tree-lined pathways displayed turrets and towers, steeples and spires. A central courtyard with sculpted gardens spread out from the keep, and a fountain of ice exhaled the same delicate mist that surrounded the castle.

This castle within a castle bustled with activity. Seekers darted through arched doorways and back again at speeds so great their flights were blurred. A few gathered in clusters, hovered for a moment, then dashed away. Beyond the keep, behind the castle, Seekers tended to their own crop of rounded ice bushes laden with diamond-shaped berries, trimming and pruning, and gently picking the delicate fruit.

Grace and Prince Owyn passed through the circle of mist. The sensation reminded her of another Seeker mound she had recently visited.

"It's just like your castle, only smaller," Grace remarked as she approached the mound.

At first, few Seekers noticed their arrival, being otherwise occupied and intent on their work. Gradually word spread through the castle and Seekers abandoned their tasks and flew to greet the visitors.

A lone Seeker advanced, breaking away from the flock, and flew up to Grace's face.

"Welcome, sweet Grace, welcome," she whispered faintly, her voice barely audible.

Grace could see she was speaking, but strained to hear her, "What? I mean, I beg your pardon?" she said politely.

The Seeker shyly blushed, and repeated louder, "Welcome, sweet Grace."

"Oh, thanks, I guess, " replied Grace.

The Seeker curtsied mid-air before joining the others.

Prince Owyn leaned over to Grace and softly said, "A Seeker has little voice compared to ours. One must labour one's ears to hear a Seeker's song."

Grace nodded, having figured as much.

"Dear Seekers of the mound," Prince Owyn softly called, acknowledging their disdain for anything loud, and knowing they would flee at any boisterous sound. "Seek out Queen Lavon and announce our presence."

Immediately the flock darted back to the castle to summon their queen. A single Seeker remained lingering alone, hovering and staring at Grace.

Kneeling, Grace beckoned the Seeker to come closer and smiled as she timidly approached.

No bigger than Grace's hand, the Seeker's form was that of a miniature girl. A short, silver robe flowed over her slender figure and delicate strands of icicle shards cascaded over her shoulders and down her back. A fine layer of clear ice covered her from head to toe as though she were wrapped in a layer of clear film, and her pale skin glistened. Long, white lashes surrounded almond eyes sparkled like diamonds when she blinked. Her chiselled cheeks glittered with silver powder and her generous smile revealed two rows of pearlescent teeth. Attached to her back, two crystal butterfly-like wings fluttered as she flew toward Grace.

"Hello," Grace softly said, "Who are you?"

In the wink of an eye, the Seeker darted to the side of Grace's head and lifted up the hat and the hair covering her left ear to check for the pearl. "It really is you," exclaimed the Seeker with wonder. "I knew it would be, I just knew it would be."

"What do you mean?" Grace asked. "Oh, I know, you think I'm the Guardian, right? Just like everyone else around here."

"Of course you are," answered the Seeker, her voice faint but clear. "I knew when I first saw you and when I glimpsed the Watchers' mark, the pearl . . . "

"You mean you're the Seeker who came into my room? It was you who found and dusted me when I was a baby?"

The Seeker nodded, pride beaming all over her glistening face.

"Well, I really wish you hadn't, 'cause I'm really not buying into this Guardian stuff," Grace said frankly, her tone suddenly turning cold and gruff. "This is all your fault. Couldn't you have dusted somebody else?"

The Seeker cowered under Grace's sharp words and hovered unsteadily.

"Grace," Prince Owyn chided her. "Do not blame the Seeker, she was performing her duty."

"Right, don't shoot the messenger." Grace sarcastically replied.

"These are delicate creatures and to offend their kind is unjust," he said.

Rejected, the Seeker darted back to the castle.

"Look at how thou hast wounded her when all she sought was an audience with one she reveres," Prince Owyn accused.

"Well, I didn't ask to be revered or whatever she thinks of me." Grace responded defensively. "Now what am I supposed to do?"

Prince Owyn heaved a heavy sigh. An audience with the Seeker Queen was next on the agenda. It was ever more pressing that he resume protocol without delay else he slight the tiny monarch. He just hadn't expected an altercation between a cantankerous Guardian and a devoted Seeker subject. "We must press on. I believe the Seeker Queen is ready to receive us in the Great Hall regardless of what has occurred here."

"What? I'm not sure I want to," Grace said with trepidation.

But Prince Owyn stuck out his arm sharply and glared at Grace until she took it, then set out toward the miniature castle.

"Er, Owyn," Grace said gingerly, not wanting to further antagonize the situation. "Did you say we were to meet Queen Lavon in the Great Hall? That's back there," and she pointed in the direction of the prince's castle.

"She will receive us in her Great Hall inside her castle," replied Prince Owyn curtly.

Grace looked at him with a bewildered expression, "But we won't fit. Her castle is too small."

"Fear not, Seekers have their ways," he said as two Seekers flew out of the castle and hovered before them.

"Ready?" whispered the pair in unison.

Prince Owyn nodded.

"Ready for wha — ?" Grace started to say, when suddenly Seekers flew up to circle Grace and Prince Owyn and sprinkle them with ice dust. They began to shrink smaller and smaller, untill finally, when the ice dust cleared, Grace and Prince Owyn found themselves to be no bigger than their hosts.

"Cool!" Grace couldn't help from exclaim in wonder.

"How does becoming a Seeker's size have to do with temperature?" Prince Owyn asked, irritated this time by her use of words.

Grace rolled her eyes. "Another expression, Owyn. It means it's neat."

"Tidy?"

"No, it means it's, ah, hmm, it means it's . . . interesting. In a good way," Grace explained, struggling to hold back her own frustration with him.

Seekers looked quizzically at Grace and Prince Owyn.

"'Tis one of Grace's sayings," he whispered, ending the exchange.

They nodded, shrugged their shoulders, then motioned for the pair to follow.

The miniature ice castle seemed just as grand as Prince Owyn's. An archway loomed overhead as they entered the Great Hall and thick columns of ice reached up from the glassy floor to the ceiling high above. The room was filled with Seekers, all whispering excitedly among themselves. Mirrors of ice with heavy, ornate frames hung on all four walls reflecting the glittering images of Seekers about the room, and creating the illusion of a larger attendance than there really was.

A hush fell as Grace and Prince Owyn entered. The assemblage parted to create an aisle allowing their guests to pass. At the end of a long, silver carpet sat a sculpted chaise with a high, curved back and a single rounded arm. Lounging on the chaise, the Seeker Queen elegantly sat, waiting to receive her visitors. As they approached, Queen Lavon rose from the chaise and opened her arms in welcome.

She was by far the most exquisite creature Grace had ever seen, more beautiful than her seeker subjects. Her skin glistened and sparkled. Frosted icicle-hair was piled on top of her head in an elaborately twisted do, and a cluster of diamond ice pendants circled her neck, casting a glow on the chiselled features of her face. Her dress, a gown of delicate ice lace speckled with tiny, clear diamonds, flowed to the floor.

"Your Majesty," said Prince Owyn as he knelt on one knee in an elaborate bow. "May I present Grace."

Grace stumbled into a hurried and awkward curtsy that flushed her face a few shades of red. She just wasn't used to all this formality.

"Your Majesty," Grace imitated Prince Owyn as she attempted to recover from her fumbled curtsy. "Pleased to meet you."

Queen Lavon nodded to Prince Owyn and slowly he rose. Gliding over, she placed her hands on Grace's shoulders to help her up. From her shoulders, the queen's hands cupped Grace's face. As she turned the girl's head to one side and back again, the touch of her glistening skin caused Grace's cheeks to tingle. Satisfied with what she saw, the queen feigned a smile.

"Although you do indeed bear a Watchers' mark, your actions are hardly what we expect from a Guardian. What's this I hear about your insulting remarks to one of my most trusted Seekers? I don't believe you're fit to be a Guardian at all."

The queen's words hit her hard, as though struck in the chest by a medicine ball winding her and leaving her speechless. Seekers stared at her and she shrank with embarrassment under their scrutiny. Queen Lavon was still faking her smile in expectation of Grace's explanation for her rude behaviour and, try as she might, Grace knew she didn't have a valid one. Prince Owyn fidgeted uncomfortably knowing he could not save her; this was Queen Lavon's domain and he wasn't about to meddle in her affairs.

"I, er, I shouldn't have said what I did," she fumbled miserably, trying to salvage the damage she'd done. "I must make it up to her."

Queen Lavon motioned for the injured Seeker to come forward. She glided tentatively from her place among her consoling sisters and landed at the queen's side.

Grace swallowed hard. "What's your name?" she asked.

Queen Lavon nodded for her to answer. "I am the Seeker known as Wynt."

"Wynt?" Grace wrinkled her forehead at the sound of such an odd name, and would hate to have borne it herself. A thought popped into her head. "You seem much more than a 'Wynt'. More like a 'Glint'. Do you like THAT name?" she prodded gently.

Puzzled by the question, Wynt looked to her queen for guidance and when Lavon returned an equally puzzled expression, Grace continued.

"It's like a nickname, a special name. I could give you one." Grace could see how this was an entirely new concept for Seekers to grasp. "I mean, you're all covered in ice, so you should be called Snowflake or Glitter or Sparkle or something."

The Seeker looked to her queen once again and, when a genuine smile spread across Lavon's face signalling her approval, Wynt blushed and returned it. "Sparkle, you say, I rather like the sound of that."

"Well then, there you go," Grace responded confidently, relieved that she had broken the tension. "From now on, I'll call you, Sparkle. Everyone can. Please, accept this as an apology."

The glow returned to Wynt's face as she curtsied delicately, indicating that she had. The Seeker and the twelve-year-old girl exchanged smiles. Any ill will melted away and both instinctively knew that a very special friendship had just been cemented — a friendship that had begun a very long time ago.

Soon the assembled Seeker flock began chatting away in their tiny voices, all excited over the gift Grace had just endowed. Wynt fluttered about, whispering to herself, "Hi, my nickname is Sparkle. Sparkle is my nickname. How do you do? I'm Sparkle . . . " Queen Lavon tipped her head in favour of Grace's act and Prince Owyn began to breathe again.

"Might we begin anew? Welcome Grace, welcome Guardian," Queen Lavon softly spoke as she herself performed a curtsy as graceful as any prima ballerina. Immediately everyone in the room followed suit, and curtsying Seekers surrounded Grace.

"Oh, er, thank you, your Majesty," Grace said, attempting to curtsy again to show no further disrespect.

"Please . . . Please, all of you stand up."

One by one Seekers rose, creating a continuous wave throughout the crowd.

"Grace, we have much to speak about, but now is not the time," spoke Queen Lavon. "Now is the time for a great celebration. Seekers!" she called out, "Let the festivities begin!"

Suddenly, the room came alive. Chairs and tables magically appeared, each set with fine glass dishes and silver goblets on lacy, white tablecloths. Seekers darted about carrying trays and silver platters filled with assorted iced canapés and frosted delights. Decanters poured clear, bubbling beverages into tall, frosted glasses and great bowls of assorted luscious fruits were wheeled in on trolleys made of ice. Musicians assembled in a corner struck up a tune and a single voice carried the melody in song. In the centre of the Great Hall, Seekers twirled their partners as they waltzed across the floor and, when it became too crowded, the dancers took to the air.

Grace stood transfixed. Everything had happened so quickly and in such a flurry — one moment she was being chided, the next redeemed, and now a huge celebration was taking place in her honour.

"What am I doing here?" she whispered to herself as she unglued her feet and fled the Great Hall to the courtyard outside. "What have I gotten myself into?" A pang of homesickness grabbed her heart. "I miss home," she lamented. "I want everything to be back to normal, and I want to go home. I WISH to go home."

Chapter Thirty-Five

How long Farren lay on the edge of the ice floe could not be measured. Time had stopped, as far as the survivor was concerned. Without a purpose to fulfill, there was little left to do and it didn't really matter if hours or days had passed. The rain had tapered off and, as the clouds cleared away, the sun's rays began to dry up the pooled water.

Farren sat up and held her knees to her chest. She closed her eyes, dropped her head and gently rocked back and forth as if somehow the motion could offer some sort of consolation. When a gust of wind ripped at her cloak, she opened her eyes. The first object she saw was the dark amulet resting on her chest. Over time, Farren had attempted to retrieve further clues that Witch Mayme had inscribed on the charm, but to no avail. Presently, with hopes dashed and desperate for direction, she recalled the Traveller's premonition that it might still have enchantments yet to be revealed. She gripped the amulet firmly in her hand and promptly fell under its spell.

In a dream, Farren was transported to a meadow of tall ice grass — a place she instantly recognised. Off in the distance, the castle shimmered in the bright sunlight as the witch's inner voice addressed her.

Trust that the path you have followed will bring you the reward you seek.

The images dissolved; Farren's eyes fluttered open. "What dost this mean?" she said to herself. "Might I still succeed in mine quest?" Farren found it odd that the witch had chosen to speak to her after all this time, and could only fathom that what Mayme had just professed might still come true. How, she was unsure.

Farren picked herself up, turned away from the dragon's watery grave, and headed toward shore. She meandered aimlessly over the frozen ice, kicking at the scattered ice-stones responsible for the dragon's demise, and quietly cursing each one as a demon of weather.

Halfway to shore, the ice underfoot became unstable. Cracks and fissures appeared in the clear pane of the lake. Even at a run, she would not make it to shore before the ice fell away and the lake would claim its next victim.

As a perfect circle grew in the ice etched in fissure lines, an eerie shattering, like the sound of breaking glass, announced an impending rift. When the ice floe was completely severed from the rest of the lake, it suddenly burst into the air like a popping cork, and flew skyward flipping over and over before crashing to the far shore. The tremendous force of the impact caused the ice to shudder and Farren struggled for balance.

Water splashed roughly against the circumference of the hole, and caused choppy waves to spill over the sides onto the lake's frozen surface. From within its depth, Percival hurtled through the water, his powerful tail thrusting and propelling him forward until he broke the surface of the water, rocketing through the air, generating spray and sending waves crashing over the sides in his wake.

Halting abruptly in mid-air, the dragon combed the lake for signs of Farren and, once she was detected, he crested back down to the ice. His astonished companion's mouth was agape. She was stunned by the dragon's spectacular resurrection and stammered for words to make sense.

"What . . . Perce . . . how?"

"Now what's the one thing dragons are most famous for?" asked Percival as he limped over, favouring a hind leg.

Farren was still too flabbergasted to answer.

"Give up?"

She nodded.

"Their breath!" he said and issued a big misty blast. "Mostly for breathing out, though we can hold it too. And I can hold mine for a very long time. Getting the ice to crack in a big enough circle was a little tough, mind you."

"Thou . . . thou wast knocked senseless," Farren finally managed to muster.

"Hitting the water revived me, although not before I sank to the bottom of the lake," Percival explained. "It's actually quite lovely down there. Lots of fish and interesting plants and . . . "

"Oh Percival! Thou hast been returned to me!" she exclaimed, rushing him and attempting to hug him in an awkward outpouring of affection. Their difference in size would not allow such an embrace, but the sentiment of her gesture resonated true.

"I thought thee lost," she lamented. "And mine quest dashed. Now we may resume once thou art fit to fly."

"I've been pelted by ice-stones, knocked out, sent to the bottom of a lake and left for dead," Percival retorted. "And all you can think about is your quest? Does everything always have to be about you?"

"I, I . . . just assumed," she stammered.

"No 'how are you? Might you be injured?'" he continued to rant, annoyed that her sudden show of concern was so fleeting. "Oh, just a bump on the head and a few other minor injuries. I'm fine, really, considering. Thank you for asking." Still dripping, Percival proceeded to shake the water from his scales like a wet dog. The resulting spray doused Farren — his action and meaning was not lost in translation.

"I see that thy manner has not suffered injury from thy peril," she said sharply, wiping away the spray. "Might I remind thee that mine quest is also thy quest."

At loggerheads with each other — again — the moment stretched out between them, both defiant in their resolve. After an appropriately awkward period of time, Farren and Percival stood down, each conceding to the other's quest.

"There is a limp in thy stride," Farren said once they started across the lake to shore. "What ails thee?"

"Oh, so now you're concerned," Percival shot back.

"Well, what is it?" she prodded, examining the dragon's hind leg by scooting under one wing. "There's a shard of ice in thy flank!"

"It's nothing," said Percival shooing her away. "It's just a splinter."

"'Tis not just a splinter."

"It's nothing to worry about."

"It will have to come out," she announced flatly. "If it doesn't, it will fester and worsen. Stand still whilst I remove it."

After a few more attempts to dissuade his would-be surgeon, Percival finally surrendered to Farren's will and offered his leg for treatment. Every time she ventured close, attempting to remove the shard, the dragon winced and recoiled away.

"It's going to hurt," he lamented after the fifth or sixth attempt. "Can't you just leave it there? It's not bothering me too much," he lied.

"Oh hush! Thou art acting like a youngling," she scolded. "Some tough, ferocious beast art thou." And with that said, she yanked the shard with one quick motion.

Percival instinctively released his frosted breath and toppled her with a spray of ice crystals. With shard in hand, she glared at him incredulously — this being the second time in one day that he had showered her with something cold and wet.

"Oh, that does feel better, thanks," clucked Percival, patting his scales where the shard had been embedded. "Much better. Coming?"

Farren let out an exasperated sigh, tossed away the shard and joined him for what she knew would be an uneventful last leg of their journey.

Chapter Thirty-Six

The sound of music and laughter wafted through the open windows of Queen Lavon's Great Hall, but in Grace's state of mind, each note, each giggle, each danced step, transmitted confusion rather than joy. She clapped her hands over her ears hoping to drown out the noise from the party and, with eyes squeezed tight, she shut out the sight of the fountain and the courtyard, hoping that once opened, her backyard would miraculously lie before her.

Perhaps this was all a dream and she would wake up in her bed, her mother gently prodding her back from sleep. Or perhaps this was just a daydream she had caught herself in, and soon she would find herself answering her father's calls. With the sights and sounds of the Ice World dismissed, she wanted to imagine herself back home. But try as she might, she could not, for the sensation caused by the fountain's mist would not allow it. As long as she could feel her skin tingle, she knew exactly where she was.

Finally, Grace opened her eyes, uncovered her ears, and looked about her, unsure of what to do next. Should she return to the party and demand that Prince Owyn find some way to right the wrong in her world and allow her to return her home? It was now very clear what he wanted of her — to accept the role of the kingdom's Guardian and somehow defend them against the Evil Ice Witch. She had given neither an emphatic yes or no to the position, and she wondered if her answer would have any bearing on whether her world would be saved. And what if her request was denied? Then what would she do? Would she be held captive, against her will? It was hard to imagine they would turn on her, and yet, who knew? This was a strange, unknown world; she could only imagine what further disaster might befall her, should she make her intentions known.

"No," Grace said out loud. "I got myself into this and I'll get myself out. I followed the quest of the Diamond Heart just like the hag said I should, so that's got to count for something."

Grace picked herself up and headed for the castle's entrance. Once or twice she looked back, wondering if anyone had noticed her departure, but the courtyard remained empty. Cursing the annoying swish of her snowpants, she dashed through the doorway, past the wall of mist, and onto the grounds at the edge of the orchard. She chose a path heading away from the Seekers' castle, past the orchard, and hoped it would lead her back to the main castle buildings. The route she and Prince Owyn had taken seemed very long. Perhaps this was a shortcut.

"If I could get back to the library, maybe Saithe would help me," she thought as she crossed to the edge of the path, not wanting to be seen going down the middle. Bushes and rocks served as welcomed camouflage as she wound her way past fallen ice twigs, scrambled over frozen boulders, and ran along the side of the path.

After what seemed an eternity of darting in and out of shrubbery and skirting fallen ice leaves, Grace looked back to see how far she had travelled. "Oh man! That's as far as I've come? At this size I'll never get anywhere," she moaned. The Seekers' castle was barely out of view and she could still make out fruits hanging from the orchard's trees. Grace sat down to rest on a fallen log covered with frost. Above her loomed tall trees cloaked in giant ice leaves that fluttered in a gentle breeze filtering out white sunlight.

Suddenly the log trembled at one end. Grace quickly jumped up as the vibration passed underneath on its way to the other end. It was then that she realized the log was hollow.

"What the . . . ?" Grace began, but her query was cut short when something appeared out of the mouth of the log. Long icicle whiskers attached to a pointed snout twitched nervously, and sensing no danger, an animal emerged.

"Hello, who are you?" Grace asked the creature. Its long body was covered in sleek white fur and its large ears and long slender tail were without colour or texture, like clear ice. "An ice-mouse?" she thought. It was almost as big as she was.

"Come here, I won't hurt you," Grace gently beckoned as she reached out her hand. Grace's experience with her two housecats, Jelly and Puck, and the other cats and dogs who lived in her neighbourhood had taught her to allow an animal to catch her scent. The ice-mouse timidly sniffed Grace's outstretched hand, then sat back on its haunches inspecting her fingers. Grace smiled at the tickling touch of its delicate, translucent paws.

"You're very cute!" said Grace as she stroked the top of the mouse's head and scratched behind its large ears. Grace was heartened by the comfort a gentle animal's attention could bring, especially since only moments before, she had felt such despair. "Hey, wait, where are you going?" she demanded as the mouse abruptly turned and sprinted away. Halting at the sound of her voice, it retraced its steps, only to sprint away again, stop and look back at her.

"Oh, I get it. You want me to follow you," Grace said. "Well I'm not sure where you're going, but maybe you can help me find a way back to the library."

Over piles of rocks, up frosty embankments, and through thickets of ice, the pair played the game of cat and mouse — or rather girl and mouse — until finally the mouse halted at the trunk of a large tree, deep in the forest. Just a few steps behind her guide, Grace stopped short and put her hands on her hips.

"You brought me to a tree?" she queried the mouse as it rose on hind legs and stretched its paws up the trunk as high as it could reach. "Is there something up there you want me to see?"

Grace approached the tree, the biggest she had ever seen. The trunk was as wide as her house and the rough bark covering it, like everything else in this world, was coated in a thin film of ice. The lower branches were thick and solid and laden with giant ice-leaves that forked out in all different directions creating a canopy of frosted white.

Pressing her cheek against the trunk of the tree, she looked up. At first, all she could see were branches and leaves shimmering in the sunlight. Then, something else caught her eye. It glided fearlessly from branch to branch, its fore and hind limbs outstretched like a four-pointed kite. The lone Flyer was joined by others of its kind and soon the tree was filled with flying creatures gliding from perch to perch.

"What are they?" Grace asked her new friend. "They're not birds, they almost look like squirrels that can fly. Flying squirrels?" Many squirrels lived in the trees in Grace's garden. She had always been fascinated by their balancing acts as they scampered from tree to tree and ran along telephone wires without fear of falling. Yet, she had never seen one fly and did not know for certain such a thing existed in her world.

"There are so many things here that seem the same as back home, but aren't." Grace reflected. "You look like a mouse, they look like squirrels, and Prince Owyn's horses look like, well, like horses — though not in the same way."

The mouse, of course, could make no reply, at least not one Grace could understand. Instead, it circled around her once before returning to the trunk of the tree. It chirped and chattered incessantly now, making demands of one sort or another, until finally one Flyer glided gently down and landed on the ground. On four legs, the creature moved as deftly as it had in the air. It regarded the mouse for a moment in a silent exchange of thoughts, then moved toward Grace. Unafraid, Grace inspected the creature more closely. Larger than the mouse and covered in silver fur, it had round, silver eyes, small transparent ears, and the bushiest tail Grace had ever seen. It swished as the creature crept then crouched before her. The ice mouse came up behind.

"Hey! What are you doing?" Grace demanded as the ice mouse nudged her towards the Flyer, pushing her onto its back. "Hey! What the . . . " she sputtered. With its tiny paws, the mouse quickly arranged Grace's arms around the Flyer's collar, and before she knew it, the Flyer took off, gliding up between tree branches toward the open sky.

Grace screamed at the top of her lungs. She squeezed the animal's throat almost to the point of strangulation and refused to open her eyes as they soared through the air. Only after the Flyer levelled off did Grace consider her predicament. One eye opened to see the tops of trees gently glide by; the second eye opened to see an empty, cloudless sky. And when

Grace finally loosened her grip, sat up and looked down, she marvelled as the whole kingdom passed beneath her.

"I'm flying!" she called to the wind. "We're flying!" she called to her mount.

Filled with exhilaration and a piqued sense of adventure, Grace secured her seat astride the Flyer and leaned forward. Clutching fur for reins, she signalled to her mount that she was ready for the ride of her life. Sensing her eagerness the Flyer reacted in kind — he veered to one side in a wide arc before diving down into the thick ice forest below. Soaring up over one branch, swooping beneath another in roller coaster mode, the pair skilfully dodged outstretched branches barring their path.

Leaving the forest behind, the Flyer climbed higher and higher, coasting on air currents, dipping and gliding like a kite attached to an endless string. The kingdom lay stretched out below and, although the castle appeared dwarfed at such a distance, Grace could make out each distinctive building: the gatehouse, the Great Tower and the keep, even the stables and the neatly tended orchard farther away.

"To the library," Grace shouted as she reigned in her mount, steering in the direction of her destination of choice. The Flyer responded and followed her lead, diving downwards, and headed through the courtyard on the way to the library turret beyond.

At that particular time of day, the courtyard was bustling with the comings and goings of the castle's subjects tending to their chores and regular duties. Quite unexpectedly, the Flyer streaked through the crowd causing heads to turn and hats to topple as unsuspecting individuals ducked and dodged the intruders. Grace and the Flyer bolted past vendors, sideswiping their heavily-laden carts, almost spilling their wares onto the ground. Children playing in the garden, abandoned their games to give chase, and a string of youngsters soon trailed below, all leaping and grabbing in attempts to make capture.

"Take me to the library," she whispered into the Flyer's ear, hoping, but not knowing whether her words would be understood. Almost immediately the Flyer whisked her away, much to the disappointment of the astonished crowd. Grace breathed a sigh of relief as the pair once again approached the library turret. The prospect of meeting with Saithe, once more, lifted her spirits. She felt confident he would have the answers she sought, and that she could convince him to help her get home.

The Great Tower loomed large, even more gigantic now than before as the Flyer skimmed along the curve of the library turret's thick blocks toward the entrance.

"Hey!" Grace called out, "slow down!"

Ignoring her, the Flyer stayed its course, rounding the turret, passing the entrance, and flying through the arched passageway that led to the back of the keep.

"Where are you going?" Grace hollered as they passed over the gardens and the oval ice terrace, startling the grounds-keepers and those having tea.

"Where are you taking me?' Grace demanded as they headed for the stables and the orchard beyond.

"Oh no! No, no, you're taking me back to the Seekers!" she bellowed at the Flyer. "I don't want to go there . . . " her voice trailed away as her captor suddenly dove into the orchard of glistening trees. Grace crouched down in her seat, afraid of low-lying branches that might knock her from her mount, but the Flyer deftly manoeuvred to keep out of harm's way.

Breaking free of the orchard, they flew through the Seekers' circle of mist, over the castle, and out through the other side.

"Where are you taking me?" Grace screamed in terror as she looked back and watched the circle of mist disappear from sight. Fearful of where she was headed — or rather where the Flyer was headed — Grace desperately wanted to dismount but knew that to leap off at this speed would be far too treacherous. She was trapped. Trapped on a flying creature on a secret mission to an unknown destination.

"Ahh!" Grace gasped out loud and clapped her hand over her mouth. A frightening thought entered her head. Was this Flyer in cahoots with Snitch? Before she could fully realize her peril, the Flyer shot into a blackened thicket so dense with brush, Grace found herself hurtling through deep woods in total darkness. She screamed, tightened her grip on the Flyer, and squeezed her eyes shut. The Flyer sped on in earnest, undeterred by the darkness or Grace's protests.

After what seemed an endless journey of ups and downs, bobs and weaves, the Flyer slowed. Grace meekly opened her eyes as a large tower came into view. The light was still low but bright enough to make out the structure, made of ice with a wide set of steps leading up to a sprawling veranda. The Flyer flew up the staircase, abruptly landed, and deposited Grace in a heap on the floor.

"Well, it's about time you got here," said an unfamiliar voice.

Chapter Thirty-Seven

Grace found herself lying face down on the veranda floor, the Flyer next to her, both panting with exhaustion from their harrowing flight.

"You know, you didn't have to just drop me like that," Grace scolded as she sat up. "I could have gotten off myself, thank you very much." The Flyer just stared ahead.

"What are you looking at?" Grace asked, as she slowly followed the Flyer's line of sight until she reached the object of its gaze.

"Oh!" Grace exclaimed.

Two gigantic laced boots stood before her, heel to heel, perfectly poised in ballet's first position — one of the five that Grace knew from her own lessons in dance. Made of soft white leather, studded with silver hooks and fastened criss-cross with silver laces, they looked more like her mother's ice skates than boots. All that was missing was the blade. The left toe was tapping in an impatient sort of way, as though waiting for something to happen. Unwittingly, Grace couldn't help bobbing her head along in steady rhythm. When the tapping ceased, Grace broke free from her hypnotic state and looked up from the monstrous boots into the face of a giant.

"There's much to be done, so let's get on with it. First things, first. Best do something about her size. Can't have her wandering around that small. Might lose her again. Seeker, if you wouldn't mind . . . "

A Seeker coasted down and floated in front of Grace.

"Sparkle!" Grace gasped, relieved to finally see a familiar face. "What's happening?"

"'Tis all right, Grace," reassured the Seeker.

"Where am I, and who is that?" Grace whispered, not so much out of respect for her Seeker friend, but more out of fear she might upset the one giving orders.

"'Tis the Ice Witch." said Sparkle.

"The Ice Witch!" Grace whispered out of the side of her mouth, fear gripping her heart. "The Evil Ice Witch?"

"No, no, fair Grace. 'Tis not the evil one," Sparkle answered as she gestured backwards. "'Tis our Ice Witch Amity."

"Oh," said Grace. "She's the, er, Nice Ice Witch? She's really big."

Sparkle laughed. "'Tis not she who is so big, 'Tis you who are so small."

"Oh right. I'm still small."

"Well, 'tis not supposed to be." Sparkle began, "Only within the walls of Queen Lavon's castle should one remain the size of a Seeker; for the moment one leaves, one returns to their original height. Except for you, and we know not why. Must be a Guardian trait."

Grace cringed at mention of the title. "That's why everything looks so ginormous," Grace remarked steering the subject away from that claim.

"Ginormous?"

"Sorry, it's an expression. It's a combo of gigantic and enormous. It means really big."

"Prince Owyn did tell of your many sayings," mused Sparkle. "I wish to learn more of them, I find them, er, cool." Grace couldn't help but grin at the Seeker using one of her expressions, and Sparkle grinned back.

"Might we get on with it?" demanded Ice Witch Amity, her left toe tapping again.

Grace and Sparkle turned with a start at the sound of her voice. Witch Amity was smiling an impatient smile as she peered at the Seeker with eyebrows raised expectantly. Sparkle nodded obediently, opened her crystal butterfly wings and took to the air.

"Grace, no longer shall we be sized the same," Sparkle called out as she circled Grace, sprinkling her with tiny handfuls of ice dust. Grace watched the spiralling Seeker shrink smaller as she grew bigger until she reached original height. Sparkle flew onto Grace's hand, her task complete.

"Thanks, Sparkle," Grace whispered. "Thanks a lot." Sparkled smiled, a slight blush glowing in her silver cheeks.

"Yes, thank you, Seeker, you may take your leave," Witch Amity interrupted. "Now Miss Grace, we have much to catch up on."

Now full-size, Grace wasn't as intimidated by the Ice Witch as when she was only six inches tall. As she studied her more closely, the witch wasn't exactly what she imagined an Ice Witch to be. The talking book in the library had illustrated both Ice Witches, and Grace just naturally assumed their appearance would still be the same, but that story had happened a long time ago. Over time, the Ice Witches had obviously changed. If this Ice Witch appeared differently, Grace wondered what the evil one now looked like.

Of all the people Grace had met in the Ice World, she expected the Ice Witch to be the most impressive. The Seeker Queen and her flock of Seekers were all incredibly beautiful, the Ice Prince was certainly handsome and sophisticated enough, and even the librarian, in his own special way, had been kind and helpful. So, much to her surprise, the Ice Witch standing before her was anything but impressive. In fact, she seemed rather ordinary, if a bit odd. She was dressed all in white — from the tip of her boots to the top of her head — in an outfit proper for a lawn bowling match. She wore the long, droopy shorts cinched at the waist with a woven belt, the oversized sweater with large, round buttons running down the front and the headgear — a cross between sun visor and baseball cap — all seemed fitting for such a sport. Except for the boots — a dead giveaway that Witch Amity wasn't on her way to a local tournament of lawn bowlers. She was neither pretty nor plain, neither too fat nor too slim, neither too tall nor too short; she was quite simply ordinary in almost every way.

"You've been waiting for me?" Grace asked, trying to recover from the Flyer's ride and her transformation back to normal height. "Saithe and Prince Owyn did tell me you wanted to see me."

"Well, that's true. How is the dear old man? So loves his books, that one," said Witch Amity. "And what of Prince Owyn? Such a charming boy."

"I guess they're both fine. At least they were the last time I saw them," answered Grace.

"And what about you, young Grace, what about you?" Witch Amity reached for Grace's hand. "Come, sit with me, and we'll get better acquainted."

The Ice Witch led Grace over to the middle of the veranda where two high-backed garden chairs sat facing a small round table set with a crystal pitcher and two delicate crystal teacups. Grace nervously took her place. That she was actually sitting down for a chat with a witch — an Ice Witch — seemed bizarre enough in itself, and she wasn't quite sure what to expect or how to act. But there was one thing for certain: she had decided against launching into her well-rehearsed tirade of the day's events. There was no telling how a witch might react to that.

"Well now, that's better," said Witch Amity as she poured a clear liquid into each of the teacups and handed one to Grace. "I thought you might need some refreshments after your little adventure with the Flyer. Tart?"

Witch Amity passed a silver plate and Grace, minding her manners, reached for the closest tart and said between mouthfuls, "Thanks. These are really good."

Witch Amity placed her cup back on to its saucer and leaned in to Grace. "Thought so. Now Grace, whatever were you thinking leaving Queen Lavon's castle? Especially without telling anyone."

"I . . . I'm sorry," Grace stammered. "I guess I shouldn't have. My mother always complains about me not telling anyone where I'm going."

"Prince Owyn and all of the Seekers were quite concerned, and of course Prince Owyn blames himself for not being more responsible. It's fortunate a Seeker saw you leave and brought it to our attention. Word was sent out immediately. Otherwise I'm not sure how long it would have taken to find you, being at such a small size and all. The Flyer was instructed to bring you here. To me. Although, it would seem that you got a bit sidetracked," she said, sending the Flyer a look. "But you're here now, and that's what's important. Now tell me, what's going on in that pretty little head of yours?"

Grace did not answer for a moment, as she collected her thoughts. So much had happened and she wasn't quite sure where to begin.

"I . . . I left the castle because I was feeling so . . . so out of place, like I didn't belong there and I just wanted to go home."

Grace struggled to keep her voice from trembling and tears from welling up in her eyes. "But I knew I couldn't because my world is all messed up and I need somebody to fix it. Prince Owyn didn't seem to know anything about it so I thought, maybe if I could find the librarian, he might be able to help."

"Grace, I understand. It comes as no surprise that what you have experienced and learned here in the Ice World must be terribly confusing for you. It would be for anybody. And, of course you're concerned for your home and your parents; it's only natural."

"So, you do understand," whispered Grace.

"Yes Grace, we all do. And we all knew that whoever our Guardian turned out to be, would need a period of adjustment."

"A period of adjustment!" Grace blurted. "I don't need a period of adjustment, I need my world to be fixed and to go home, back to my old life."

Witch Amity reached for the crystal pitcher and refilled both teacups. "Grace, are there Seekers and witches in your world?" she asked, remaining calm.

"Well, no. Just in books and stories. It's all make-believe."

"Are there talking books and black demons and magic to make you small?"

"No." Grace answered.

"Do your people live in ice castles surrounded with gardens of ice?"

"Well, no. Except in the winter when it's carnival time and all sorts of ice things are made. But nobody lives in them."

Witch Amity returned the pitcher to the table. "And what do you have in your world that you can't find here?" she asked.

"I don't know, there're lots of things," Grace said, frustrated that the witch was forcing her to think off topic. "Like cars and computers and shopping malls. And colours."

Witch Amity picked up her cup and saucer and took a sip. "So it would seem there are a great many differences between our two worlds?"

Grace fidgeted in her seat, her snowpants swishing. "Yeah, I guess so. So what?"

"In the same way that our worlds are different, so are the people who live in them," said Witch Amity as she replaced her cup and saucer on the table. "The talents I possess are not the same as the talents you possess. I perform witchcraft, and you, you have abilities I lack."

Grace cocked her head to one side, annoyed that the witch was making some sense. "Well, I guess I never thought of it that way . . . But you know what your powers are. I don't," she said quietly. "And what about what's happened in my world? Who's going to fix that?" Grace demanded, standing up.

Ice Witch Amity knew a crossroads had been crossed and hoped she had managed to gain Grace's trust. But, she was also aware that what she was about to tell her just might set her off again. "Your world was returned to its former state the moment you entered the Ice World."

Grace stared at the witch incredulously, taking a moment for this news to sink in. "What? You mean you're the one who did this? Why would you do such a horrible thing?"

"When you wouldn't come willingly, we had to take drastic measures to force you to come," explained Witch Amity. "You gave us little choice in the matter."

"What happened to 'dark forces crossing over from your world to mine'?"

"Oh, make no mistake, that still rings true," answered Witch Amity gravely. "Someone did tamper with your gift of extraordinary sight, and since we know not who, proves the threat still possible. It's fortunate that we were able to get to you in time."

Grace's head was spinning; she plunked herself back into the chair and fell silent. The knowledge that her parents were fine and her world righted was a tremendous relief. She thought she should feel overjoyed but, instead, she was furious with the Ice Witch for having deceived her. Grace wondered if she should believe anything the witch had to say. She was quite fed up with playing the pawn in their game.

"I don't believe you," Grace said challenging the witch. "Prove it. That my world is back to normal."

Witch Amity heaved a heavy sigh. "Do you have the mirror Prince Owyn gave you?" she asked.

Grace nodded and pulled it from her jacket pocket.

"Now, wish to see your world."

Grace did as instructed and the clear glass clouded over.

"You will see the exact moment you left, as if nothing had happened."

The mirror displayed her parents' room where they both lay soundly sleeping, her father softly snoring and her mother gently nudging him to roll over.

"But they're still sleeping," Grace exclaimed in protest.

"Of course they are," answered Witch Amity, casually picking up her cup and saucer and taking a sip. "Weren't they when you left? They will wake once you have returned. Remember, time does not follow when you enter our world."

Grace stared into the mirror at her sleeping parents, then glanced at her watch displaying nine forty-five — her departure time. She could only hope the witch was telling the truth, that everything was all right in her world and she could worry a little less about her parents' welfare. For now.

Grace rose from the garden chair, walked over to the edge of the veranda and looked out at the dense thicket she and the Flyer had flown through. The intertwined branches and twigs gleamed with dark, icy shadows lurking within. "So I can go home now," Grace stated, rather than asked.

Witch Amity set down her cup and saucer and joined her. "Well, not necessarily," she responded. "If Watchers believe you have completed the task you have been summoned to do, they will allow you to return to your world. If not, there's one way to find out."

Grace looked up at the witch, eyebrows raised in fear and asked, "How?"

"Ask through a wish and, if the Watchers grant it, you'll find yourself home." Witch Amity replied.

"I'm ready. Thanks, Witch Amity. Say goodbye to everyone for me. Tell them I'm sorry, but I really have to go."

Witch Amity nodded graciously and withdrew.

Grace took a deep breath, closed her eyes in expectation of blinding white light that would engulf her as she was whisked away, and said, "I wish to go home."

A few seconds later, a smile spread across her face, as she was about to open her eyes to find herself in the backyard. But when she did, the dark thicket beyond the veranda stared back at her.

Sighing relief, Witch Amity approached, put her arm around Grace's shoulder and squeezed her tightly. "It would appear that it's not quite time to leave, Grace. There must be more expected of you."

For the second time that day, Grace was speechless. Initial shock turned to panic when she realized that she was indeed trapped in the Ice World no matter what.

Chapter Thirty-Eight

A Seeker suddenly streaked across the porch and halted at the witch's ear. Her whispers were inaudible to Grace. Once her message had been delivered, the Ice Witch nodded and the Seeker flew off again.

"What did the Seeker say?" asked Grace, resigned to her fate.

"Pieces are falling into place according to plan," she replied.

"What pieces? What plan?" Grace asked.

"You shall soon see," Witch Amity answered cryptically. "The Festival is fast approaching . . . "

"Festival?"

"And you play an integral role and must be prepared."

This revelation surprised Grace. "Now what? As if being Guardian wasn't enough," she thought.

"Come, we must return to the castle," Witch Amity ordered.

Before Grace could object, Witch Amity bolted across the veranda and hurried down the stairs. Grace sat fastened to her chair, somewhat dumbfounded at the witch's sudden change in demeanour and hasty departure. When Witch Amity realized that Grace's footfalls were not following behind, she looked back at Grace and with the snap of her head motioned a silent "come on!"

Grace took the cue and leapt to her feet, hurrying to catch up to the lawn-bowling attire disappearing from view.

The path from Witch Amity's residence was lined with bushy hedges and dotted with tall, crystal flowers that swayed in the slight breeze as Grace and the Ice Witch quickly passed by.

The appearance of Grace and the Ice Witch in the courtyard caused quite a stir. A visit from Witch Amity was not a common occurrence, and the workers knew well enough that her presence there meant something was amiss. Caught off guard at the unexpected guests, castle folk interrupted their chores to catch a glimpse at what the matter might be.

"Good people," the Ice Witch called, sensing the tension. "There is no need for concern. All is as it should be, so please, let us not detain you from the duties you so well perform." Comforting words to be sure, however her manner displayed the opposite, and a murmur spread through the crowd as she continued to wend her way. Grace followed behind.

"Come along, Grace," motioned Witch Amity. "The kitchen is through here and I must seek out Mistress Baker Cass."

The Ice Witch led her through a vestibule and into a large room filled with counters and tall cupboards. In the centre stood a long table filled with bowls and dishes of assorted shapes and sizes, while crystal-clear pots and pans dangled on hooks above, waiting to be put to use. At the far end, on a wide sideboard, sat rows of casseroles, each steaming a fine white mist into the air. On the other side, a curved faucet set in the wall gently spilled water into a large, clear basin atop a solidly built washstand. Dishes and cooking utensils — stirring, scraping and scouring — clattered and clamoured above the voices of the kitchen staff as they prepared the day's fare.

A short, portly woman in a long white apron entered the kitchen from the pantry, barking, "Mind the ice berry pie. If there's not enough sweet added, it'll be so tart we'll all be knocking about for days with pursed lips, wrinkled noses and squiny eyes. Ooooh, what have we here? My, my, such distinguished guests."

"Mistress Baker," said Witch Amity. "I'm sorry for the interruption, I know how busy you are."

"Tut, tut!" the Mistress Baker clucked. "I'm never too busy for the likes of you," and embraced Witch Amity with a hug befitting an old friend. "Would this be the one?" she whispered softly, eyeing Grace.

"It would appear so," Witch Amity whispered back.

"Yup, that's me. Miss Guardian Grace," Grace cut in dryly. The Mistress Baker and the Ice Witch exchanged glances.

Witch Amity reached into a pocket and pulled out a sheath of paper. "Here's the menu and you'll have hurry if you're going to make it all in time."

"Never in a hundred teaspoons did I ever imagine that such a grand event would be served from my humble kitchen," Cass said reverently.

"What event?" Grace attempted to interrupt.

"I realize it's a tall order," said Witch Amity ignoring Grace's query and speaking directly to the baker. "I trust you shall do us proud."

Cass nodded as she held up the list, perused the items and promptly whisked away to rummage through a cupboard.

Witch Amity turned back to Grace and said, "Follow me."

"Where . . . ?" Grace attempted, but the Ice Witch had already disappeared through a doorway and down a hallway. Grace hurried to catch up.

Witch Amity led her up a flight of stairs and out into a large studio with windows on three walls. On the fourth, bolts of fabric lay neatly stacked on shelves from floor to ceiling. Spindles of thread and yarn lined the lower shelves of the flanking walls. A large rectangular worktable sat in the middle of the room surrounded by individual stations where workers fed freshly-cut pattern pieces into purring sewing machines. A curio cabinet in one corner displayed scissors of various sizes — from the tiniest clippers to large, jagged pinking shears — all of gleaming silver. Watermelon-sized pincushions, pierced with assorted needles and stickpins, sat stoically. Amidst the whir and hum of spinning wheels and threads intertwining by needles and bobbins, a very tall, slender young woman wrestled with wafer-thin pattern paper at a large drafting table.

"Mistress Tailor, " said Witch Amity. "Nadelle, she's arrived."

At the sound of her given name, Nadelle smoothed the unruly paper with the palm of her hand. She turned toward the witch but her eyes rested on Grace as she quit the drafting table and advanced. Her stride was long and exaggerated, each foot fluidly crossing in front of the other with graceful precision while her arms swung at their sides in opposition to her legs. With shoulders back, head slightly cocked and hips forward, her runway strut made for quite a dramatic approach.

Grace had never seen such an elegant person and at the same time, one so severe. Her jet-black hair was cropped at her ears, short bangs bluntly lined her long forehead and dark, long-lashed eyes framed by manicured black brows gave her oval face and high cheekbones a distinctively cold appearance. Grace stood nervously before her, not knowing where to look, and cast her eyes up at Witch Amity, hoping she might explain Nadelle's scrutinizing inspection. Only when Nadelle directed Grace to turn around did she speak.

"I see what you mean, Amity," said the Mistress Tailor as she perused the twirling girl. "Unusual costume." She reached out and squeezed the arm of Grace's quilted jacket.

"It's called a snow jacket and snowpants." Grace said quietly, hoping she hadn't spoken out of turn.

Nadelle raised a manicured brow at the witch. "Is that so? Well, she'll have to remove them, whatever they're called."

Grace wrinkled her brow, wondering what to make of the request, but the witch nodded encouragingly, "Go on, take them off."

Grace pulled off her hat and her woollen gloves expecting the tips of her ears and fingers to redden and sting. Balancing, she reached down and pulled off her right boot and pant leg in one clean motion. She hesitantly placed her stocking foot on the icy floor, anticipating the cold to leak through her sock and the same numbness as when she had spent too long at the skating rink or outside with her friends.

"I . . . , I don't feel anything," she said, bewildered. "I mean I don't feel anything at all. I'm not cold, I'm just right. How can that be?"

Standing on one leg, she reached down to withdraw her left foot. Suddenly, she lost her balance and, despite flapping her arms wildly, she toppled over onto the floor. Landing with a thud, feet thrown up into the air, her left boot sailed across the room into a bin of remnants. "Oww!" she exclaimed, suffering from more than just a bruised bottom as Witch Amity rushed forward to help her up.

Witch Amity put her arm around Grace's shoulder and gave her a squeeze. "'Tis the way of our world, young Grace. You'll get used to it."

"So here I don't have to wear my snow clothes. I can wear whatever I want?" Grace asked.

"To answer your question in a word, no. You may not wear your regular clothes while you are here in the Ice World," replied Witch Amity. "A Guardian must look the part. That is why we are here to enlist the skills of our Mistress Tailor," said Witch Amity.

"You mean I have to wear a uniform? Sheesh, it's just like school."

"Oh, it's no ordinary uniform. Whenever you travel in our world you will wear these garments. When you return home, you will wear what you left in," replied Witch Amity. She then turned her attention back to Nadelle. "One set will do for the time being."

Nadelle nodded and withdrew a pair of half-moon spectacles from her smock, placed them on the tip of her nose and inspected Grace again. A thin sliver of crystal spiralled from the centre of the spectacle lenses and traced a perfect copy of Grace in the air. When finished, Grace stood with her crystal twin shimmering alongside her.

"Just like the stars outside my bedroom window," she whispered to herself.

"Nadelle, please deliver the Guardian robes as soon as they're finished," said Amity. "Grace will need to wear them in order to activate their magic. She will be waiting in the royal apartments."

Nadelle nodded. "Shan't be too long," she said as she began to drape a fine fabric around the crystal manikin, pinning it into place. Almost instantly Grace could see a shape beginning to form. She noted that anything resembling snowpants were not under design.

Suddenly the doors flew open and Prince Owyn rushed in with such force he nearly toppled both Grace and Amity to the ground.

"Your grace, and . . . and Grace," he gasped. "I was concerned for thy welfare and safety. It is rumoured the Guardian had been taken captive by a rogue Flyer."

Grace laughed. "A rogue what? Owyn, I wasn't kidnapped, I just had kind of a wild ride, that's all. Somebody's been pulling your leg."

"I assure you I have not been attacked. Mine leg remains as it should," declared Prince Owyn.

"I believe you have been caught in one of Grace's expressions, Your Majesty," said Witch Amity. "True enough, Grace?"

"Yeah, it's an expression, all right." Grace answered. "It means someone has fooled you into believing a story that isn't true."

"I shall have to have words with the Mistress Baker," he said stiffly in an attempt to recover his dignity. "After all, am I not her future king?"

"Your majesty, the Mistress Baker treats all with fairness and respect," Witch Amity assured him. " Do not take this too seriously. She's just having a bit of fun."

Prince Owyn began to object but before he could, the witch raised her hand and silenced him. "There is much to do. The Crystal Ice Spirits will be arriving soon and we must be ready. Your Majesty, please take Grace to the royal apartments where she can change her clothes," she instructed as she started for the door. "I'll be in the courtyard if you need me."

Chapter Thirty-Nine

Leaving the frozen lake behind, Percival soared up through a clear white sky with a bright shining sun and was soon sailing gently over a meadow of tall ice grass. Gliding to the crest of a hill he landed, lowering his wing for his rider to dismount, before collapsing to the ground. Farren clumsily fell off and rolled a few times in the tall grass before coming to a halt face down. Both were so exhausted from their harrowing experience that a silent understanding had crossed between them, and their decision to rest was mutual.

In time, Percival rose to his feet, stretched out his wings and breathed deeply, swallowing the fresh meadow air. Wading through tall grass, he snatched at a blade and ran it through his chiselled teeth. Meanwhile, Farren had wandered off a distance to the top of a hill. So steep was the grade of the hill, it was only after Percival reached Farren that the vista beyond was revealed. A deep valley spread far and wide, covered in the same ice grass as the hill, waving and swaying in the gentle breeze. A river of clear ice meandered its way through and, at the foot of the valley, a great mountain towered overhead, its snow-covered peaks glistening and sparkling. Farren stared intently out over the valley and when Percival followed her line of sight, his gaze came to rest on a glistening castle of ice nestled into the gentle slope of the mountain.

"'Tis quite beautiful," said Farren, breaking the silence. "More beautiful than I remembered."

"Mmm," murmured Percival as he sat down on his haunches beside her. "It is indeed splendid. It is no wonder you have been so determined to complete your quest of returning."

She nodded wistfully and sighed deeply.

"I would have thought you would be a little more excited at finally seeing this kingdom," noted Percival. "Instead, you seem quite withdrawn."

Turning to the dragon, Farren said, "So many years have passed since I took mine leave that mine greatest fear is that so much has changed that I might not be welcomed."

"What you say is absurd," said Percival. "If they are the good people you have spoken of, it will make no difference how long you have been away. They will surely welcome you with open arms."

For the first time in their long journey Farren actually smiled. "I thank thee Percival, for thy words of encouragement. I trust thy wisdom will prevail."

"A dragon can sense such things. We are blessed with powers of premonition. Had you not heard?"

"Indeed I have," she said with a smirk.

"Well, let's go find out whether I'm right."

They decided to walk through the valley as both had had their fill of flying for one day. Though it was quite steep, they easily climbed to the valley floor and were soon wading through ice grass en route to the castle. Off in the distance, the castle shimmered under its protective veil of glitter. Its tall towers and turrets stood lightly shrouded, the castle walls softened and the gatehouse slightly blurred. Cloaked in this fine crystal haze, the whole castle appeared more like a mirage than a solid structure made of ice and snow. One wondered if, in a glance, it might disappear.

Finally they reached the foot of the mountain, and the castle loomed ahead in all its splendour. The drawbridge in the gatehouse had been lowered across the moat, but the protective veil still blocked the entrance, barring passage. Farren clutched the dragon's arm and squeezed it tightly.

"Perce, the time has come. Draw breath and be done with this mask of evil," she implored. "Destroy that which impedes mine entry. Fulfill mine quest and I shall fulfill thine own with the Diamond Heart."

Percival bowed his head. "To be reunited with my beloved is more than I could have ever hoped for. My heart is filled with such joy I know not why it has not already burst," he said softly. As he turned toward her, their eyes locked and, in a single moment, everything they had experienced together flashed between them — their bickering and arguments, arrogant tempers, the obstacles lain in their path. None of it mattered anymore. Only this — the moment at which they were both to be granted what they most desired.

"A promise made is a promise kept," whispered Percival, and he launched into the air.

After Prince Owyn had escorted Grace to the royal apartments, loud calls from outside breached the glass-paned doors. Grace and Owyn rushed out onto the balcony where, down below, the courtyard buzzed with a flurry of excitement.

"Someone's coming! Make ready! They're here!"

Witch Amity stood in the centre of the courtyard calling out instructions and shouting orders. All around her castle folk scrambled as the Mistress Baker burst out from the kitchens yelling frantically. "'Tis too soon! 'Tis too early!"

"What's happening?" Grace asked.

"Must be the arrival of the Crystal Ice Spirits for the Festival," Prince Owyn answered. "'Tis odd, the Spirits are not expected until much later in the day. Something must have been seen through the veil."

"Witch Amity mentioned a festival," Grace exclaimed. "What is it?"

"Forgive me, Grace, but as thou can very well see, the castle is quite unprepared for this early arrival," said Prince Owyn. "I'm afraid I must leave and offer mine assistance. I shall recount the story of the Festival another time."

Grace nodded, "You're right. What can I do to help?" she said as a knock sounded on the door announcing the arrival of her new clothes.

"Change quickly and meet me down in the courtyard. Witch Amity will explain what is expected of thee," Prince Owyn said as he dashed from the room jostling the maid who held the new robes.

Opening the bundle Grace was pleased with what lay inside. The pair of smoky-grey riding pants and matching cropped jacket suited her just fine and she quickly slipped them on. The fit was perfectly tailored to her slight frame. The chambermaid brought her a pair of tall riding boots of the same colour and only when she offered a long flowing cloak did Grace raise her eyebrows sceptically.

"It's a bit much, don't you think?" she said.

The chambermaid shrugged, drew the cloak over her shoulders and fastened the button under her chin.

Chapter Forty

Percival soared up into the sky, flapping his great wings. As he rose higher and higher, he stoked his resolve to honour his beloved one last time. He banked over mountain peaks and streaked downwards to circle the castle, skirting around turrets and diving between towers. Skimming the shroud that embraced the castle, his tail skipped the surface like a pebble over still water.

Touring once around the castle, Percival finally slowed to a hover mid-air. Down below, through the misty veil, he could faintly distinguish the castle folk bustling about the courtyard, oblivious to their impending fate. Little did Percival care that Witch Amity stood fixed in the centre of the chaos, calling out instructions and shouting orders, nor that Grace had donned appropriate Guardian attire and was about to leave the royal chambers while Prince Owyn assisted Mistress Baker Cass with her chores. That librarian Saithe had left the library to join in the festivities, and Queen Lavon and her flock flitted to and fro were of little consequence, for the focus of the dragon was the task at hand.

Outside the castle walls Farren anxiously waited at the drawbridge, her eyes to the sky, following the dragon's every move with great anticipation.

Drawing breath deeply and forcibly, filling his chest to capacity, Percival arched his spiked spine backwards as his powerful wings rose to their widest expanse. With a sudden lurch forward, he unleashed a cone of icy frost from his powerful jaws with such thundering force the ground trembled.

Thousands of minute, crystallized ice pellets exhaled from the dragon's breath blasted the protective veil engulfing the castle, scattering and skittering as though pounding a tin roof. The invading breath quickly released its destructive power, penetrating the veil and viciously eating away layer after layer. Churning, white steam bled from the veil's open wounds as it swiftly disintegrated and fell away, crashing down to the ground below, leaving the castle unshielded and exposed.

In the courtyard, all activity ground to a halt as startled castle folk looked up and watched in horror as the dragon's breath destroyed the protective armour of their kingdom. In an astonishing blink, the one sterling constant in their lives assuring their safety and immunity from harm, crumbled to the ground.

Upon hearing the blast, Grace had raced to the balcony and strained over the ledge to see events unfold. Above her, the dragon still hovered in the open sky. Below her, in the courtyard, a wave of bewildered wonder washed over the faces of the people who had so generously embraced her that day as their Guardian.

Unflinching, Witch Amity remained stationed in the midst of the scene. The genteel manner Grace had come to know suddenly transfigured into something completely different. Straightening her spine, she threw back her shoulders, appearing much taller and forceful than before. Flinging off her cap, her white hair tumbled onto her shoulders as she wrenched her head up to the sky, glaring at the dragon. With eyes blazing and brow furrowed, she brandished one arm up at Percival, her fist tightly clenched.

"Who dares strike this kingdom with such fury, and with what right?" she demanded, her voice thundering up from the courtyard to the dragon above. Grace's eyes widened at the sight of Witch Amity's now commanding presence. Never would she perceive her as ordinary again.

On cue, Percival swooped down to face the Ice Witch.

"Dragon of old, dragon of legend," Witch Amity bellowed sternly. "Why have you destroyed the veil that shields us?"

As the great beast attempted to land, people in the courtyard scattered quickly, mothers herding away children and men shielding loved ones. Witch Amity, however, held her ground, her fists now firmly set at her hips in defiance.

Folding his wings, Percival set down before her and bowed his scaly head. "Revered Ice Witch," he began with much pomp and ceremony. "I am honoured . . . "

"Enough!" interrupted Witch Amity. "What is the meaning of this intrusion? I demand to know."

Percival raised his head and frowned. "There is no need for such harsh words. I was merely carrying out a great service for your kingdom."

"A great service? What great service is that which leaves our doors open to evil threats?" Witch Amity shouted angrily.

With a great flourish Percival stretched out one wing and waved nonchalantly to the archway of the gatehouse. "One that allows you to welcome back one of your own."

All heads turned in the direction of the gatehouse. Above, on the balcony, Grace peered at the scene unfolding below with pent breath. The dragon's appearance and the veil's disintegration proved devastating enough. The prospect of yet another intruder was overwhelming.

"What did it mean, 'welcome back one of their own'?" she thought to herself as she watched and waited.

From the gatehouse, a hooded figure emerged. Percival grinned, feeling quite pleased with himself, and smugly crossed his arms over his chest as he imagined the adulation and praise he would receive from the people of this kingdom once her identity was revealed.

Slowly, she approached Prince Owyn. Then reached up and withdrew the cloak's hood as all eyes stared unbelievingly at her familiar face. A collective gasp swept through the crowd.

"Art thou not pleased to once more cast thy gaze upon thy sibling?" asked Princess Farren.

Cheers and applause erupted from the courtyard and the crowd rushed the princess as Prince Owyn lifted her up onto his shoulders.

"Behold, good people!" he shouted. "Mine beloved sister has finally returned to us! Hail the Ice Princess! Hail Princess Farren." The crowd exploded again and joined in the chant and soon the courtyard was filled with shouts and cheers.

Percival smugly leaned over to Witch Amity and whispered, "Did I not tell you true?"

"Indeed. However, it does not justify destroying the veil," she said curtly as she turned from the dragon and focused her attention on the princess.

Relieved, Grace leaned over the banister for a better view. "Owyn never told me he had a sister," she thought. Looking into the face of this new stranger, she was met with something completely unexpected — it was like looking into a mirror, the resemblance was so strong. Her mind raced as she tried to comprehend the meaning of such a coincidence.

Realization seeped in; she was suddenly conscious of certain pieces falling into place and of matters making sense that couldn't possibly be true. Ones like Owyn commenting that someone was amiss in her heart, the hag mistaking her for someone else, her own obsession with a phantom sibling, the pull on her heart watching the destruction of the castle in her dream.

Just when she thought she had figured everything out, something else dropped into her lap and she felt as if she was back at square one in the Ice World's game.

Distracted by Witch Amity hushing the crowd, Grace turned her attention back to the courtyard as Witch Amity approached Princess Farren and bowed, "Your Majesty. Welcome home. But, how is it that you have come back to us in this way after so many years?"

Prince Owyn gently lowered his sister to the ground and the crowd stood silent, anxiously waiting her response.

"I longed to return and yet I heard tales of the castle's destruction and the shrouding veil that barred all who hoped for passage through," she began. "'Twas rumoured to be the act of evil and I feared for the safety of mine kin. Thus began mine quest to seek out one who might offer a way through. 'Twas when I discovered the powers of this dragon, Percival of the Glenn, that I knew he would be my salvation and enable my return home."

Witch Amity chuckled and shook her head. "It was I who installed the veil. You needed not to have enlisted the powers of an ancient dragon to come home," she said taking Princess Farren's hand. "You could have entered at any time. All you had to do was make a wish."

"Again with the wishes," Grace said to herself from her perch.

"I knew not!" exclaimed Princess Farren. "A simple wish wouldst grant passage?"

Heads nodded. Momentarily the dragon and loss of the veil were forgotten when suddenly Princess Farren's eyes rolled back into her head, her body grew limp and she fainted away, collapsing into Prince Owyn's arms. Quick to react, he caught her, then gently laid her on the soft grass where she remained motionless, barely breathing.

Witch Amity rushed to her side. Stroking Farren's forehead, she whispered, "Princess, what ails you?" Her face drained of colour when she spied the dark amulet around Farren's neck and she turned to Prince Owyn. "Something is not right. I fear the worst."

Suddenly, the ground began to shake and the air to rumble as though a thousand pounding hoofbeats approached. Dark ominous clouds emerged in the sky, swirling wildly, swept up by a cold, ripping wind that raced through the castle and slapped at those in its path. The crowd drew back, struggling against the wind and wrestling to stay balanced, grabbing at each other and anything else to hold on to. Grace clung to the bars of the balcony as she braced against the wind, trying desperately to make out the strange occurrences below.

A great gust of wind roughly shoved Witch Amity aside and flung Prince Owyn away from his sister. A dark shadow escaped from the amulet and washed over Princess Farren. It wrapped her body with a thick, black mask. Now enveloped in a cloak of darkness, Farren began to shiver and shake uncontrollably.

A strand of ghostly filament emerged from the charm, gaining in length and breadth as it streamed across Farren's frame to join the shadow. When the two became one, the entity lingered momentarily above before slowly floating to the centre of the courtyard. In a flash of black and a thunderclap, it exploded, sending an ebony spray over the courtyard before raging, howling winds swept it away.

"A simple wish wouldst grant passage?" said Evil Ice Witch Mayme mocking Princess Farren's last words. "Certainly not a simple wish from my lips!" she bellowed sarcastically.

Grace froze. Here was the Evil Ice Witch in all her infamy — her robes billowing about her body, her long silver hair dancing wildly in the frenzied wind and snow. Grace immediately recognized her from the librarian's history book and wondered if she was about to relive the tragic story of her dreams.

Visibly shaken, but undeterred, Witch Amity picked herself up to face her sister. "You are not welcome here," she seethed with contempt.

"Not welcome? Are you quite sure?' retorted Witch Mayme. "Not so, dear sister. There is change in the wind, for I do believe I shall welcome myself. This kingdom is mine to rule now and there's naught you can do to dissuade me."

With the snap of her hand she jettisoned a spray of fine, black crystals, their edges pointed and sharp. They showered the courtyard and, as they bore down on Witch Mayme's victims, those gathered in the courtyard were rendered frozen in their places, covered in an icy film — all but Grace and Percival, the dragon.

Witch Mayme wended about the frozen statues, laughing wildly as she swept through the courtyard until she came face to face with her sister.

"Where is your protective veil now?" she taunted. "Nothing to protect you from my charms, is there?" she paused. "But there is one tiny detail I really must attend to before I begin my rule," she said as she tapped herself on the chin. "And what might that be, you ask? Why that would be your demise!" she taunted. "While this lovely little spell has caught you in this state, alas, it will not keep. I fear something more permanent is in order for today."

Unable to respond, Witch Amity stared blankly through the film of ice in which she was imprisoned.

"Dragon!" Witch Mayme shouted. "Prepare your breath once again and make ready your vapours."

Percival stomped over to the Evil Ice Witch, leered down at her and asked in a mockingly, curious tone, "Who are you?"

"I am your mistress and you will do as I command," she casually said.

"I will not!" retorted Percival.

"Ah, but you must."

"No, I must not. I was promised the Diamond Heart — "

"Ahh. Of course. The Diamond Heart," she interrupted.

"And I demand to have it now!"

"Here is your Diamond Heart, you ancient fool!" she said as she picked up an ice rock and threw it at the dragon's scaly chest. "Now do as I command or you will never see your beloved Diamond Heart."

In disbelief, Percival peered down at the spot where the rock hit his scales, denting a few and tarnishing their shine. "I was promised. I was promised, I was promised!" he moaned incredulously.

"The promise was made by a princess, and I doubt she is capable of fulfilling it," Witch Mayme spat, waving to Farren's motionless body. "You shall get your Diamond Heart but not before you do as I command!"

Up on the balcony, Grace anxiously watched and listened to the arguing below. Although the witch's spell had not touched her and she was left unscathed, the image of all who were frozen scared her immensely and she was quite frantic at what to do. Again, a haunting realization seeped into her mind, and as much as she would have liked to brush it away, she could not. In her heart she knew that the kingdom's salvation was now in her hands. "But how? With what?" Grace said to herself.

"I demand the Diamond Heart!" bellowed Percival angrily.

"Do as I command!" shouted back Witch Mayme.

"The Diamond Heart!"

"As I command!"

Witch Mayme was becoming increasingly angrier and impatient with Percival. From under her breath she uttered strange-sounding words, her lips twisting and twitching grotesquely in an incantation. Deeply entranced in the oration of her spell, the Evil Ice Witch began to transform. Her arms rose at both sides, elbows arching along the way, tracing an invisible circle until the back of her hands touched above her head and she slowly began to increase in size.

Larger and larger she grew, stretching and spreading in all directions. Her arms swelled like tree trunks, ending in hands larger and thicker than pitchforks. Her shoulders broadened to gargantuan proportions, while her head ballooned enormously and her features adjusted to her enlarged face. The long silver tresses flowed down her back becoming strands of thickly twisted rope. By the time she has ceased growing, her massive frame exceeded that of the dragon and she loomed so large in the courtyard there was barely room to move. Her voluminous robes billowed in the wind, now the size of circus tents, toppling innocent castle folk unkindly to the ground. She reached down and plucked Percival by the scruff of his neck and dangled him precariously in front of her gigantic nose.

"Unbeknownst to you I journeyed to your lair where I released a potion — a powerful potion of obedience," Witch

Mayme hissed into his face. "And you are still bound under its spell and must obey my every command."

Percival struggled to break free from her grasp, but her grip was too tight.

"Because we are kin, my powers are limited against my sister," she sneered, pinching Percival between her fingers. "So, you must do the deed. With your frosted breath, crush her, and I just might reward you with your precious Diamond Heart."

"Wait a minute," Grace thought to herself as realization crept in again and the purpose of her knowledge of the stone became clear. "That's it!" she exclaimed as she scrambled to her feet, mindful to stay low as she furtively darted through the balcony doors.

Quitting the apartment, she raced along the long corridor of the east wing. Bolting down the imposing ice staircase, gripping its carved banister at irregular intervals, ricocheted her down ever faster. At the foot of the stairs she hurtled into the Great Hall.

"This has to be it. It's just got to be it," Grace said to herself as she dashed across the polished mirrored floor to face King Roarke's throne. A sense of propriety struck her suddenly, after all this was a royal throne and some decorum should be upheld, but she quickly banished the thought. The fate of the kingdom was at stake and she had no time to fret over manners and the like. Grace scrambled up onto the king's throne, stood up on its seat and faced the jewel embedded in its back.

"I hope I'm not going to get into any trouble for this," she said as she frantically began to pick and pry at the stone; it refused to give way. No amount of chiselling by her slender fingers would free the diamond. It simply wouldn't budge.

Outside in the courtyard, the giant Evil Ice Witch had dismissively flung the dragon into the air and Grace could hear her voice echo loudly, "Do as I command!"

Consumed with the devastating prospect of losing the Diamond Heart and conflicted with terrible guilt at maiming Witch Amity, Percival spiralled out of control. If succumbing and crashing into the rocks below would somehow hinder or even foil the Evil Ice Witch's plan, Percival concluded it would be worth losing his life for such a noble cause.

"The spell cast compels you," Witch Mayme shrieked, "You cannot refuse!"

Percival continued to free fall, desperately fighting the forces trying to control him, but the power of the spell prevailed and he finally surrendered. Soaring upwards, narrowly missing the jagged rocks at the foot of the mountain, he managed to right himself in flight. After circling the castle, he once again hovered mid-air and prepared to release his breath.

Through an arched window, Grace glanced at the dragon hovering above and picked at the stone even more feverishly. "It's got to come out," she said desperately. "Come on. Please come out." Her small fingers worked at the edges of the stone trying to pry it from its setting but try as she might, she couldn't.

"How am I going to get it out?" she fretted anxiously. "How, how, how?" She looked up at the dragon again and fear gripped her heart at Witch Amity's impending demise. Then she remembered what Owyn had told her in the garden and, finally trusting in what she knew would come true, Grace took a deep breath. "I wish to hold the Diamond Heart jewel." She cupped her hands. The back of the throne quivered briefly and out popped the stone. "Yes!" she exclaimed triumphantly.

Up in the sky, Percival again arched backwards, his powerful wings rising on both sides as he inhaled. Grace crashed through the doors of the Great Hall and bounded out into the courtyard, "WAIT!" she screamed as she ran.

The Evil Ice Witch turned with a start at the sound of Grace's voice. "Who goes there?" she demanded, catching a glimpse of Grace as she darted between the frozen statues of the castle folk. "So this is whom you employ as your Guardian," she said sneering at her sister. "A mere child! 'Tis hardly suitable competition," she jeered, her evil laugh echoing off the castle walls.

"WAIT!" Grace shouted again as she crossed the courtyard.

Witch Mayme turned in her direction, raised her beefy arms and pointed at Grace while uttering a spell. Daggers of black ice flew from her fingertips, exploding as they stabbed the ground, missing Grace by inches.

"You may have eluded Snitch's capture but you cannot escape my powers, you urchin," Witch Mayme frothed. Yet Grace was too fast, too nimble and too small a target — and the Evil Ice Witch's enormity slowed her from reacting with the accuracy required to hit her mark.

In order to distract Percival from destroying the Ice Witch, Grace ducked and dodged to reach her. When she finally did, she gasped in astonishment at Amity's frozen face. Her eyes were fixed and vacant.

"Witch Amity!" Grace shouted. "I've got the Diamond Heart. We can stop the dragon." The witch stared blankly. When an incoming dagger suddenly exploded at her feet sending shards of ice everywhere, Grace turned toward the sky. "Dragon! Look!" Grace pleaded, thrusting the jewel skyward high above her head for him to see.

Time was not in her favour; her actions had come too late. Percival had already lurched forward, directing his powerful head down toward the castle, and unleashed a second cone of icy frost from his powerful jaws with the same thundering force as the first. Ice pellets hurtled at Grace and Witch Amity with lightening speed and Grace watched in terror as the cone of frost sped toward her. Grimacing, she closed her eyes tightly and braced for the impending impact of thousands of pellets painfully stabbing her skin.

From somewhere deep within her, an instinct compelled Grace to keep the jewel aloft — above her head. With tremendous speed and a blinding white light the crystal stream hit its mark, but not the target Witch Mayme had intended. Instead it struck the Diamond Heart jewel, bounced off and instantly ricocheted onto the looming figure of the Evil Ice Witch.

"NO!" screamed Witch Mayme, as ice pellets mercilessly pummelled and pelted her. Once completely enveloped, her enormous frame began to shrink. Her trunk-like arms withered and recoiled, her head and shoulders narrowed and drooped as her body dwindled to customary proportions. A crystal haze lingered before seeping into her skin, leaving her petrified and covered in a clear film of ice, her mouth agape from her last spoken word.

Immediately, the howling wind blew itself out and the ground stopped trembling. A wave of calm washed over the kingdom as the sun broke through the departing clouds and bathed the castle in glistening, white sunlight that melted the ice from all who had been frozen.

With the Evil Ice Witch's spell now broken, the courtyard teemed back to life. Everyone stared unbelievingly at the statue before them.

Chapter Forty-One

As if caught in a trance, and with the jewel still tightly cupped in her hand, Grace slowly walked over to face Witch Mayme. "It worked," she whispered.

Prince Owyn approached and knelt on one knee. When he rose, he turned back to his subjects and called out. "The Guardian has prevailed! The Guardian has prevailed!"

On cue, the people of the kingdom exploded with cheers and applause as they rushed forward to honour their Guardian, Grace. Everyone wanted to touch her, to shake her hand. In the midst of the pandemonium, Witch Amity wove her way through and reaching out for her, Grace fell into her embrace.

"Might you have surprised yourself?" Witch Amity whispered into her ear, the one with the pearl nestled on the lobe, "with powers of your own?"

Grace nodded and caught her breath. She looked at the frozen statue of the Evil Ice Witch. "Is she . . . ?"

"Dead?" said Witch Amity. "No, she's alive. The dragon's breath will keep her this way for a very long time. Eventually the effect will fade and she will be as she once was."

"What will you do with her then?" Grace gasped.

"We'll worry about that when it happens," Witch Amity assured her. "As long as she harbours evil thoughts, the longer the spell will hold. Given enough time, perhaps she will decide to lose those thoughts and come back to us with good in her heart."

Prince Owyn stepped forward. "Farren has awakened," he interrupted, "We should tend to her needs."

Cass was mopping Princess Farren's forehead with a damp cloth as Grace, Witch Amity, and Prince Owyn approached.

"She's quite shaken, she is," Cass said gravely.

Still feeling faint, Princess Farren attempted to speak. "Mine thoughts are clouded and I am at a loss at what hath happened," she struggled to say.

"Dear sister," soothed Prince Owyn. "Thou hast been bewitched by Evil Ice Witch Mayme."

"Bewitched?" she gasped. "By what means?" Still dizzy, Princess Farren sat up and with help from Saithe, managed to stand.

"By this," said Witch Amity snatching the dark amulet from Farren's neck. "A channelling charm that bears her mark." Barely visible to the eye, the shape of a black icicle was etched onto the bottom of the amulet.

"The day I fled, Mayme gave it to me to use as a guide," Farren explained. "That it would aid me on mine quest. I thought that the stone given by the Seeker Queen so long ago might be the stone of dragon Percival's desire. I hoped that if I could unite the two, its power would restore the damage done when I conspired with Mayme. But never in mine journey did I ever encounter her."

"You would not have had to. Such is the power of the amulet," Witch Amity explained. "As long as you were wearing it she could see everything you saw, see everywhere you went, see everyone you met simply by consulting its twin." She walked over to the petrified witch and pointed at the matching amulet that lay frozen around her neck. "Only if she needed to change the spell would she have had to come in contact with you. Did you ever let anyone touch it?"

Princess Farren thought back to the encounter at the rest stop and nodded. "En route I came upon a fellow traveller, a Seer — or so I thought."

"You did not recognize her?" asked Saithe. "Did you not know she was evil?"

"Nay. Nay, not at all," answered Princess Farren. "She was blind and feeble and gave sight to where I might find the dragon's lair."

"My sister is a master of disguises," said Witch Amity. "It would not have been difficult for her to deceive the princess. Only I can see through her trickery."

Saithe nodded in agreement.

"What spell would she have cast anew?" asked Prince Owyn.

"One that would allow her to travel through the amulet and appear wherever Princess Farren was," Witch Amity explained. "And without the protective veil she would be free to enter the castle."

"That's pretty creepy." Grace said, speaking for the first time in the presence of Princess Farren who gave her a quizzical look.

"Creepy?" asked Prince Owyn curiously. "As in the act of moving close to the ground?"

Grace nodded her head, "That's exactly what it means — crawly — low like a snake."

"Pray tell? Who is this child?" Princess Farren asked softly as she reached to touch Grace's cheek and stroke her hair. "Has the queen given her king another heir in mine absence?"

"Allow me to introduce our new Guardian, Grace," Prince Owyn quickly intervened. "The resemblance is not from our mother, Farren, but from one from the past."

"Nicely done, Prince," complimented Witch Amity. "We must wait for the Watchers before more can be revealed. There is no other option."

Grace gazed into the Ice Princess' face. She, too, wanted an explanation for the similarities they shared, but it would have to wait until the festival began; the witch had been adamant. But she felt an extraordinary connection to Princess Farren as they locked eyes. Caught in the moment, she forgot what she was holding and when she looked down, she still clutched the Diamond Heart.

"What about the dragon? And the Diamond Heart jewel?"

Unnoticed, Percival had quietly landed in a corner of the courtyard and lay panting against a wall, tired and spent. His huge wings dangled listlessly at each side, his head drooped on slouched shoulders and his scales had lost their lustre. Small puffs of mist trickled from his mouth and he whistled and wheezed with every laboured breath. Without the strength to fly, Percival could not escape the castle nor his own demons. Betrayal and defeat had replaced pride and confidence. He recoiled in shame at what he had been forced to do against the good people of the kingdom.

Grace stepped forward and held out the stone. "Is this what you're looking for?" she asked as she approached the dragon.

Princess Farren joined her and quickly explained Percival's story to everyone listening, although it was one Grace already knew. "If 'tis truly the Diamond Heart of his cherished mate, it is thy obligation and thy duty to return it," she said solemnly. "This dragon is of a good heart, and his only failing was to become the unwilling servant of the Evil Ice Witch."

"My obligation? Why me?" Grace asked.

"Trust me," said Princess Farren. "As Guardian it is thy calling."

Together, Grace and Princess Farren ventured closer. Grace had never seen a real dragon before and despite his size and his obvious power, she was unafraid. He looked quite harmless as he lay against the wall, defeated and helpless. Grace could only feel sadness and pity for this once great beast.

"Mighty dragon, Percival of the Glenn," said Princess Farren. "Do not despair. Thou hast been mine friend and mine salvation, and hast delivered me to mine kingdom. For that, I am most grateful and in thy debt. Nary a grudge will be held by mine people. We know 'twas neither thy choice nor thine intention to cause our kingdom harm."

Percival looked up, sheepishly at first, but heartened by the princess' kind words, drew strength and was humbled by her compassion.

"A promise is a promise," she continued, motioning to Grace to offer the stone. "With all mine heart, I hope this is truly the treasure thou seek."

Cradled in her slender, twelve-year-old hands, Grace held the stone up to Percival's face. The diamond twinkled and sparkled in the white light, reflecting the sun's rays and bouncing glints of light about the castle. Reaching out with a talon, the dragon delicately plucked it from Grace's grasp. Crystal tears streaked from his eyes, and his mouth quivered slightly as he carefully studied the stone. Then he thrust it to his chest where his own heart lay pounding.

Suddenly, a blast of white light exploded from the stone showering and engulfing Percival with its brilliance. His dull scales now shimmered and his drooping wings opened impressively to their full span. With shoulders back and head held high, he slowly lifted off the ground. Gone were the tears, gone was the shame and humiliation; all replaced by the power of love emanating from the Diamond Heart.

Still shimmering, Percival hovered in the courtyard for all to see, before settling back down to the ground. Never was a moment more touching and more intimate, as when Percival joined with Brynn's heart. The Ice Princess smiled. Grace smiled. Everyone smiled — even the librarian.

"Your Majesty," said Percival quite formally as he bowed his head. "You have kept your promise. This is the Diamond Heart of my beloved. My greatest treasure."

Approaching the dragon, Princess Farren placed her hand affectionately on his forearm. "Percival," she began. "Mine quest has ended, and hence mine journey, thanks to thee."

"Princess, my quest has also ended," he replied. "My thanks to you."

"Nay, nay. 'Tis I who am in thy debt," disagreed Princess Farren politely.

Percival was about to protest further but caught himself. "Princess, had I known I was in the company of royalty, I might have acted more honourably. Might we not begin our friendship anew?"

Farren blushed and a silent understanding passed between the young princess and the ancient dragon.

"The Guardian has prevailed. Now is the time for celebration," Witch Amity called out. "We have a festival to prepare. Everyone back to work. The Crystal Ice Spirits will be arriving soon. Send word to the king." With a clap of her hands, the courtyard suddenly teemed with activity again as castle folk returned to their duties and hurried to complete the preparations.

Standing alone with Prince Owyn, Grace turned to him. "She called me the Guardian."

"Yes, Grace. She did," he answered. "Art thou still not convinced?"

"Oh, I don't know. It all happened so fast," she said as she plunked down on the bench circling the fountain. "Maybe I was just lucky. This time."

Prince Owyn joined her. "This time and every time, Guardian Grace. Luck played no role in what thou didst. 'Twas thee and only thee who saved us from a terrible fate."

Grace took a deep breath, "I'm just glad it's over, 'cause I never want to go through that again. I hope Ice Witch Mayme stays frozen forever." she exclaimed. "Well, I guess I did what I came here to do, even though I really didn't know what it was," her voice become quiet and reflective. "Owyn, I want to go home. Do you think the Watchers will let me?"

"Not quite yet, Guardian Grace," said Prince Owyn. "The Festival draws nigh and thy presence is required."

Chapter Forty-Two

"What exactly are we waiting for?" Grace whispered to Prince Owyn who was standing next to her among the castle folk now gathered in a circle. "And why is everybody looking up?"

Prince Owyn leaned over to her, "The Spirits hail from our northern skies and 'tis considered a good omen to catch their first glimpse."

"Look! There they are!" shouted a single voice. "The Crystal Spirits!"

A tiny speck of light appeared in the distance, high above the mountain peaks, glinting on and off like a mirror reflecting sunlight as it travelled toward the castle. It reminded Grace of the speck that had appeared at the back of her garden. Soon other voices joined in, calling out excitedly. The light blinked more rapidly, until it appeared no longer as a speck but as a sliver of light. It passed over the moat, through the gatehouse, and into the courtyard, then swirled around the frozen Evil Ice Witch before gliding up over the keep and down into the gardens. The circle of castle folk parted, allowing the sliver to reach Witch Amity.

"Welcome Spirits. Welcome Watchers," she said reaching out with an icicle wand and piercing the light with its tip. The sliver of light slowly spread out as it dissolved into a cloud of tiny, white crystals sparkling and twinkling. Dividing in two and two again, the shape of four ghostly, male figures faintly materialized, their phantom forms appearing almost transparent. The spirits appeared to be kin — their chiselled faces resembled each other. Their celestial bodies, although pale and translucent, looked strong and fit under veil-like garments that clung to their sheer skin. As they lingered near the ground, their feet never touching it, they looked more like mighty warriors than wistful spirits made of crystals and light.

"We feared the worst," one Watcher said gravely. "But it would seem the Guardian has succeeded."

"And why wouldst ye have feared the worst?" asked Prince Owyn, stepping forward.

"For quite some time we have been following a cloaked traveller and an ancient dragon." said the Spirit. "As Watchers, we attempted to overtake the pair to discover their true intentions, for they seemed to be journeying in the direction of this castle."

"Alas, we were never able to catch up," continued a second. "And we knew they would reach the castle before we were able to warn you. So we took what measures we could."

"Measures? What measures?" asked Witch Amity.

"We sent barriers to impede their travels. To slow their pace."

"Barriers of what sort?" piped in Princess Farren knowingly. "Barriers, perhaps, in the likes of a forest of elder trees, an avalanche, or a sudden snow squall lasting for hours and ice-stones of monstrous proportions?"

All four Watchers stared at Princess Farren in disbelief, "Your Majesty, how could you know this?"

"This I know, for it 'twas I who travelled with the dragon, bewitched by the Evil One and it 'twas I who encountered thy barriers," she answered. "Along with this dragon."

"We had no way of knowing it was you, your Majesty," said a Spirit. "The traveller was shielded by dark magic that clouded our view. We hope we did not cause you any harm."

"Thy barriers were indeed impeding and challenging," answered Princess Farren. "Have ye glimpsed any other dangers in thy travels which might trouble our kingdom?"

"Although there are curious stirrings farther east, there is nothing that we may speak of at this time," a Spirit replied. "But we will keep our watch, just the same."

"And now that Witch Mayme no longer poses any threat, thanks to the Guardian," said Prince Owyn gesturing to Grace, "our kingdom is assured of its safety, at least for some time to come."

At the mention of her name, the Crystal Ice Spirits drifted over to where Grace stood. She could almost see through their ghostly figures, and when one Watcher reached for her hand, she felt only a slight brush — a touch barely there — as he held her hand in his.

"Grace," he began. "You have indeed proven yourself as a rightful Guardian. Honour us with the joining of hands. Our pact to serve you and serve with you will be honoured for all time."

With each Watcher's caress, a serenity infused Grace's being and she welcomed the embrace with a keen understanding that she did indeed have a role in this world. And that she could finally head home.

Chapter Forty-Three

Meanwhile, Searchers had been sent to intercept King Roarke's riding party with news of the Guardian's triumphant defeat over Evil Ice Witch Mayme, and the return of the monarchs' daughter, Princess Farren. The king immediately reversed his course and headed home, driving his horses hard to arrive quickly. Queen Isolte's spirit lifted from the malaise it had endured for so long, and the king's heart warmed at the signs that his wife was returning to the woman she had once been.

Charging over the moat and across the drawbridge, the carriage careened into the courtyard and came to an abrupt stop just shy of the steps to the keep. Stepping out of the carriage, the king and queen rushed to the terrace where their subjects were assembled listening intently to one of the Watchers. Not wanting to interrupt such revered guests, the royal couple quietly mingled with the crowd.

" . . . And after the fall of the dragon's mate, Brynn, we were forced to send the Guardian back to his world with his memory cleansed," answered the Watcher. "He remembers nothing of his Guardian days and of the creature he watched over."

"You really mean you sent him back because he caused the dragon's death," Grace accused defending one of her own kind. "Like a punishment?"

"It is uncertain whether the Guardian could have prevented the tragedy. He had already thwarted many attempts and his presence might have made the difference had he been there, but it is something we will never know for sure. We sent him back without memory, out of compassion. To live with the guilt, deserved or not, would have destroyed him."

Grace had to admit the Watcher made sense and the Watchers' actions were honourable. It all seemed so incredible and she wondered if there was more they hadn't told her.

"When did this happen?" Grace pressed further. "And why wasn't he there when it did?"

"Of this I can answer," interrupted Queen Isolte as she stepped forward.

Before speaking again, Queen Isolte embraced the princess and a quiet moment passed between mother and daughter as they reconciled, both heartened to be reunited again.

"Many, many years ago," began Queen Isolte, "it came to pass that a young man, a Guardian, was summoned to watch over a pair of sacred dragons who faced extinction. They bore distinct and unique powers of enchantment and the love they shared became legend. Those unlucky in love often sought the dragons out, hoping to be blessed with a sliver of their passion. One was an unbetrothed princess from a distant kingdom desperate to be smitten. She not only chanced upon the creatures, but their Guardian as well, and fell deeply in love with him. Knowing her father would never sanction such a reunion, she and her lover stole away, casting aside their reputations and responsibilities to be together."

As she spoke, Queen Isolte reached out to Princess Farren and caressed her cheek. "In time she grew heavy with child and at the moment of the birth, one of the Guardian's dragons was viciously slain. Instantly, Watchers knew of its demise and their only course of action was to send the Guardian back to his world. Distraught at the loss of her love and alone with an infant, the princess returned to her home. She begged her father to forgive her and to take them in. The king acquiesced because she had brought an heir — albeit not pure royal blood — but it was of some consolation and he accepted the child on the condition that she marry a royal from the north."

Stepping to her side, King Roarke took his wife's hand and gently brought it to his heart, knowing how difficult it was to tell her story. Although tears trickled down her face, she was determined to finish.

"The princess agreed, and soon after a son was born and, although my new husband was not the first love of my life, he was kind and caring and I soon grew to love him in return."

Spellbound by Queen Isolte's rendition of her secret past, everyone was bereft of speech, not knowing how to react to her admission. Witch Amity, however, was well versed in social graces and knew the proper approach; she was the first to speak. "Your majesty, we are honoured that you have chosen to share such an intimate experience. We applaud your courage. Our place is not to cast judgment here, for we all have our own regrets. Rest assured that you remain our beloved queen."

From the onset of the queen's speech, everyone had held their breath, and now they heaved a collective sigh as Witch Amity conveyed their sentiments as befitted their sovereign. With the ice finally broken, cheers of adulation swept through the crowd. The royal family embraced one another and graciously waved to their subjects, beholden by the kingdom's continued allegiance.

But a Watcher stilled the crowd. "There is still one final detail," he said as he beckoned to Grace and Percival to join him. "Grace, by following the quest of the Diamond Heart jewel, you have not only lifted the curse cast when Brynn of the Glenn was slain, you have returned the heart back to its rightful owner. What was lost to this dragon by one Guardian is now found by another — and all is as it should be."

Cheers rang as the crowd dispersed, everyone leaving to mingle in the garden, to sample the fare, and to excitedly discuss the events of the day. Children scampered from their parents' sides, and headed for the pitched white tents where games and contests began. Eager riders jumped onto their mounts as a carousel of ponies began its trek, circling the paddock. Musicians took their places on a makeshift stage and soon a spirited melody filled the garden, coaxing partners of all ages to take to the dance floor.

Prince Owyn, Ice Witch Amity, and Princess Farren had gathered with Percival. They spoke in hushed tones and when Grace joined in, all talk immediately stopped.

"What's going on?" she asked curiously. "What are you talking about?"

"We are conferring about thee, fair Grace," said Prince Owyn.

Grace wondered what mysterious plan they had in store for her this time. The librarian, the Mistress Tailor and Baker approached and Sparkle the Seeker hovered nearby. Assembled before her were all of the people she had come to know during her day in the Ice World. Even the Flyer streaked in and settled at her feet.

"Owyn, you're giving me the willies," she said.

He cocked his head to one side, puzzled.

"No, no," she corrected herself, not wanting to explain the meaning of "willies". "I mean, you're making me a little bit nervous. Like, you've got another plan for me."

"A plan," said Prince Owyn. "Now that is something I do understand. We do indeed have a plan for thee, fair Grace."

"We have asked Percival to remain here with us and he has graciously agreed," continued Prince Owyn. "Together with the Crystal Ice Spirits as our Watchers, and Ice Witch Amity's magic, he has also vowed to be our protector. So you see, the kingdom is now well guarded."

"So does that mean you don't need me to be your Guardian anymore," Grace asked.

Witch Amity stepped forward and took Grace's hand in hers. "Grace, we know how much you wish to return to your world, and it would be unfair to ask you to stay as our Guardian, along with the others. Besides, it's clear the Watchers have given their blessing. That's not to say we still won't need you and the special powers you possess one day. And when we do, we want to be able to call for you and for you to call on us. To that end we have devised a way for us to reach you, and for you to reach the Ice World," she said as she took Grace's other hand and held them out together in front of her. "Percival . . . " she called softly.

The huge beast squeezed between the prince and princess, and towering over Grace said. "Fear not. I shan't harm you. Ready?"

Before Grace could answer, the dragon inhaled deeply, his chest filling with breath as he arched his great head back before lurching forward and releasing a single stream of frost.

Stunned, Grace stared helplessly as the ice pellets sped toward her hands.

Instead of striking her, the stream veered off, and drew a perfect line of frost along her palms, ending at her fingertips. Individual ice pellets melded together, crystallizing into a solid shape that dropped into her hands.

"Oh!" Grace exclaimed with a sigh of relief. And soon a broad grin spread across her face. "It's an icicle. An icicle just like Witch Amity's."

"It's not quite like mine, Grace," corrected Witch Amity. "Its powers are unique, and rightly so," she began to explain. "Whenever we should have the need to call for you, the icicle will quiver at your touch. And because you live in a world in which darkness falls, it will also softly glow."

"Nice," Grace said approvingly. "It's like the Ice World's version of a cellphone."

Her friends exchanged glances at the mention of yet another set of strange words.

"But how do I get here?" she questioned. "And how do I get back?"

Prince Owyn put his arm around her and gently squeezed. "Grace, I am surprised you should feel the need to ask."

Grace blushed a smile knowingly. "Everyone," she quietly said. "It really is time for me to go home."

Prince Owyn nodded, reached for her hand, and as he bowed to kiss it, he whispered, "Make a wish."

Surrounded by blinding, white light, Grace was engulfed in a swirling cyclone of brilliance, just as she had when first entering the Ice World. This time, however, she was not afraid and knew exactly what would greet her on the other side.

The light exploded in the same blinding flash, and her world emerged. The boulevard appeared busy, with buses on their routes and cars on their way as traffic lights turned from green to yellow to red and back again. The freezing rain had stopped and ice melted everywhere, fuelled by the warm rays of the bright winter sun that shone in a clear, blue sky.

Grace landed in her backyard. She looked up and saw lights beaming through the windows, ones mistakenly left on during the power failure. She padded up the back stairs and entered the house, then tiptoed up the staircase and peeked into her parents' room where they both lay soundly sleeping. Her father softly snored and her mother gently nudged him to stop. Grace's heart swelled at seeing them again and she resisted the urge to clamber onto their bed and rouse them. But too much had happened and she was too spent to explain. At least for the time being.

Grace quietly closed the door and made her way to her room. She was exhausted from her stay in the Ice World. Grace felt as though she could sleep for a week — well, a few extra hours at least — and knew that her mother would let her. Slipping out of her clothes, she crawled under the covers and closed her eyes.

J.L. SCHARF is the Creative Director of an advertising agency, and her written work has earned her awards in Canada and in New York, Chicago, and London. This is her first novel.